Time to Talk

Roderick Hart

First published in 2013 by The Portable Press
Copyright © Roderick Hart 2013
First edition
This book is a work of fiction. Any resemblance to actual events, or persons, living or dead, is entirely coincidental.
The author asserts the moral right under the Copyright, Designs and Patents Act 1988 to be identified as the author of this work.
All Rights reserved. No part of this publication may be reproduced, stored in a retrieval system, or transmitted, in any form or by any means without the prior written consent of the author, nor be otherwise circulated in any form of binding or cover other than that in which it is published and without a similar condition being imposed on the subsequent purchaser.

ISBN: 1484929055
ISBN-13: 9781484929056

for Audrey

1

When I was young I had opinions, too many and none of them earned. Yet I was happy to share them, and looking back on it now I really don't care for the person I was then: impatient to make my mark, an eager dog wagged by its tail. But hormones changed all that, hitting me with a painful self-consciousness which led me to merge with the wallpaper, whatever its pattern or colour. Suddenly a low profile became attractive. I felt a reluctance to make myself available, both in the flesh and in the mind, and that had one significant result. People talked to me because I didn't talk back. Maybe because they sensed I was selling them nothing, had no designs, they started to open up. Sometimes I'd just met them for the first time and they spilled, sure that what they said was safe with me. No doubt some were thinking, *This guy has no life, I'll lend him some of mine*, but mostly all they wanted was someone to lighten the load. And as we know by now – it is, after all, in the public domain – I went on to make that my vocation.

Susan, for example. We attended an evening class and sometimes went to Dean's Diner afterwards. Not the classiest place but the nearest. Too much Formica by far. I hardly knew her, yet one night over a hot chocolate she told me about a man who'd stayed with her for several days the week before and hadn't made a move. Walter. There he was in her spare room under his duvet and only himself to play with. What was he thinking? How did he imagine that made her feel as a woman? I remember considering what a strange question that was. Did she expect any man who stayed with her to make a move and, if so, how was he supposed to know? Perhaps it was listed on a nightly tariff posted on the bedroom door beside what to do in the event of fire.

She was attractive if somewhat plump, past the first flush of youth but, by her account, so was he. Yet this was a man she described as a friend. Did she really want to change a permanent friend into a temporary lover? Sex is more trouble than it's worth, clouding the judgement and overwhelming reason. It is also exceptionally boring which is why, in my career as a therapist, I have avoided cases majoring in that area. And it hasn't been easy. If Dr Freud is to be believed, everything comes down to sex. If I'd accepted that I'd have had no clients at all. No income. Nothing. Some cases are sexual in nature, of course, but many are not, and I soon built up a list of relationship counsellors, sex therapists and the like to whom I could refer such people on. Anything to get them out the door.

Mention of the door leads me to a problem I had at the outset: where to practise. A client is entitled to expect a commercial environment of some sort, however well tricked out with easy chairs, artwork and tasteful lamps. What would a prospective patron make of a practitioner whose home was also his office? That he was an amateur, a small-time operator who couldn't afford a genuine consulting room. Not the impression I wanted to give. But then, as so often after, fortune smiled on me and I smiled back.

I refer to the Collective. Its members rented workshops in a renovated warehouse by the banks of the Esk. In an imaginative masterstroke, they had called it The Warehouse. The rents were reasonable bordering on low, and all I had to do to qualify was discover a latent artistic tendency. I took advice from Colin, a print-maker of some note, an out-going, paint-spattered individual very easy to like.

'Whatever you do avoid heavy gear,' he told me over a beer. 'Ceramics are out, and weaving, and as for metal sculpture, forget it mate.'

We toyed with large knot macramé, crochet, knitting and lace-making, but none of them seemed quite me. Then Colin hit on photography.

'It's not like the old days,' he assured me, 'when you required a darkroom, safelight, enlarger and chemicals. All you'd need is a computer, which you'd want anyway, and a professional-looking digital camera.'

And some materials for mounting and framing. No need to use them, just so long as they were there, useful props to give the right impression. And a portfolio was a must. When I suggested I would need a lighting rig and a couple of white umbrellas Colin just smiled.

'You're not getting this, Max. You're a landscape photographer using the studio as a base.'

If the man from the council came round, the prints on the wall didn't have to be mine. Neither did those in the portfolio. But, he told me with a cheerful smile, I had to know the locations. And he added, more worryingly, have a modest handle on the technicalities.

'You know, depth of field and all that.'

I nodded sagely. No doubt he knew what he was talking about.

There were two units available, a first floor studio on the north side and a ground floor studio facing south. The south was larger and needed less done to it, but faced onto the courtyard where people parked their cars. An intimate tête-à-tête punctuated by the slamming of doors and revving of engines, that wouldn't do at all. But the north-facing workshop was just the ticket. Two large windows overlooking the river: coot, moorhen, mallard and swans all clearly visible. What could beat the therapeutic sound of gently running water burbling its way to the sea? Even with both windows open you couldn't actually hear it, but you knew it was there, and in my mind's ear I was already playing the gentle plash of water into my consulting room via artfully hidden speakers.

The trouble was the previous occupant, a graphic designer who had filled the available space with drawing boards and plan chests. Useful as these items were, their owner was nowhere to be found, though rumour had it his girlfriend had received a nice-while-it-lasted card from Guatemala. Putting these items in storage would cost, but Colin had a solution: sneak them into the other empty space for the time being. If someone else rented it at a later date that would be their problem, right? Artists are so creative when they get going. And I was all fired up to go myself till I opened the toilet door. The place would have disgraced a downmarket disco: chipped bowl, cracked seat and tiny basin. Besides which it was too small.

Empathy is important. Imagine what it's like to be a client arriving for the first session. About to discuss their problems with someone they've never met before, they're going to be nervous. Comparable to a job interview in some ways, where your average candidate will want to visit the rest room, relieve bladder and bowel, and buff up in front of the mirror to present a bold front to the world. Hardly possible in these conditions. But, as I like to tell my clients, problems are there to be solved, and what was the value of this nostrum if I couldn't apply it myself?

Colin knew an architect who came down the next day and ran an eye over the place.

'Well,' he began. But he said it in such a way I knew money was involved.

He proposed borrowing space from the main area to extend the toilet and sketched a plan on the wall to help me visualise his suggestion. We stood there, the three of us, admiring his work. And it was good alright. I felt like asking him to sign it.

'On the plus side,' he pointed out, 'the plumbing's there already: cold supply, hot supply and waste. But you'll want to replace the fixtures and,' he added, 'the room has no window. You'll need ventilation, so we're talking additional wiring.'

If I was interested, he'd draw up plans. Since he hadn't mentioned load-bearing walls I agreed on the spot.

What I failed to consider was why we needed plans in the first place, the answer being the Planning Department. Like it or not, I was in the hands of bureaucrats which meant, as it always does, rising costs and lengthening delay. For example, the planners wouldn't sign off the plans, modest though they were, on the ludicrous grounds that I didn't own the premises to which they related. For all they knew, the owner might object. So the architect approached the owners who (surprise, surprise!) were delighted that any tenant would be stupid enough to spend his own money improving their property.

The next few weeks were an ordeal by chaos, and though the architect doubled as a project manager he didn't seem so organised to me. He hired a plumber, electrician and a tiler, who were sometimes on the premises at once with competing transistor radios all on music stations. And though I wasn't sure it was necessary, he insisted on a sander for the main area.

'Those floorboards are too rough by half. You don't want your clients picking up skelfs.'

I didn't want them coming in bare-foot either, but the man was adamant. He had standards – which aren't as difficult to hit with other people's money as they are with your own. Every time I checked, which I did with increasing anxiety, my small pot of savings had dwindled further. I consoled myself with the thought that the outlay was a necessary investment which I would start to recoup as and when the clients rolled in. The architect agreed, and was ready with tiresome references to little acorns, mighty oaks, and the priming of pumps. But I knew that when those clients came they would sit on chairs I had ordered from IKEA and put together in the teeth of the diagrams (I am by nature a verbal person) with assorted Allen keys, cross-head screwdrivers and not a little sweat. I could just imagine them reclining on the Jönköping or curling up on the Umeå, thoroughly at home and ready to talk.

But when it was finished it looked good. Not only was everything tasteful and welcoming, but the newly painted walls were starting to look the part. Colin had leant me two of his prints, botanic subjects, very intricate, in a restricted range of greens and browns, and put the feelers out for suitable photographs. He had contacts and it was just a matter of time. He also produced a tattered book on digital photography so that I could 'bone up'. Starting at the back, I began leafing through it but soon realised I would end up as I always did - learning from experience. Trial and error. The heuristic approach. Inefficient perhaps, but you can't learn from your mistakes if you don't make any.

Wonderful as my studio was, something was missing and it took me a couple of days to figure out what. Plants. I shouldn't have told Colin I was going to the garden centre that Saturday afternoon, but botanics were a must and I had to have them. Living things grow, and where there is growth there is hope. That, at least, is what I intended my clients would inhale with the soothing aromas subtly tingeing the air – provided I chose wisely. They wouldn't be conscious of it. Just an encouraging subliminal effect similar to the smell of newly baked bread in a supermarket bakery. It's the result that counts, not the trigger which brings it about. But not for the first time I hit the limits of my knowledge. I loved the smell of privet in flower but I could hardly plant a hedge in my consulting room. I needed advice, and not from the web. Attractive shots of flowers are all very well, but how do they smell? The web couldn't tell me that, much as it might try.

The moment I arrived I knew the garden centre for what it was, a haven of a peace blessed with an excellent café. Before getting down to business, I ordered a coffee and bulked it out with a slice of fruit loaf. Delicious. Seduced by the background hum of middle-aged and elderly diners (myself a few years down the road) I came close to nodding off. Then my mobile pinged: a text from Colin wanting to know when I'd be back. Something had come up, nothing urgent. He'd speak to me later. I estimated six, but really had no idea. Reluctantly, I left the café and headed for the greenhouse. The display of plants and flowers was a work of art in itself. I doubt if any of the talent in the Collective could have done better. For the first time in years I wished I had a camera and began to see some future in photography after all.

The first person I asked wasn't strong on indoor plants but pointed me to a woman who was. According to her badge her name was Eva, and it was soon clear that she came from Latvia, Lithuania, Slovakia, or some such place, but try as I might I couldn't pin-point the accent.

'You realise of course that some of these plants have properties.'

I agreed. That was something they shared with everything else. But when I told her the nature of the space they were going to improve she really took off.

'This is good, I am enthusiast.'

The scent of plants could affect the mental state, did I know that? Well no, I didn't, and the more she went into it the more I saw myself replaced by exotic blooms which, by purely chemical means carried on the air to the nose, would sort out my clients more quickly – and much more cheaply – than I could hope to do. But my panic soon subsided. The advantages were clear. I would sit there listening attentively, taking notes, and making encouraging observations. The plants would take the strain and I would take the credit.

Eva walked me round the stands with my trolley, her first port of call being the herbs. Holding a specimen at eye height, she extolled the virtues of rosemary which, she claimed, and I'm translating here, improved cognitive ability and protected the brain from free radicals. This was a new one on me: where diluting free radicals was concerned I relied on generous amounts of red wine.

'And you may be excited to know that rosemary gives out the essence of its oil into your room.'

She explained what she meant with touching emphasis.

'You don't need to boil it, you don't need to make tea!'

She gave me some basil too which, I might like to know, reduced carbon dioxide. She used it at home herself. (I wasn't sure what she meant by this: where she was living now, Riga, Vilnius?) Thus far so leafy. When I hoped for a touch of colour she led me straight to lavender, which would suit my purposes since it helped you relax if you suffered from anxiety.

'You will be dealing with the anxiety, yes?'

I left the garden centre with a supply of rosemary, basil and lavender, together with some jasmine (love the dinky white flowers) and geraniums for added colour. I left with other things as well, after Eva pointed out that the plant pots had holes in the bottom, so if I put them on the window sill and watered them, guess where the water would go? I was no more a gardener than a photographer, but everyone has to start somewhere. So I bought some black plastic saucers to match the pots, and a bottle of Babybio the lady talked me into. Apparently, plants were just like people: they needed nourishment too.

I parked my clapped-out Panda in the courtyard, opened the boot and lifted out some of the plants. I'd have to come back for the rest. The ground floor seemed strangely quiet, but no doubt artisans clocked off early on a Saturday. And it was still quiet on the way up the stairs. The reason was obvious the minute I opened the door to my studio – there they all were, every last one of them, for the studio-warming party Colin had secretly arranged. Hence the text. Before I had time to draw breath I was surrounded by artists emoting, not one of them without a glass. The plants were wrested from my hands and taken to the windowsill, and in their place an empty glass and a plateful of savouries: rice, potato salad, coleslaw, samosas, halves of boiled egg. Mindful of the free radicals I asked for red and watched in dismay as someone filled me up with white. I mentioned the car, boot wide open, key still in the ignition, and the rest of the plants. No need to worry, they would take care of all that. And someone did, though it took me till ten o'clock that night to track down my car keys in his jacket pocket.

I had seen some of them through open doors, and recognised a few, like Antonia and Vicky who collared me from the off. Since

Antonia was a glass artist and Vicki a jeweller, I supposed they must compete with one another, but they soon set me straight. Vicki worked in silver, a burnished example of which graced her hair even as she spoke, and based her designs on Pictish symbols. Not straight copies, of course: the originals were more of a starting point. What into, I wondered silently, a journey of self-discovery? Antonia was nodding, she'd heard it all before and knew the party line. They seemed so close I wondered if they were an item, but decided probably not: more of an arts and crafts double act. William Morris would have had his hands full with this pair. To keep my end up, I pumped them on the other guests Colin had so thoughtfully invited. For instance, who were those two standing by the window? One was Steve, a lovely man (said with feeling). His studio was at the far end of the first floor; hand-crafted musical instruments, violins, violas, cellos. I'd probably heard the odd note. As for the other one, he was the famous Ceramick. He'd come up with the name because he threw pots and was Irish. Very witty, he thought, though for everyone else it soon wore thin.

And so it went on till Colin came over, at which point Antonia and Vicki started circulating – straight to the trestle table with the food and drink. He apologised for setting me up, but knew I wouldn't have come if I'd known. Then, to my dismay, he tapped his glass with a tuning fork (thanks for that one, Steve) and called for order, which eventually he got. As they all knew by now, I was the newest member here at the Collective and, as they probably also knew, a photographer to trade. He put 'photographer' in heavily inverted commas and was rewarded by a ripple of laughter. I couldn't believe it. What was he thinking about? We'd gone to great lengths to arrange my cover and here he was blowing it. He hoped we'd all get on famously and, given the artistic temperament, no doubt several of those present would end up in need of my therapeutic services. Despite the evidence before him right now, the bottle wasn't the answer to everything.

'Speak for yourself,' Ceramick shouted from the sidelines, swaying just a little in the breeze.

I ended up with Janice, whose ground floor studio housed, among other things, a couple of knitting machines. I asked the obligatory questions and learned how she made ends meet: garments of her own design run up by her and sold at craft fairs and other outlets, and by the sale of knitting patterns to magazines. So I would see her name in print if I looked in the right places? Unfortunately not. Comely Janice of the copper-red hair was a ghost-writer of patterns. Other women claimed the credit. This seemed patently unfair to me, but she shrugged it off. That was life at the commercial level, accept it or opt out. Oh, and about my sink.

Near my newly refurbished and beautifully tiled bathroom was a Belfast sink, together with a fridge, and a single kitchen unit with kettle, toaster and microwave. The bathroom was lovely, as was the studio, but these things stood out like a sore thumb, completely out of keeping with their new surroundings. The sink was only where it was because of the plumbing, surely I realised that? It had occurred to me before, but neither Colin nor the architect had been troubled by it, and the disruption of concealing my little kitchenette behind stud-partition walls was more than I could bear. I'd had enough of tradesmen for the time being. Janice heard me out and smiled. There was another solution: simpler, cheaper, and much more elegant. If I came down to her studio she'd show me what she meant.

2

The following day, Sunday, I regarded as a day of rest, though not for religious reasons since I am not that way inclined. They tell me there is Good News out there. I hold my hand to my ear. Either there is nothing to be heard or, as a helpful reverend once had it, I am tuned to the wrong wavelength. Since being tuned at all is an achievement, I'll go with the reverend.

For me, rest has never meant freedom from work, which I like and find relaxing. So after a late breakfast, I went back to the bedroom and attempted to sort my books. They were lying in no discernible order on the floor, on chairs, under the bed and on the window sill. I needed shelves or a bookcase, but space was limited. If my enterprise took off I'd move to a larger flat. In the unlikely event it took off big time I might consider buying one.

Because there are many approaches to psychotherapy, keeping books on the same technique together was the obvious way to go. But the real dilemma facing me was marketing, and I knew this book-sorting caper for what it was, a displacement activity allowing me to avoid the problem. The room might look a mess but I knew where everything was. I had a handle on my subject, yet no one out there knew it. Unless that changed, my book-learning wasn't worth a row of beans.

I stepped over some magazines (Psychology Today, Psychological Science), moved a pile of books off the chair and switched on my computer. I had drafted a leaflet promoting my services but was far from satisfied with the content. I knew that many in the field offered a first consultation free, giving each party an opportunity to assess the other before committing to a course of treatment. I had also noticed a growing tendency to offer a bulk discount – for example, ten sessions for the price of eight. I could see why the driving lesson approach might be attractive to the client but it seemed sharp practice to me. A client might pay for ten and need only six. But unless I went along with this trend, market forces would freeze me out. Money talks alright, but seldom makes much sense.

What troubled me most was the biography: how much personal background to include, how to list my qualifications and, most worrying of all, whether or not to add a mug shot. There are no photographs of me or anyone else in this house. When I bought it from the second-hand shop, my wardrobe had a mirror inside the door. Not a good idea. Some use alcohol, others drugs. I use sleep. It's simple, cheap and non-addictive. You go to bed, you sleep, and in so doing escape from yourself. However, when you can't go for a clean shirt of a morning without being surprised by your own image in the wardrobe door, it defeats the purpose. So I removed the mirror. But I couldn't do the same with the image in the leaflet: the therapist had to be there looking reliable, approachable, or both.

I added a short code of practice based on several, all much the same, which I found online, then revised my potted biography, giving less away and changing both the town where I grew up and the year I graduated, tips I had read to counter identity theft in the social media. Funny that. I had to suppress a smile. No one can steal what you don't have. As for the photograph, I scanned the shot on my driving licence and inserted a copy to fill the available space. A temporary measure, I knew it wouldn't do. I'd have one taken at The Warehouse - The Therapist in His Studio. But what, exactly, does a therapist look like? Artists have it easy, posing in front of an easel or whatever, draped in a smock, tools of their trade in hand, background busy with their work.

When the phone rang I was tempted to ignore it on what was, after all, a day of rest – rest for me meaning rest from other people. Colin wondered how I was shaping up after the events of yesterday. He hoped I didn't mind the speech. I'd never have got the photographer thing past them anyway, and in that place every rent counted. One empty studio was one too many and put them all at risk. They'd happily play along, partly for the fun of it but mostly out of self-interest. Though he was probably right, I saw no virtue in unnecessary risk. Some of them might have suspected, now they knew for sure. But the cat was out of the bag and couldn't be put back, so I reassured him, thanked him for his thoughtfulness, and hung up.

Twenty minutes later I heard the double honk of a car horn, the signal Colin had used since the Entryphone died. I went to the living room window and looked out: the usual cars parked nose to tail. Colin waved up, his working clothes replaced by a white linen jacket and chinos. I could only assume that, despite my best efforts, my tone had cast doubt on my meaning and Colin's accurate ears had picked it up. Added to which he was at a loose end.

I cleared some space on the kitchen table and made him a cup of tea, realising too late that he added sugar I'd forgotten to buy. He said he didn't mind, I was doing his teeth a favour, and we talked for a while about the eccentricities of Ceramick till he moved the conversation on to Janice. How had I found her?

'She found me.'

'Come on, Max, you know what I mean.'

I did. He was match-making. Being an easy-going person he wasn't putting much effort into it, but that's what he was doing.

'I liked her.'

'Good.'

When I mentioned the leaflet he asked to see it. Picking our way past obstacles on the floor, we went through to the bedroom. He was used to the mess and didn't comment on it. I parked him and his tea in front of the screen, went back to the kitchen and raided the biscuit tin. The least he could expect was a bourbon cream or a chocolate digestive. Given his artistic bent, I expected him to query the typeface or question the use of colour, but he surprised me.

'That's odd.'

'What?'

'There's something missing here.'

'Such as?'

'Contact details. Not much point advertising your services if no one can get in touch.'

This was so obvious I couldn't believe it hadn't occurred to me, so here already was the benefit of an innocent eye. But he had been through it himself and knew the score: two email addresses, one reserved for business, and an online presence, in my case based on the leaflet. Oh, and a second mobile phone. Apparently that was a must, but I didn't like the sound of it: a recipe for confusion.

'You don't have two.'

'I don't have the occasional fruitcake bending my ear for an hour.'

Neither did I, not yet. But he was right, it could easily happen. Then his own phone rang, his girlfriend wondering when he was coming over. I couldn't hear her end of the conversation, but his tone was affectionate. They plainly got on well. I'd learn more when I saw them together. I hadn't studied body language for nothing. As Colin was leaving he said I'd need fliers and should figure out where best to leave them when they were ready.

After he'd gone, I thought back to the party and my reaction to it. At the time I'd felt under attack, though I tried not to show it. An adverse reaction which confirmed my view of myself. I have never cared for the unexpected. As for groups and how they work, I already knew this was beyond me. Books have been written on the subject, but where does that get you if you don't have an instinct for it? All the books in the world won't give you that. A group of people in their place of work is hard enough to fathom, but those same people letting their hair down at a social gathering defies understanding.

I know there is a door and social skills are the key, but for someone like me, not fully socialised, the key won't turn in the lock. I hear the party-goers through the wall as they sit and talk, stand and talk, stand and talk and drink. I see them, as it were, on the other side and know that all is not as it seems. Through the dividing wall I hear them speak, make out the rise and fall of sentences and phrases, the cadence of their conversations, but the meaning eludes me. Language is a fluid medium, a stream with undercurrents opposing the surface flow. So yes, I usually know that something is going on, but nine times out of ten I don't know what it is.

When it comes to pleasure, though, these people don't fool me for a moment. Their laughter is too loud. They have to make sure we hear it. They have to make sure they hear it themselves. They are not only insecure but kidding themselves. The time they're having is not as good as they would have us believe. Why do they bother? What's the point? Yet knowing all this doesn't help much. Groups may leave a lot to be desired but the fact remains I am not at home in them. Given that man is a social animal, this is a major failing. There is an upside, however. Two people talking is something else again. If one of them is me I can cope with that, so my choice of profession makes perfect sense. It is the level at which I function best.

3

It was a lovely day. Sunlight came streaming in through the windows, both of which were open. Looking out I could see couples strolling along the riverbank, people walking dogs, and children exhibiting irrational behaviour ranging from chasing pigeons on the grass to kicking balls into the water and wailing as they floated off. The more I observed children the less I liked them, and very early in my brief career I added them to those with sexual problems as unsuitable cases to take on. Apart from anything else, the presence of a parent would have been required and for me, as I have explained, three is one too many.

My first consultation went much as expected. To protect their privacy, I have changed the names of my clients, so the middle-aged man I shall call Mr Brown came in and sat on the chair of his choice: on this occasion, the Jönköping. Since he hadn't shut it behind him, I closed the door and sat down near him: not so close as to be threatening, and definitely not behind my desk. The client should feel there is nothing between himself and the therapist, and certainly no barrier of any sort. I remember feeling a lot was at stake, and not just for him. If this first session went badly my confidence would take a knock and, just as damaging, word would get round. So I was as nervous as he was, though I did my best to conceal it.

According to my leaflet the first consultation was free, was that correct? Confirming this, I told Mr Brown that it would last half an hour and commit him to nothing.

'So,' I asked, almost hoping not to find out, 'what seems to be the problem?'

'It was different when I was young.'

No doubt, I thought, but who could not say the same?

'What was?'

'I used to dream.'

'I see.'

He used to dream a lot, in great detail and in glorious Technicolor. As recently as three years before he'd filled notebooks with his dreams, usually when he woke in the morning, but also when a dream was unusually vivid and woke him up in the small hours. He kept a notebook on his bedside table. He called it his dreambook.

'How can you tell,' I said, asking the obvious question, 'that you're not still dreaming as before but simply don't remember on waking?'

Since there was no way he could disprove this I thought he might show signs of doubt, but he didn't. Waking now, he assured me, wasn't the same as before. In the past when he woke, he felt at the end of an enriching experience, even if he couldn't remember what that experience had been. Now when he woke, everything was flat, stale and profitless. He opened a bleary eye on the world and wasn't impressed by the dawn. He woke up tired and listless. Before, when he used to dream, he would wake refreshed and leap out of bed with a spring in his step. Except when the dream was a nightmare, which happened very rarely. And, he added as a clincher, he had conducted an experiment.

Over a period of three weeks he had set his alarm for various times when dreaming could reasonably be expected: two, three, or four in the morning. When it went off he immediately interrogated himself, searching for vestiges of dream activity which were never to be found. How did I explain that, he asked, in a slightly triumphal tone? I was the therapist, the expert, and he'd backed me into a corner.

'I'm not saying I can explain it,' I admitted, 'but there are two possibilities at least. The first is that you're correct, you have no awareness of dreams because you haven't been dreaming.'

'And the other?'

I advanced an alternative view with some diffidence, thinking his explanation was probably correct. How often did a person set an alarm and wake up before it rang because the brain was on edge against the ring? The mere act of setting the alarm kept the person more wakeful than usual and so less likely to dream. I could tell he wasn't impressed.

'You don't seem to understand, Mr Frei. The colour's gone out of the world!'

He pointed to the lovely cyclamen in bloom on my desk, a gift from Janice.

'Flat as a pancake, doc,' he said, though he knew perfectly-well I wasn't a doctor and didn't claim to be. 'What do you suggest? What's the way ahead?'

For him it was unclear but for me it was obvious. I would give some thought to the matter and we would discuss a possible strategy at our next meeting. If I couldn't come up with one I'd let him know by text, in which case our first session would also be our last.

'By the way, Mr Brown, if you don't mind me asking - what's your occupation?'

'I'm an optometrist, though I don't see what that has to do with it.'

As he stood up to leave, his business over for the time being, he glanced round the studio, his gaze dwelling on the walls.

'Nice pictures.'

I had told no one, not even Colin, that my first appointment was that morning. The last thing I needed was a chorus of good wishes beforehand and a succession of post-mortems afterwards. Plainly, I had failed to conceal my moves. Mr Brown hadn't climbed a drainpipe and entered unseen by the window: he had driven into the courtyard, parked, and asked directions on the way in. From that point on, word had spread rapidly - though it needn't have bothered, since it had half an hour to do its work in a two-storey building full of ears. Shortly after my first client left, my first fellow tenant arrived. She was wondering how it had gone and I was wondering where Vicky was: I'd thought they were joined at the hip? Oh, she was hard at work, not to be disturbed. She had an order to complete by tomorrow.

Antonia Hamilton was a bottle-blond and proud of it, happy to let her roots show, which may have been a declaration of attitude but fell some way short of a Major Statement. She looked at me enquiringly, furrowing her brow. She smiled a lot too, so I could see those creases becoming established and the fair Antonia lining up the Botox at some point down the road. But maybe she didn't care, in which case she had my respect. The fight against the ravages of time is a losing battle. If you will insist on fighting, pick a fight you can win.

I was tempted to run the case past her. It even crossed my mind that Antonia might be a small part of the solution. If all colour really had gone out of Mr Brown's world, then some of her lovely glass artefacts designed to hang in windows would be an excellent antidote: coloured light streaming into his room whenever the sun was shining. She was particularly strong on flowers and garden birds, blue tits a speciality. But I told her, as I told everyone else who asked, that the session had been satisfactory, but what with client confidentiality and all that . . . She quite understood.

Next up was Ceramick, who hadn't the least interest in how the session had gone but had come up with a marketing masterstroke. (I should perhaps explain that Michael, despite his doubtful sense of humour, failed to conform to other stereotypes: he did not have red hair and didn't bang a bodhran in Biddy Mulligan's on folk nights.) From behind his back he produced with a flourish a dog-eared sketchpad and brandished it in front of me. I could almost hear the trumpets and drums. Prominent text at the top of the page posed a question. PROBLEM TO SOLVE? Below that was a picture of an exotic bird with a large beak. And below that again was the legend, ONE CAN'T BUT TOUCAN! Mick thought his idea as witty as it was relevant.

'The client can't solve it by himself, he needs your help!'

When the last visitor had gone I reviewed my notes. If Mr Brown was still dreaming but could no longer recall anything he dreamt, that would surely indicate a growing disassociation between his conscious and unconscious minds - which would give rise to stress, the more so the longer his condition persisted. But if Mr Brown was correct, the problem lay with the hippocampus, which was no longer reviewing the events of the day and processing them to memory. (I should say here that in order to make this account accessible I have kept jargon to a minimum, but there are no everyday terms for areas of the brain.)

Clearly, there was no point seeking a solution to both of these problems without knowing which needed to be solved and which did not. (Something stirred in my mind concerning an equation with two solutions only one of which applied in the real world, but I couldn't call to mind what it was.) First we had to know whether or not the client was still dreaming, and that could easily be achieved by hooking him to an EEG brainwave monitor. When we had readings from that, then could we consider how best to proceed.

I went over to the window, leant my elbows on the sill and looked out. The same play with a different cast. Life goes on and carries us with it to the sea. And it occurred to me then, when I was not consciously thinking of Mr Brown at all, that his profession might have a bearing on his condition, that spending all day in darkness with red and green lights might be good for his customers but not so good for him. When he fell asleep of a night, part of him was rebelling. It didn't want to see things any more. It needed a break.

When Colin got back from a meeting at the Printmakers Workshop he came straight up to see me with lunch in mind, wondering how it had gone. I told him as much as I reasonably could and watched as he picked up a crumpled flier from Mr Brown's chair.

'So it worked.'

'Yes.'

'Where did he pick it up?'

He couldn't believe I'd forgotten to ask. We needed to know which venues generated interest. Surely I could see that? I should have asked Mr Brown where he'd found the flier. Colin was an eminently practical man who, when perplexed, ran his hand through his generous head of brown hair as he was doing now. Yes, after the event, when I had begun to relax, I could see he was right. But I have yet to meet the person who functions at full capacity all the time. The best I could do was apologise and cover this angle in future.

4

The man from the council came sooner than I had expected and proved to be a woman. I didn't realise she was in the building till Janice ran upstairs to warn me. It wasn't obvious why she was coming at all, but there were regulations to do with proper use of space. What they were I didn't know and Janice, who was one hundred percent bona fide, hadn't bothered to find out since she had nothing to hide.

I heard a melody from the other end of the corridor which Steve (the lovely man) later told me had not been played by him, as I had supposed, but by Miss Craig trying out, at his invitation, one of his hand-crafted instruments. She had recently renewed her interest in the violin and he had hopes of a sale.

As I later discovered, Miss Craig was a woman of many parts, most of which moved. Steve, on the other hand, was a married man with three children at least, but Miss Craig spent quite some time with him anyway and I was left on tenterhooks for twenty minutes, which I put to use making as much as possible of the few photographic objects I had – leaning my portfolio against the desk, fighting my second-hand tripod into an upright position, and hauling out the battered guillotine which Colin had given me when he bought a new one.

I had a craft knife in the top desk drawer and brought it out for added effect, but seeing it lying there was strangely unsettling. What, I wondered, if a client who turned out to be psychotic got his hands on it and slit his wrists or slashed my throat? Unbidden thoughts like these may take unexpected turns. This one led to a greater appreciation of the sanded floor, now varnished: much easier to clean than blood-soaked carpet.

When Miss Craig finally arrived she was less officious than I expected and lacked a clipboard. Either she was reasonable by nature or she was softening me up. She flashed her ID: Lyndsay M Craig, Administrative Officer. The photograph showed a serious young woman with shoulder-length auburn hair.

'Good to meet you, Mr Frei. This may be an official visit but I want you to know that I'm here to help not, as some people seem to think, to cause trouble.'

'I'm sure no one thinks that,' I said, hoping to keep her sweet.

'You'd be surprised.'

I later found out that Ceramick had called her a nit-picking pip-squeak, a pen pusher and a jumped-up jobsworth when she pointed out that the trailing four-gang cables he tripped over every day were a safety hazard.

She walked slowly round the studio taking everything in and coming to a halt in front of Colin's prints.

'Colin Kirkpatrick?'

'On loan.'

'A very distinctive style.'

I was thinking the same of Miss Craig, who was wearing a white panelled shirt with large collar, open at the neck. She was wearing other things as well, of course – jacket, skirt, and boots perhaps on their first autumn outing – but the blouse took my eye. And the skin, which was lightly tanned, either from the sun or a lotion. She seemed the outdoor type.

Miss Craig had a theory. According to her, an artist was more likely to be popular if his style was easily recognised. The act of recognition gave an extra element of pleasure, a warm feeling of expertise however superficial it might be. It sounded plausible to me, but I must have taken too long to respond.

'You don't agree?'

'I'm a slow thinker. Takes me a while to get there.'

'But you do in the end,' she said, with a disarming smile.

'I like to think so.'

As she moved on, the heels of her boots clicked on the floor, the sound amplified a little as it bounced off the walls and ceiling. Too many hard surfaces, too little in the way of curtains (none) and cushions (two). She cast her eye over a series of landscapes, officially mine, of the Ardnamurchan Peninsula. I'd never been there, but I'd done some reading against just such an event, so I was ready to hold my own in a question and answer session. One picture in particular she lingered over so long I began to think she had taken it herself. But it was the scene she recognised, not the photograph.

'Am I right in thinking that's Loch Sunart?'

I was sure I remembered the name, so I took a risk and agreed that it was. For what is a loch but a body of water and anyone could make a mistake.

'I take it you use a DSLR?'

If I said 'no', she'd ask what sort of camera I used instead. If I said 'yes' she'd no doubt ask me which one, so I was trapped either way. For her, this visit was an escape from the office, a sightseeing trip taking in the sights and sounds – photographs, cameras, violins.

'It's the only choice really. I'd be happy to let you see it if I hadn't left it at home.'

To my dismay, she removed a smart-phone from her jacket pocket and starting taking pictures.

'Hope you don't mind. So many studios, so much to remember.'

She assured me that they were aide memoires for her use only: none would make it into the public domain via the social media or by any other route.

'Might save me coming back and annoying you all again.'

By this time she had reached the desk and something on it attracted her attention.

'So where are you off to next?'

I hadn't a ready answer for that and heard myself mentioning Orkney and Shetland if the budget stretched to it.

'You realise smoking isn't allowed in this building.'

She was right, it wasn't, which explained the large numbers of cigarette ends in the courtyard.

'I've never smoked in my life.'

'It's just,' she said, pointing to my desk, 'that you have an ashtray. I couldn't help wondering why.'

The studio-warming party had brought with it several small gifts, one of which was an ashtray lovingly hand-crafted by Ceramick. It was a highly glazed affair with splashes of primary colour, but his line in ashtrays had bombed when the smoking ban came in, so offloading them as gifts was a smart move on his part. Hearing this explanation, Miss Craig's expression softened considerably. It was then she told me about her run-in with Mick, including the names he had called her. Though she was trying to be dispassionate I could tell she was upset. And now, thanks to

Mick, we had something in common: we were on one side and he was on the other, which made me feel a little safer. If I'd had alcohol on the premises I'd have offered her some.

Mindful of her weight, which didn't look too bad to me, she declined the offer of biscuits but accepted a camomile tea. She was surprised I had such a thing, and I could hardly explain that its relaxing properties had an obvious use in calming an agitated client. (I am not endorsing this use of the product, having no empirical evidence that it works as advertised, but there's no harm in hoping.) When we retired to our respective chairs sipping the healthful brew, she hit me with another of her theories, namely, that the rapid advance in mobile phone technology would soon make the dedicated camera redundant. I knew what she was doing. The woman was noising me up: depriving me of my trade and my income at one fell stroke. When her prediction came to pass, how would I pay the rent then?

To her way of thinking, it wouldn't be long before everyone would be a landscape photographer: all they would need was a jacket with a phone-sized pocket and the latest high-tech mobile device inside it. I knew even less about mobile phones than I did about cameras, but it seemed unlikely to me.

'But surely, Miss Craig . . .'

'Lyndsay, please.'

A lens of any quality needed physical depth, exactly what a smart-phone couldn't have. If that wasn't a limitation I didn't know what was. But before I was able to articulate this point, inching as I was with crab-like motion towards it, she hit me with something else.

'And if you're out and about hiking or hill-walking, and you happen to get lost, your phone's GPS will fix your location to within two metres or so! Also,' she added, tightening the screw, 'let's not forget that mobiles have maps. No more stopping your soggy ordnance survey taking off in a high wind.'

It crossed my mind, listening to all this, that digital cameras might have GPS too. But because I didn't know for sure and couldn't afford to be caught out, it was an argument I couldn't use. I have seldom felt so frustrated, yet what was I doing defending an occupation I professed but didn't follow? Strange that it provoked such strong feelings. I knew then that I had to get to grips with the subject. Putting it off any longer wasn't an option.

Time to Talk

For my own protection, if nothing else, I had to study photography in much the same way as I had studied psychology, but compressing the time taken from years to a couple of months. A camera, no matter how advanced, cannot compare with the complexities of the human brain which created it.

Meanwhile Miss Craig was flitting effortlessly in the meadow of thought, alighting on one flower for a second, on the next for ten and constantly changing direction without apparent reason. As with the butterfly there is always a reason, of course, though we have no way of knowing what it is. But ever since she had touched on photography and mobile phones I was finding it difficult to keep up with her, and was relieved to hear loud noises on the stairs, which continued along the corridor till they reached my door. Two men had arrived with a Chinese screen. Instead of a utilitarian solution to my kitchen problem, Janice had proposed something more attractive which would, as she put it, add to the ambience – and for my own benefit rather than the owners', since I could take it with me if and when I moved on.

We had spent a day touring auction houses, all of which I found intimidating. The art of valuation was beyond me but, worse than that, I felt I was drowning in a sea of objects: tables, chairs, mirrors, clocks, paintings, prints, fireplaces, fenders, and even a piano or two. As for the smaller items, the jars, vases, decorative figures, knick-knacks and so on, there seemed to be no end of them. Were human beings really so insecure that they needed to surround themselves with such things? And who dusted them? Not me. Life was too short.

As the day wore on I became increasingly fatigued, and only several rests in watering holes and the quiet determination of Janice kept me going. It was late afternoon when we finally tracked down a selection of screens which would be auctioned off the following week. One was a small table screen and so of no interest, which left two. I was instantly taken with the black lacquered one with assorted Chinese figures, as always accompanied by calligraphy. According to the catalogue, the screen concerned events by the river during the Qingming Festival, when Chinese people bearing doomed roosters visited the graves of their ancestors. The catalogue also listed a reserve price in the cardiac arrest range. The remaining item, now being delivered, was a six-section rosewood screen with rice paper panels showing a branch of cherry blossom, once across the first three panels, again across the second.

The experience was nerve-wracking at the time, but looking back on it the auctioneer, complete with bow tie, played into our hands by setting a ridiculously high opening price. He was soon obliged to drop to his reserve and was only able to increase it by small increments. He kept glancing at the man behind the laptop (internet bids) and the lady on the phone (telephone bids) but to our relief there were no takers in either of these directions. So in shelling out just shy of £240 we felt we had done well.

'My goodness, what have we here?'

I explained to Lyndsay what the intended purpose was as the men carefully stood the screen in the middle of the floor, ensured it was stable, and produced a document for me to sign. I put my copy in the top drawer of the desk and placed the craft knife on top of it. Presumably it had been noticed and done its work.

Lyndsay leapt to her feet. 'Want a hand with that?'

Together we moved it to the kitchen area and arranged it three times before she was satisfied. It should make a good impression when people came in, she said, screen off the offending area but also allow ease of access for the user. I had to assume that in its final position it met all known official requirements.

We had just finished when Janice arrived looking slightly flushed.

'I saw the van leaving. How does it look?'

She walked up to the screen and inspected it for possible transit damage, then stood back and surveyed it from several angles.

'Well I must say I think you've made the right choice, Max.'

'Thanks to you.'

She still looked slightly flustered, perhaps because another woman had got there first and muscled in on her project. And then it occurred to me that Janice might regard Miss Craig as competition on the more personal level. It had never crossed my mind that she might have me in her sights, and even now it seemed improbable. I was plain as they come, while she was accomplished and attractive. But the fact remained I had no interest in her body, which put her in a large group, since I had no interest in anyone else's either. And for me that came close to guaranteed peace of mind, something I have always valued highly.

5

Three weeks after Lyndsay Craig's visit, Colin appeared in the studio managing to smile and look worried at the same time. The feeling in the Collective was that while they were happy with my presence they thought it wouldn't last much longer unless I brought in more punters (their word, not mine). It is amazing how artists, apparently hard at work, notice visitors passing their open studio doors or, in my case, hardly ever passing them at all. Even the quietly-spoken gentleman in the neighbouring studio had been asking questions. Albert was an older man who made toys out of wood and painted them himself. Many of them moved, and not always on wheels. The wings of his brightly coloured birds flapped up and down by means of weights and pulleys.

We agreed that something had to be done or, more accurately, I agreed with Colin. Although the problem was less easily solved, it had to be tackled as actively as the camera question had been. I was slowly coming to realise that Colin was as much an unpaid arts administrator as an artist in his own right, and it was on the way to a meeting with fellow printmakers that he passed one of the several shops which had sprung up in the city since the hard times began in 2008. Apart from prominent offers of payday loans (not a useful service to those of us who never have a payday) they specialised in all things technical: watches, mobile phones, exercise gear, golf clubs, sound equipment, musical instruments and cameras. They were fast becoming the Aladdin's Caves of the times.

The cameras were second-hand. More often than not, the owner was short of cash, went to the nearest branch of the Cash Machine and sold – though not before checking the market value of his camera on Ebay to ensure he wasn't being ripped off. At the other end of the spectrum was another type of person altogether, the man (and it was always a man) who had to have the latest gear, had the money to pay for it and, as part of the process, wanted to off-load his existing equipment which he now considered obsolete.

As far as I could see, some of these men would have made ideal clients, having swallowed whole the concept of 'trading up' to the point where they were selling ex-cellent equipment at a loss, despite the fact that it already met all their requirements and more. There was status involved in this, and also a fear of being left behind. It didn't occur to them for a moment that being left behind might come as a welcome relief.

When we went back the next day to buy the DSLR Colin had put through its paces and reserved in my name for twenty-four hours, I overheard one of these men running strings of make and model numbers past a bemused assistant. He knew so much he didn't know anything at all. There was a horizon, but he never looked into the distance far enough to see it. That was his problem. Mine was to generate more interest or, as Colin would have it, to put myself about more. According to him, most of the interest I had generated so far had come from an outlet which promoted alternative remedies. His proposal, to which I naturally agreed – especially since it included pubs and restaurants as well as shops – was that we take a day to tour such places, pin promotional material to their notice-boards and leave fliers. I remember he was unusually direct.

'You've got to understand, Max, there are plenty of people out there with problems but nearly as many offering solutions. You don't have the field to yourself. This is a competition, and from where I'm standing you're not winning.'

Despite a definite nip in the air it was a pleasant day. We started out in the Grassmarket, browsed in Helios Fountain, moved on to The Lot, and made our way past the shops, pubs and restaurants on the north side of the street leaving fliers in several. Having laboured up West Bow and Victoria Street to the top of the hill, we turned onto George IV Bridge and made for the Central Library. If my forward planning had been better I could have borrowed a book or two on photography, but my card had expired. I had no idea then how important this building would turn out to be, that Faith Gordon worked there, or that she would figure so large in my life. It's even possible I caught a glimpse of her in the corridor or behind a counter, or that she caught a glimpse of me.

Displaying a flier in the library wasn't as simple as we had hoped. They had a suitable notice board, but staff approval was required before anything could be added to it. So we handed it to an assistant and left for a refreshment break in The Elephant House. I noticed some papers on the window ledge and borrowed one to relax with as I ate my quiche and savoury rice, but much good it did me. I had just made it to page two when Colin returned to the attack, taking out the notebook he kept in his leather shoulder bag, a most impressive affair he had no doubt acquired when he swung by the Venice Biennale, the Rangoon Printmakers Expo or the Bonnyrig Market.

It was then I noticed, for the first time, that the end of his nose was a little bulbous and I was seized by a childish desire to squeeze it between thumb and forefinger. In my mind's ear I heard the gratifying sound of the klaxon on a vintage car or a U-Boat preparing to dive. I believe that at one level this embodied a reaction to the word 'hooter', but in the main it was an irrational response to Colin's attempts to help which, being overly vigorous, I experienced as harassment.

'I don't know if you've noticed, but it's mad out there. Absolutely mad!'

This was reassuring. 'Plenty of work for me, then.'

But Colin was streets ahead of me. Not only had he deposited fliers, he'd collected them as well from the many examples we had come across in our tour of the morning's venues. He spread them out on the table and drew up a list.

'Right, I'm not saying this is all of it by any means, but it's a start: aromatherapy, reflexology, Butekyo, cranio-sacral therapy, holographic repatterning – whatever the hell that is – Indian head massage, manual lymph drainage, polarity therapy, Thai foot massage, zero balancing, thought field therapy, neuro-linguistic programming, kanpo, copper bracelets, magnetic wrist straps, crystals, shiatsu, and wait for it – yes – Hopi ear candles!'

'Good God!'

'That's just a little of what you're up against, Max, and we haven't even made it to the herbalist yet.' Napiers was next on our list. 'Have you any idea how many remedies are available by mouth?' I hadn't, but pointed out that most of them would be for physical conditions, alternative remedies to those recommended by the medical profession.

'Most but not all. Take St Johns Wort.'

Having enough problems as it was, I decided not to.

Perhaps the most methodical print-maker in the city, Colin began quizzing me on my client list, which was far too short. I had advised Mr Brown that there wasn't much I could do for him since there was no known cure for a failure to dream, but he insisted on further sessions. He wanted me to review the literature with him, which was fair enough, but by the third session he was showing an unwelcome interest in drugs. With the right chemical stimulus, he believed he might kick-start his stalled subconscious. He mentioned LSD and mescaline both of which, it is true, have mind-altering effects. I had two problems with this: I had no access to either of these substances and they led to hallucinations rather than dreams. Surely Mr Brown didn't want to dream while awake? In any case, the dangers of both were so well documented that it would have been foolish to consider them.

The only thing for it, I felt, was to set him off down a different track. There was another possibility, I suggested: the Edinburgh Sleep Centre. If Mr Brown explained his problem to them they might agree to monitor his brainwave patterns as he slept and establish with certainty whether or not he still dreamt. For all I knew their research had advanced to the point where they could stimulate dreaming. (I thought this highly unlikely but not impossible.) I didn't have to sell this idea very hard. From where he was sitting, the mere existence of a Sleep Centre was the answer to his prayers, so I wrote a letter for him in which I outlined his plight and expressed the hope they might be able to help.

I was short of money at the time and Mr Brown was the first of my clients to offer to pay by credit card. I remember staring at blankly at it, knowing very well that some people used them for every transaction, large and small. Since I had no way of dealing with it I had to let him leave with the promise of cash to come. Since then I have always explained to clients at the outset that I can only accept payment by cash or by cheque, at which point some clearly assume I am secreting large sums in the Cayman Islands. The truth is less colourful. I have always completed my tax return accurately and on time, and in the current proceedings against me there is no suggestion whatsoever of financial impropriety on my part.

Time to Talk

So much for Mr Brown. I had also been retained by Mrs Blake, a young lady who consulted me not on her own account but on her husband's. He was spending so much of the family income on books that she had trouble making ends meet. If her attire was anything to go by they hadn't much left for clothes so I could see she had a problem, but surely this was one for Citizens Advice? Anyone less suited than me as a debt counsellor would be hard to imagine. In any case, her husband wasn't present. His side of the story might be different, I couldn't afford to assume that hers was accurate or complete. But I was inclined to believe her when she revealed that her husband was a sociologist and the books in question were academic textbooks which could usually be found in the university or departmental libraries. Yet he had to have them round him – an interesting expression. She made his many volumes sound like blocks of stone in a castle wall. And I wouldn't believe how many titles he had or how expensive they were. What finally persuaded me of her case was the fact that some were in foreign languages with which he had little or no acquaintance.

When Mr Blake himself turned up, this was my starting point. Why did he buy books he couldn't read? Well, he told me with a defeated gesture, he was taking an evening class in Finnish and, in the meantime, selecting passages and typing them into Google Translate. The whole thing was ludicrous. Since he couldn't understand the original he couldn't possibly know which were the passages he might find significant: he was selecting paragraphs at random and living in hope. At this first meeting, with Mrs Blake awaiting the outcome on a bench in the courtyard, I made the mistake of going into the technicalities. Had he foreign language symbols on his keyboard? How did he cope with Cyrillic, Chinese and so on? I then felt a bottomless pit opening up when it transpired, against all expectation, that he had answers to these questions to which I was obliged to listen. I have never come closer to terminal tedium. But he was on my books and paying, though the couple could ill afford it.

I had also had an enquiry from a jobbing gardener (have trowel, will travel) whom I expected to sign up the following week, but as I was explaining this to Colin I saw his attention was elsewhere. A young woman had just arrived in search of a table and I have never seen a waist so narrow. Since I didn't attempt it I can't be sure, but I think I could have encircled it completely with my hands, which are not unduly large. She may have been slim to start with, but this extreme effect was achieved by what looked to me like a lace-up corset, which she made no attempt to hide, pulled painfully tight.

'I knew her at art school. She was going that way then.'

Thanks to Annie, Colin knew about steel bone corsets.

'I didn't think it would come to this,' he said, shaking his head. 'She's had her lower ribs removed!'

If Colin was correct, and it seemed he was, Annie, not content with drawing and painting, was moulding her own body into an art-work. Why she would want to do that I couldn't imagine, and none of my reading to date has offered so much as a clue.

6

The following days were a relief after the hectic activity of the week before. Colin was hard at work preparing for an exhibition at the City Art Centre, though Janice dropped by from time to time to see how I was doing, sometimes bearing gifts from the baker.

Autumn was well under way by then, the leaves were changing and any landscape photographer worthy of the name would have been out there. I already owned a small pocket camera, but though I used it I hated holding it a foot in front of my face, and the on-screen menus were so complicated I gave up on them entirely. All I did was point and shoot and, needless to say, the hoped-for opportunity to strike it rich never arose: no action shots of a heist as it happened in the city centre, no revealing images of the latest celebrity spilling out of her dress as her dogs wrapped their leads round her ankles.

So out I went with my DSLR round my neck and tried my hand again, this time with the luxury of a genuine viewfinder. At first I wandered along the Esk, took some pictures of the river, and attempted one or two of ducks and swans. But I noticed a tendency towards stock images – the river flowing on under a bridge, part of which framed the shot, the branch of a tree serving the same purpose. Not original, then, but my aim was competence, nothing more. When I got to know my new DSLR, creativity would follow. (I was fooling myself, but knew that at the time.)

As my walk took me closer to the High Street the noise of traffic grew, and with it the number of people appearing in the frame despite my best efforts. You can only get close to nature by steering clear of people, so I gave up on the attempt for the time being, slung the camera over my shoulder and strolled along Bridge Street to the theatre. Pictures of the current show in the foyer were good enough to put my gas even farther on the peep – well composed, well lit, punchy contrast – so I went on to the Bistro for a coffee with a feeling of relief.

When the phone rang I reached for the wrong one. Colin's notion of having two was all very well, but neither rang so often

I could yet tell their ringtones apart, and even then I seldom knew which was where. On this occasion it was the antiquated flip phone I used for personal calls, but by the time I found it Colin had given up and left a message. Where was I? Someone had arrived on spec in the hope of consulting me: could I get back quickly? I returned his call, left my coffee half drunk and started back in what, for me, passed as a jog.

I have always assumed that men and women are unlikely to differ much when it comes to mental health but also that women, being more given to talk and less likely to pretend everything is alright, would seek help more readily. So I was surprised to find yet another man waiting in the studio. This one was above average height and wearing khaki dungarees with many pockets. He strode towards me, hand outstretched.

'Mr Robertson, I phoned you last week. You do remember?'

'Very clearly.'

He hoped I didn't mind him dropping by; he'd been working in the area.

I assured him I didn't, wondering how to protect my new chairs from attack by dirty overalls without seeming rude.

'Please take a seat,' I said, seeing no way out.

But, as so often happens, the client solved the problem for himself, taking a folded newspaper from a back pocket and spreading it on the Umeå.

'Don't want to ruin your upholstery, do we. Enough trouble in the world as it is.'

Mr Robertson was a gardener who enjoyed his work but was increasingly beset by problems of a doctrinal nature and hoped that I could help. This seemed unlikely to me, innocent of doctrine as I was, but a preliminary chat would soon make that clear and he would depart in peace, never to return.

'Do you mind if I record our conversation?' I asked, indicating the mini voice recorder I'd picked up in the Cash Machine when Colin wasn't looking, 'my memory isn't all it might be.'

He nodded, though I wasn't convinced he'd taken the question in.

'You have to understand,' he said, becoming more agitated, 'that from my perspective God created all living things.'

I smiled reassuringly. 'A commonly held view.'

'So you can see I might have a problem when someone tells me to remove all the weeds from a flowerbed.'

'Not at first blush, no.'

I was tempted to remind him he was a gardener, but he knew that already.

'Come now, Dr Frei, it must be blindingly obvious to a man with your qualifications. If God created all living things then God created weeds.' I was about to remind him that I wasn't a doctor but didn't have the chance. 'In fact, I have some trouble with the very idea. When you come to think of it, a weed must be an inferior type of plant. Troublesome. To be entirely removed.'

'I see what you mean.'

'Which clearly implies or suggests that God created inferior plants. Now He wouldn't do that, would He? Nothing He created would ever be inferior. That must be true in the nature of things, don't you think?'

Looking at Mr Robertson – tall, angular, weather-beaten and balding – I saw reason to doubt it. But he appeared to have swallowed whole the ontological argument for the existence of God, the starting point of which was perfection. Plainly Mr Robertson could conceive nothing greater. Faced with this philosophy, which cannot be argued with on its own terms, I was at loss how to proceed and fell back on the tried and tested device of asking a question. Unfortunately, I asked the wrong one.

'Is there nothing in the Bible which sheds light on this point?'

'A very good question, Dr Frei. In this case the answer is yes.'

He proceeded to recount the parable of the wheat and the tares, quoting directly from the Gospel of Matthew, which he knew by heart from the King James version.

'So you see, Dr Frei, when Jesus refers to good seed he's really talking about men. That's what makes it a parable, after all. And,' he added, pointing at me with a long and bony index finger, 'you'll have noticed that when the servants offer to pull the weeds up Jesus doesn't say go right ahead chaps, haul them out, like we gardeners are always expected to do. In fact, he tells them not to!'

When I later checked the Gospel for myself I found this was true, but only until the harvest, when the weeds would be gathered and burned. As many disputatious people did, Mr Robertson quoted the verses that suited his purpose best. And then an odd thing happened. I'd forgotten ever having seen it but, thanks to Mr Robertson, a painting came into my mind, a small oil on canvas entitled Still Life With Bible and Scissors. I had wondered about the scissors at the time, but now it all became clear. The owner of these items, possibly the artist himself, used the scissors to excise from the Good Book those passages with which he disagreed. Or if that wasn't it, then he excised passages particularly to his liking. Despite what young people think, the days of cut and paste long pre-date the computer, as did the wonderful Cow Gum, now departed the scene.

'And that's not my only problem, Dr Frei.'

He was increasingly concerned with the idea of vermin, which he also felt to be totally at odds with a beneficent creator.

'It's as clear as the nose on your face that God wouldn't create such a thing. But we've already agreed that God created everything,' I didn't remember agreeing to that, 'so God created rabbits, rats, and crows, therefore they can't be vermin. And another thing: how can pigs be unclean when God created them? Are we really to believe His creation is unclean? I don't think so.'

I knew I was onto a loser here, and resisted the temptation to hit him with deadly bacteria, lethal viruses, mosquitoes, scorpions, poisonous snakes, deadly spiders, tape worms and the whole panoply of parasites which prey on well nigh every living thing. Had God created them too and, if so, why?

The flow of words stopped for a moment, some of his internal pressure being relieved, but I noticed him rubbing his hands together as if he were cold. Which made me realise that as the heat I'd worked up from my rapid return wore off, I was feeling it too. The studio had several 13 amp sockets but no heating. Since it was then mid October I made a mental note, as a matter of urgency, to buy a couple of heaters, and not of the fan type which would create a noise problem for my clients and myself. But my only recourse right now was to offer him a hot cup of tea or coffee, which he gladly accepted. He'd left his flask in the van.

He joined me in my little kitchen, which I didn't mind at all since he was a working man and knew where the things we take for granted really come from. And when we sat down again to resume our discussion, mugs warming our hands, he moved the conversation to another bone of contention.

'I've asked several of them, you know, and none of them could tell me.'

'Perhaps you could give me an example.'

'Well, there's my dog, for a start. I asked the minister if Glen would go to heaven when he died and he couldn't tell me. According to him, scripture isn't clear on that point. So I began to wonder what heaven is really like. I mean, Dr Frei, can you imagine being trapped for all eternity in a place with no animals and plants, no wind in your face, no rivers and seas?'

I could, and I didn't like it one bit. (Not much scope there for a landscape photographer!) And I could see very easily why an outdoor person such as Mr Robertson would be troubled by the prospect.

'I even asked a professor of practical theology and he couldn't tell me either.'

'Not so practical, then.'

I made myself a light lunch from the fridge and sat down at the desk to write up notes on my clients. I found transcribing from recordings of what had been said, even selectively, a laborious business and was soon entertaining fantasies of a computer programme which would do it for me. I was still working on the Robertson transcript when Janice knocked and entered. If Colin was one wing, Janice was the other, and I was taken under both. She sat down in silence till I finished the section I was working on.

'How did it go?'

'Fine.'

'You realise you'll need a filing cabinet.'

'I don't have that many clients.'

'It isn't a question of numbers. These sessions are confidential, right? That's what you tell the clients. So you can't just leave your notes lying about where anyone can see them.'

She was correct, but I hadn't seen any filing cabinets, lockable or otherwise, in the Cash Machine so where would I get one cheap? Until I acquired a cabinet of my own Janice offered me a drawer in hers. My confidential files could share a space with her latest patterns, still under wraps.

Late that afternoon, when I'd finished updating my diary, my mind returned to Mr Robertson. Before he left, he'd wandered round the studio looking at the photographs.

'You don't need to go far to get good pictures round here.'

He recommended Lord Ancrum's Wood at Newbattle Abbey: full of seasonal wildflowers and lovely willow trees. It suddenly occurred to me how strange it was that Mr Robertson, a gardener, a man who had praised the wild flowers in a local wood, should have twice passed by my rosewood screen and not been struck by its vivid representation of cherry blossom. I was reminded of Thomas, my cat now passed away, who took no interest in the moving image of a bird even as it whistled and sang on television. Both for Mr Robertson and Thomas, only the real thing would do. How would one construct a heaven for creatures such as that?

7

The select few invited to private views take some trouble with their appearance. Colin's show at the Art Centre was no different. There were the inevitable arty types, understandable given the nature of the event, and for the most part the men were well turned out though, unlike like male birds, less colourful than their female counterparts. A few were sporting cravats, one or two had large handkerchiefs spilling out of their top pockets and there was, I think, a greater percentage than usual of eye-catching waistcoats – coloured satin, tweed, suede.

Despite these efforts, the females outdid the males on every front: colour, range of styles, adornments depending from earlobes, resting on necks, clinging to wrists. The fact that, unusually in our species, display is concentrated in the female sex was most evident in the use of cosmetics. How could these ladies improve on nature? If they failed, it wasn't for want of trying, though with some the application of war paint had become a habit which had overtaken vanity: they felt uncomfortable leaving home without it, just as we would all feel uncomfortable leaving home with no clothes on. And there were always a few who dispensed with the stuff entirely, saving themselves at one fell swoop a great deal of money and, over a lifetime, many months – perhaps even years – wasted in front of the mirror. According to Ceramick, most of this group were lesbian, but I didn't believe it then and don't believe it now.

I attended Colin's private view because he'd invited me and because no one was more deserving of support. My wardrobe, minus mirror, gave me little choice of clothing: either the suit I kept for meetings and other formal occasions, very seldom worn, or a jacket and slacks. My guiding principle being to attract as little attention as possible, all the items available to me were neat, plain and dull. With any luck, voluble arty types would get the message and steer clear, but that was not how it worked out.

The Collective was there in its entirety. Since I was one of them, they included me in everything they did: selecting food from the buffet, looking at the prints on display, appraising their arrangement on the walls, discussing Colin's pricing, wondering how many he would sell and even, on occasion, discussing the quality of the work. But many other guests already knew one or more of the Collective, they moved in art circles too, so sometimes I found myself included on the periphery of an even larger group. And the more they used them, words which once had meanings dissolved into a stream of noise. I envied Albert, who could turn his hearing aid off and nod agreeably if anyone spoke.

I saw things, though: the forming and re-forming of groups of guests; the people who returned to the buffet too often for their own good; Antonia and Vicky moving as one and charming everyone they met; Ceramick keeping the troops entertained and laughing at his own jokes; and the red head of Janice doing the rounds. At one point I noticed her circulating on the ground floor from my vantage point on the first floor gallery. As far as I could see, she favoured some more than others, and one in particular.

I had offered to drive Colin to the gallery and take him home afterwards. I knew perfectly well that drink lubricated the social wheels, and knowing I was driving left Colin free to keep his glass topped up till the last guest left. But the last guests left somewhat later than the gallery staff would have liked, and even then groups of them gathered on the pavement outside as if what they had to say wouldn't keep. A few wanted to move on to other venues, though thankfully Colin did not. But by the time I got him back to his first floor flat in Bath Street, he had set his mind on coffee and didn't want it alone.

He had plenty of work on his walls, mostly gifts from fellow artists. His own was nowhere to be seen. On various flat surfaces, including the top of his upright piano, were photographs of family and friends. He talked non-stop, both when he was making the coffee and when we went through with it to the living room. He thought it had gone very well. He was fortunate to have a show at the Art Centre, though it was modest as exhibitions went. He'd never had made it at the gallery across the road, which went in for the challenging, the cutting edge, the ground-breaking. I detected a rare note of self doubt and assured him that whether or not his

Time to Talk

work was challenging (whatever that meant) it was aesthetically pleasing, no easy feat to bring off. There was an almost infinite variety in plants, in their structures, shapes and colours, to say nothing of their botanical complexities. And it wasn't as if his prints were straight representations.

'Do you ever play that thing?'

'It's out of tune.'

Antonia and Vicky had been unusually lively, didn't I think? They'd moved on to a club, though where they got the energy he didn't know. Neither did I. Ceramick had been on good form too. Some of his jokes had gone down well: a testament to the relaxing effect of alcohol. He had been one of the waistcoat brigade, though having slicked back his hair with an oil of some sort he called to mind a snooker player on a bad day. But the major talking point had been Janice, who'd turned up with a boyfriend no one knew she had. Bernard Henderson worked for Creative Scotland if, as she said herself, you could call that work. She'd kept him under wraps for his own protection, fearing some of her colleagues might pin him to the wall on the sensitive subject of grants. Did he, perhaps, have some influence in that direction?

As Colin explained all this I couldn't help thinking, rather ruefully, how foolish I'd been to believe that Janice had any interest in me. Why would she? I couldn't think of a reason and now, it turned out, neither could she. And then it occurred to me that what was interesting in all this was the subject that hadn't come up, Colin's girlfriend. Where was she? Why hadn't she been there?

I looked across at one of the photographs, Colin and a girl, smiling for the camera, arms wrapped round each other. He noticed.

'We're going through a bad patch right now.'

'I'm sorry to hear that.'

'She's a chartered accountant.'

I had no way of knowing the relevance of this. It was a fact, but it is also a fact that there were twelve inches in a foot, so I did what anyone would do, encouraged him to talk without saying much myself. I learned that she did his books which, for an artist, were in unusually good order. However, it also seemed that Catherine was interested in breeding and specifically, breeding with Colin. There was some question of a biological clock, the lady having fears of an early menopause. Colin was in hand-wringing mode. He was sympathetic to her plight, which he knew was entirely genuine. But he did not want children, who would take up too much of his time, energy and mental space. Before he knew it they'd be rampaging round his studio, getting their little fingers into everything and making meaningful work impossible.

They had discussed all this in a civilised manner but reached an impasse, for the obvious reason that though they, as individuals, were compatible, their objectives were not. If Colin kept saying no, the opportunity might pass Catherine by. The only solution for her was waving goodbye to Colin, thus ending a six-year relationship, and signing up someone else who would meet her requirements. Breaking up with Colin, though wasteful and upsetting, was the easier part, since there was no guarantee that a suitable replacement could be found. In that event she would lose everything. It wasn't as if she was taking a faulty garment back to the shop and leaving with a replacement. For one thing, as she said herself, they always asked for a receipt and she didn't have one for Colin. (I took this to be an example of accounting humour at work.)

I finally left in the small hours. Colin felt better, but only because he'd got things off his chest. Nothing had changed. The situation was every bit as difficult as it had been before he opened his mouth. So, sadly, we had achieved nothing. I went to bed late but rose at the usual hour, though with an unaccustomed feeling of emotional exhaustion. And it was on this very morning that I received an email concerning my flier from Faith Gordon, an assistant librarian at the Central Library. She expressed an interest but needed more information and hoped to meet at my convenience (not an expression I like). This was too much effort by far to expend on a single document: I couldn't imagine what I could possibly add. Had there been anything else on my agenda, however small, I wouldn't have gone. As it was, we arranged to meet that afternoon.

She was in the Scottish Library when I arrived. Leading me to a vacant desk, she removed my flier from a folder and laid it down.

'You probably saw the notice board when you came in.'

I had passed it, yes, and very busy it was.

'Most of the fliers we accept are from official bodies or community groups. We can take personal fliers like yours, but there are so many people out there we could double the size of the board and still not cope. And really, it's the law of diminishing returns. The larger the board, the more each notice gets lost in the crowd.'

'Too much competition for the eye.'

'Exactly.'

I had the feeling she was sizing me up, or maybe down.

Miss Gordon was a trim young lady in a charcoal grey trouser suit, her dark hair up and skewered to her head with workaday grips (a definite opening for Vicky and her silver hair ware). Her glasses were light on the nose, the lenses in a thin metal frame, and her blue eyes, tending to grey, appeared and disappeared with reflected light as she moved her head. Was she as severe as she looked? She had asked to meet me for a reason, though as far as I could see it was only to tell me why she couldn't display the flier.

'We have had instances,' she said, evidently recalling them with displeasure, 'where fliers have not been entirely accurate, but I can see this really is a photograph of you.'

Colin had taken several in the studio and this one, while a good outward likeness, gave nothing else away.

'So I should hope.'

'Actually, Mr Frei, there was something else I hoped to discuss with you.'

In fact, there were two something elses, but I only discovered the second one later. On reading my flier, Miss Gordon had checked the library catalogue and come to the view that it was short on recent titles in my subject area. She knew it was asking a lot, but she wondered if I might consider checking their stock for omissions and recommending titles. She could read reviews like anyone else, but lacked the professional expertise to adjudicate between them. The same went for her colleagues, none of whom was qualified in psychology.

I listened with interest. What she was saying made sense, but I doubted if anyone on the staff had a handle on particle physics, polymer chemistry or microbiology either. There had to be a process by which library staff cleared this hurdle when ordering titles from the many available, but waiting for someone to wander in off the streets with a flier could not be part of it. However, the only way to know where an unmarked road is going is to follow it, and I had no other call on my time, not even a meter. I'd come by bus.

'I'm not sure how long it would take.'

'I appreciate that. I really shouldn't have asked.'

She was approached by a member of the public with an enquiry regarding maps of the Old Town in the time of George IV and, having dealt with this request as best she could, returned her attention to me revealing, with some diffidence, that she had recently been taking an interest in psychological conditions and their associated therapies. This was a hint lightly dropped, but she moved on from it so quickly I almost failed to pick it up.

'I take it you're self-employed.'

'That's correct.'

'Well I'm sure we could arrange a one-off payment: two days, six hours per day at your standard hourly rate?'

In the absence of her boss, presently on extended sick-leave, she probably could, and her plan was simple: one day to check the stock, a second to compile a list of titles plugging the gaps. I would do the best I could in the time available. How I used these hours was up to me. Whatever worked best with my current commitments. She looked at me enquiringly but decided not to wait for my response. A busy woman doesn't have all day.

'We'd need an invoice, of course.'

8

There are days you will never forget till you're trapped by a sagging armchair in the eventide home wondering who you are. I was sitting at my desk in the studio. A watery sun was shining low in the sky but the windows were shut to keep out the biting wind. My new oil-filled heater was pleasantly close to my legs though Miss Craig, of council fame, would have frowned on the extension cable. Still, it was on castors and easy to move to the nearest socket in the event of a snap inspection. My laptop was open at the library catalogue but the news wasn't good – well in excess of five thousand titles on psychology. As the man said, who'd have thunk it?

Colin had been pleased to hear about my new offer of work, a small one-off though it was. He was still in contact with Catherine, who had evidently referred to it as a new income-stream, a phrase he wouldn't have used himself. It was strange to think that, given their problem, they should waste time talking about me, but they probably did so after the bell in a break between rounds.

I needed a break myself. There was no way I could work through so many titles. Some would be out of date, others catchy but superficial books aimed at the popular market, but a proper analysis was out of the question in my few allotted hours. My anxiety grew when I checked an online retailer: it listed well over two hundred thousand titles. Who read all those books? Why, apart from lack of money, had I let myself be bounced into this crazy project? If I had thought about it even for a moment . . . but, as already mentioned, I am not greased lightning between the ears.

After spending some time in a state of panic, interrupted by a session with a new client and visits from Colin and Janice, I returned to the drawing board – a piece of equipment some of my colleagues actually used. Cutting through the morass, I concluded that the best way to proceed was relatively simple: draw up a list of books which the library should have, check whether the library already had them and, if it did not, add them to the list I would give to Faith Gordon.

Having settled on a method, I was sufficiently relieved to visit the mews workshop off Pilrig where Charlie did his best to keep my car on the road. He was given to throwing off technical terms like 'wishbone' and 'trunnion bush', but he knew what he was doing. Every time he saw me he came over with an oily rag, a cheerful expression and the same joke. You know what FIAT really means, don't you Max? And I would say No, Charlie, what does it mean? According to him, the answer was Fix It Again Tony, which he found very funny. But he could afford to laugh, he had far more business than I did.

'You're good to go,' he said, clapping the bonnet as though my Panda was a horse.

'How much do I owe you?'

Looking at the bill it was suddenly clear to me why I'd accepted the job: it would take all my library money and more to keep the old rust-bucket on the road. But Charlie had kept his best joke till last.

'A new one would save you in the long run, you know.'

Driving back to the studio I thought of turning right, parking in Chambers Street and dropping in on the library. Since I had nothing to report, the only reason would have been the off-chance of bumping into Faith. But I carried on down the straight and narrow (thanks to bus lanes, much of the route was both) thinking as I drove. I could picture her clearly and realised in retrospect what had struck me most about her. Set off by the dark material of her suit, her skin was unusually pale. I also realised that was something I liked. Perhaps I was suffering from the Ice maiden Syndrome (if such a thing does not exist, it should) whereby the sufferer desires what he cannot attain precisely because he cannot attain it. A mind-set such as that would afford a degree of mental pleasure while protecting the subject (me) from the dangerous complications of a relationship. As I drew up in the courtyard, I was visited by the outline of a paper on amour courtois, in which I would seek to explain the advantage to both parties of their unrequited love, but this time from a psychological rather than a social standpoint. Here was surely a notable example from history of the games people play though, for obvious reasons, not included in the book of that name.

I'd been studying psychology textbooks for half an hour or thereabouts when a man knocked and came in. Reviews of The

Time to Talk

Science of Mind and Behaviour were so laudatory I had begun to wonder whether they had been posted by friends of the author or staff at the publisher working from home. I had reason to know that some things are not as they seem. On the other hand, they might all have been genuine. Short of reading the book it was hard to tell.

'I hope I'm not disturbing you.'
'Not at all. Please take a seat.'
'I believe you know a Mr Robert Brown.'
'I do.'
'The day before yesterday he was hit by a car in Raeburn Place.'
'I'm sorry to hear that.'
'He died at the scene.'

Until he set me straight, I assumed my visitor was a relative or friend come to warn me that the unfortunate Mr Brown would not darken my door again and, if I was really unlucky, to ask for a rebate on behalf of the estate. In fact he was a Detective Constable Hunter following up on the death. Mr Brown had been seen immediately prior to the accident walking in an erratic manner. He had staggered onto the road, giving the driver no chance of evasive action. Yet no trace of alcohol was found in the body, which led the pathologist to look for a pre-existing medical condition that might have caused Mr Brown's erratic behaviour. None was found. But a search of Mr Brown's flat revealed a small quantity of LSD and, as a medical man myself, I didn't need him to tell me that all it took was a very small quantity. This last statement rang alarm bells. Since everyone knew I was not a medical man, DC Hunter was fishing.

'I have no medical qualification.'
'So you wouldn't be prescribing LSD.'
'I wouldn't be prescribing aspirin, let alone LSD.'
'It's just that I found a diary in his flat.'
'I see.'
'Mr Brown refers to you as Doc Frei in his diary.'
'And I refer to him as the Tooth Fairy in mine.'

He looked at me sharply, noting the resistance he had every reason to expect.

'He also mentions his troubles with dreams and seems quite taken with the idea – how did he put it? – of freeing up his brain.'

'He ran that past me too.'

'And you said?'

'I advised him strongly against it. LSD isn't available legally. If you find a source on the street it may not be LSD at all. Even if it is, it will probably be cut with other substances. In any case the side-effects are dangerous in the extreme.'

DC Hunter produced what I assumed was the diary in question.

'But we know he got hold of some.'

'So it would appear.'

'My problem is,' he said, rifling through the pages, 'he doesn't say here where he got it.'

'Then you don't have a problem at all.'

'I'm not sure I follow you, Mr Frei.'

'To explain Mr Brown's behaviour it's only necessary to know that he had taken LSD, not where he got it.'

'You regard that as a separate issue.'

'Don't you?'

On his way out, DC Hunter thanked me for my assistance and hit me with a parting shot.

'By the way, Mr Frei, you didn't ask to see my ID. Given what we were discussing was confidential . . . I don't normally use bad language, but for all you knew I might have been a journalist. And if you don't mind me saying so,' he added, making parting doubly sweet, 'your car's seen better days.'

So had he, but I wouldn't have commented on it. Then I experienced another moment of panic. How did he know it was my car? Had he been checking up on me, and if so why?

My alarm subsided when the probable explanation occurred to me. He had spotted the sticker on my rear window proclaiming a partial truth – IT'S ALL IN THE MIND.

9

As the days went by and the clients with them, the visit from DC Hunter gradually faded into the background. A report in the Evening News gave the impression, without saying so directly, that Mr Brown had been under the influence and there was little the driver could have done. The driver was quoted as saying that Mr Brown had come out of nowhere (that would be the pavement) and she would remember the noise of the impact as long as she lived. Since she was already eighty-two, that might not be long. Like Mr Brown himself, I expected the story would soon run out of legs.

I took me a further week to complete my list for Faith Gordon. I read it through several times in an attempt to satisfy myself that it was adequate, then printed it out. It wasn't costed, but buying so many titles wouldn't come cheap. Jean Ritchie, a new client, was just coming in as I sent an email to Faith to arrange a meeting. As had happened with Mrs Blake, this lady was acting on behalf of someone else. She assured me that her daughter, Zoe, had serious mental health issues which were adversely affecting her life but which she was unwilling or unable to face up to. She had been diagnosed with BPD but refused to accept the diagnosis.

Our conversation got off to a bad start. I assumed the problem was bi-polar disorder and tried to establish which mood-stabilising drugs had been prescribed. Since none had been, I asked if Zoe was refusing medication. On hearing that she hadn't been offered any, I began to suspect our lines were crossed.

'When you say BPD?'

'Borderline personality disorder. What did you think I meant?'

My limited reading on this subject led me to believe it was uncommonly difficult to treat, the biggest obstacle being the patient herself. Non-cooperation was the norm, the patient taking the view that out of the whole regiment she was the only one in step. If anyone was at fault it was always someone else, never her. And in those cases where the patient agreed to therapy, a typical pattern was that the first session went well, perhaps even the second, then the patient stopped attending when the therapist questioned her narrative, even by something as simple as asking a question which gave rise to an alternative view.

'I have to wonder why Zoe isn't here herself?'

There was more than one possible answer. Zoe was scared to risk opening up before yet another stranger. Added to that was the further possibility that, from Zoe's perspective, the people who needed therapy were those who were at fault, not her, so what was the point of coming?

The more Miss Ritchie described specific behaviours, the more I suspected the problem might be intractable. She drew a picture of a girl with a perfectionist streak who was, at the same time, afraid of failure. Zoe had concluded that if she didn't try, she couldn't fail – which was obviously true, but not without its drawbacks.

'The thing is, Miss Ritchie, if she doesn't try she can't succeed either.'

'I've told her that, Mr Frei, believe me. Many times.'

As things stood, and for whatever reason, Zoe was refusing to come: there was no escaping the fact that progress was impossible if she had set her face against it.

Miss Ritchie reached into her handbag and brought out a photograph, as if producing a picture of her daughter meant she was now present.

'Lovely girl,' I assured her.

She was looking directly at the camera and smiling.

'My daughter on a good day.'

'She does have them, then?'

'Oh yes.'

When she left I started playing back our session because I couldn't remember a single allusion to the father, or any role he might have in his daughter's life. Then there was the fact that the mother referred to herself as 'Miss'. It might simply be that the couple, as is increasingly the way, and despite having a child, had seen no reason to marry. They might well have been living together in the family home doing their best to support her, yet I had the impression that Miss Ritchie was a single mother coping with the problem alone. What had given rise to that feeling? Was it something she said? Was it the way she said it? I tried to remember if she had metalwork on her ring finger and failed. I felt, at several points during our talk, that the poor woman was on the verge of tears, and I tried to avert them by assuming a detached tone, as if her feelings were those of a third party not in the room. This tactic appeared to work, and saved her the trouble of mascara running down her cheeks. But it was clear that many years of dealing with her daughter's condition had taken their toll.

I was getting nowhere fast when my mobile rang (business candy-bar model). It didn't recognise the number, but instead of another cold call from Personal Injury Advocates 4U, the lady at the other end was selling me nothing.

'Dr Frei?'

It happened so often I was beginning to feel like a hospital consultant, correcting everyone who called me doctor.

'He's out at the moment, I'm afraid. Will I do?'

'Who is this?'

'Maxwell Frei. I am not a doctor.'

'Ah, right. OK. My name is Maureen MacNeil. You recently spoke to a colleague of mine, DC Hunter.'

'Concerning Robert Brown.'

'DC Hunter tells me you met him several times. I was wondering if you might assist us on this one?'

They already knew who had driven into Mr Brown, so the only help they could possibly require was on the drugs angle. Since I knew my hands were clean I saw no harm in agreeing. In effect, I was being consulted. There was always the remote chance of an ex gratia payment for my services or, if I made an impression, becoming an occasional expert to the force. Not likely but possible, therefore an avenue worth following. DS MacNeil invited me to meet her at Leith Police Station any time before five. Was this feasible? I plotted an easy route in my mind by way of Seafield Road, a metal alley of car showrooms flying commercial flags.

The station was situated on Queen Charlotte Street, though whether she ever knew of this honour is doubtful. Too recent a period for me, all I could remember was that she had made the mistake of marrying George III by whom (we like to think) she bore fifteen children. A productive life in one sense, then, though not one many would like. As I approached the front of the building with its four large pillars, I noticed a green telecoms cabinet on the pavement to the right. For a second, thoughts of phone tapping crossed my mind, but surely the force wouldn't be as brazen as that? Its location had to be fortuitous. Seeing the large welcome sign as I entered reassured me a little, irrational as that was.

DS MacNeil ushered me into an interview room.

'Glad you could come, Mr Frei. We should get some peace here. Please take a seat.'

She took some papers from a file and sat down opposite me, placing great strain on my ability to read upside down. We already knew that Mr Brown had expressed an interest in mind-altering drugs. We also knew that he was an optometrist working from a shop on Stockbridge High Street. Hoping to shed more light on his demise (given his profession, an interesting way to put it) she had visited the shop and spoken to the receptionist. According to her, he had shown no signs whatever of erratic behaviour in the days leading up to his death. She had mentioned one thing, though: he'd been asking some of his customers to describe their dreams, with special reference to colour.

She handed me several pages of notes found in a drawer in his consulting room. It would help her to know what I made of them. She appreciated I would need a little time. Which would I prefer (said with a smile) tea or coffee? Left alone for a while, I glanced round the room. It was functional but far from relaxing. What was I doing here with a sheaf of papers in a dead man's jumbled scrawl? A uniformed officer came in with tea and left, the string from the bag hanging over the edge of a white polystyrene mug. My mind wandered to the oceans, filling with plastic fragments from the farthest reaches of Antarctica to the Sargasso Seas of human debris accumulating in the Atlantic and the Pacific. If there was any hope I couldn't see it.

Most of Mr Brown's notes consisted of clients' responses to questions, but towards the end he was arriving at conclusions, two in particular: without a brain to receive incoming information from the eyes there was no vision whatsoever and, when dreaming, people saw things without recourse to the eyes at all. His thoughts read like a long-winded syllogism resulting in the proposition that where vision was concerned the brain was more important than the eye, albeit that in his case the brain was letting him down. His reasoning was sound but, in optometrist speak, blindingly obvious.

When, after a decent interval, DS MacNeil came back, she had an opinion on that.

'Comes across as a bit desperate to me. Obsessive.'

'It can happen,' I agreed. 'Wanting something too much reduces your chance of getting it.'

'That would explain my love life.'

Maybe it would, but I was starting to suspect this woman was working me over, resorting to the personal to soften me up. So, in line with my existing policy for clients, I ignored her love life and referred her to insomniacs, whose fear of sleeplessness only made matters worse. Anxiety saw to that.

'They could always stop worrying and take a sleeping pill.'

'Not a solution, more of a short-term fix.'

'So why are they prescribed so much?'

Her line of questioning was nearly as unobtrusive as she was. Everything about her was average: average height, average weight, average mid-brown hair of average length – all conspiring to give the wholly false impression that Maureen MacNeil was of average intelligence as well.

'Would you say you have a conventional view of narcotics, Mr Frei?'

It wasn't clear why she was asking me this when I was there to answer questions about Mr Brown.

'That would depend on your definition of conventional.'

She pointed to recording machine at the end of the table by the wall.

'There's something I'd like you to hear.'

I couldn't remember exactly when it had been, probably March or April of the previous year. I'd caught the programme by accident, listening to the radio as I tidied the flat. The fact that I'd phoned in had slipped my mind.

'We have another caller, Max from Edinburgh. What's your take on this one, Max?'

'With all due respect to the doctor, you have to wonder how effective anti-depressants actually are.'

'OK. And why do you say that?'

'Well, for a start, you don't find people queuing up for them on street corners.'

'Because people aren't buying them from dealers you're telling us they don't work? Hardly a clinical test.'

'There will be some people out there who benefit. But the real problem is they're being over-prescribed by the medical profession. Pop them a pill and show them the door whether it's any use to them or not. Something your listeners might not know . . . over the last few years the number of people on anti-depressants in this country has risen to one in seven! Do we really believe that one in seven of the population needs these drugs?'

'Good question. What's your response to that Dr Foster?'

DS MacNeil stopped the programme in its tracks.

'I agree with the presenter here, Mr Frei. I find what you have to say very interesting. You appear to know what's available on the street and what is not.'

She had me on the back foot. Surprised by the recording I had to think quickly, but I have never done that well. How did she know I'd taken part in this broadcast? Why had she gone to the trouble of obtaining a recording?

'You think I supplied Mr Brown.'

She looked at me without a trace of an expression.

'I had occurred to me, yes.'

I rose to leave. This officer had lured me to the police station not to seek my help with the case but in the belief that I'd provided LSD to Mr Brown. That was serious in itself, but since he probably died as a result of taking it the outlook was even worse.

'You're trying to fit me up as a supplier.'

DS MacNeil pretended to look surprised. The thought had never crossed her mind.

'I have no interest whatever in fitting anyone up, Mr Frei. You're free to leave whenever you wish. I do think, though, that it would be in your own best interests to hear me out.'

I resumed my seat. If she had a case, I needed to know what it was.

She produced some photographs taken in Spey Street Lane. They showed Charlie and I concluding our business, my Panda clearly visible in the background.

Time to Talk

'You had me followed!'

'Following suspects is a costly business, Mr Frei. Our budget doesn't run to it where minor players are concerned.'

I was getting the idea. I was a suspect but she hadn't marked me down as Mr Big. On the contrary, she thought I was small fry and was appropriately condescending.

'So where did these come from,' I asked, indicating the photographs, 'Amateur Photographer?'

'We've had several locations under observation for the last two weeks. This is just one of them. Known dealers have been active in the Pilrig area.'

'And you're telling me Charlie is one of them!'

'Mr Caldwell has more money in his account than we would expect, and that's just the account we know about.'

'For heaven's sake, have you seen what he charges?'

She removed a document from her folder and showed me a copy of my last bill. It was fully itemised and totalled £416.17. I was astonished.

'How did you get hold of this?'

'Mr Caldwell's financial affairs are currently under investigation by HMRC.'

'You got the tax man onto him?'

'I'm afraid I can't comment on operational matters.'

She sat there quietly, awaiting a response beyond my understandable shock.

'Detective Sergeant, you already know where he makes his money. You've just shown me one of his bills.'

'A bit steep, wouldn't you say?'

'Maybe, but what are you supposed to do? My MOT was coming up, the car is old, the work had to be done or I was off theroad.'

'I put it to you, Mr Frei, that the bill was large because part of it covered narcotics supplied to you by Archibald Charles Caldwell.'

'Archibald!'

I couldn't blame him for using his middle name. I'd have done the same.

'It's wonderful in its simplicity, wouldn't you say? Everything's documented, leaving a paper trail with all the outward appearance of a legitimate business transaction. As, indeed, some of it is. Clever, I give you that.'

I had set off on my journey to Leith entertaining fond thoughts of ex gratia payments, and now here I was, implicated in a criminal investigation. I sat there mulling over this sobering fact and DS MacNeil gave me the time to do so, though she probably thought of it as letting me stew in my own juice. Then DC Hunter knocked and came in with a piece of paper. Seeing me sitting there he couldn't resist it.

'Hi, doc.'

When he'd gone, the duplicitous MacNeil scanned the paper and put it down.

'I had a colleague from traffic look your bill over. He informs me you've been overcharged to the tune of £120. And that's making certain benign assumptions.'

'Such as?'

'That your oil was actually changed. Have you checked?'

I had to admit I hadn't. Like most people, I never did.

'That your hydraulic brake fluid was actually changed. Well, you could hardly check that, I suppose. But you see where I'm going with this?'

'Charlie was ripping me off.'

She looked at me in evident disbelief.

'Let's get real here, Mr Frei. Coming on for half the amount you paid Caldwell was intended for another purpose altogether, and we both know what it was.'

10

Troubled by my treatment at the hands of DS MacNeil, I was heading back to The Warehouse when I realised I couldn't cope with anyone else, not even Colin. Small-talk was out of the question, and as for her outrageous allegations I needed a couple of hours to think them through for myself.

Back in my flat I distracted myself by listening to the news, switching to the History Channel for a while (The Sinking of the Royal Oak) and putting together a simple snack of ham, coleslaw and mashed potatoes. I have never been so restless. I checked my email on autopilot, just for something to do, and it proved to be more significant than I could have imagined. Faith Gordon had replied.

It was then approaching six. She could see me at any time till eight that evening or any time the following day till five. Why I grasped at this I still don't know. I had no intention of explaining my problem or asking her advice. Perhaps an hour analysing book lists in a neutral environment was just what I needed. But if it was, I can't recall harbouring that thought. Whatever the reason, I replied at once, offering to meet her first thing the following morning.

With more experience of full time employment, I wouldn't have made this suggestion. When professionals arrive at work they are hit by everything at once: colleagues with questions, phone calls, voice mails, texts, and so many emails it takes several minutes just to figure out which ones to junk. And before all that comes the daily ritual of logging on, which lets management know, like it or not, how early they have arrived, how eager they are, how wonderfully conscientious. So just after eight that evening I received a reply asking if I wouldn't mind meeting her at eleven the following day.

As it was, I arrived a little early, headed upstairs to the reference library, selected an empty desk, took my papers from my briefcase and spread them out. As environments go it was unusually peaceful, morning light streaming down through high windows which reminded me of a church. I had always admired the spacious vaulted dome, but what I liked most was the gallery (staff use only) well above head height, running round the room above the bays. It called to mind the promenade deck of an old-style liner or the well-known painting, The Gallery of HMS Calcutta. (We don't want our librarians falling overboard in a heavy sea onto the reading public.)

My booklist was complete, but my notes on the case against me were something else again. I thought I would while away the time till the appointed hour reading up relevant points of law – it was, after all, a reference library – but I soon realised I hadn't a clue where to start. Law was beyond me. To make matters worse, legal language had a marked anaesthetic effect. After ten minutes reading the law as it applied, say, to capital gains tax roll-over or the treatment of deferral reliefs, a dentist could safely have removed a mouthful of teeth. Even subjects of potential use to living and breathing human beings, such as pre-nuptial and cohabitation agreements, looked remarkably hard going. Glancing through this stuff I couldn't help feeling that the legal approach might prove the kiss of death to a previously loving couple.

I was on the point of nodding off when I felt a light tap on the shoulder, and there she was, Faith Gordon.

'We could go to my office, or stay here if we keep it down.'

It was still relatively quiet, so we stayed put. Pulling a chair from a nearby desk, she sat beside me. To my surprise she had a modest list of her own, and it soon became clear we had several titles in common. As she examined my recommendations I examined her. She was wearing the same suit and a similar blouse, perhaps the same one laundered. Her dark brown hair was still up, and cosmetics would have been easy to detect on that distinctive white skin. Not a fashion victim, then, and all the better for that.

'This is excellent,' she said, when she finally looked up.

She liked the listings by category and had just one regret, that it wasn't hierarchical – her fault, she said, for not asking me in the first place. I had just offered to annotate it when a worried library assistant approached her with a problem. An incident had occurred in the fine art library. Her presence was required. Out of respect for our privacy the library assistant took a step back,

Time to Talk

but remained nearby looking anxiously towards the entrance and checking her watch. The woman was a living study in the non-verbal application of pressure.

'I'm really sorry about this. Perhaps I could leave you for five minutes while you're marking up your list? I'll be back as soon as I can.'

'Scale of one to five?'

She nodded. 'That would be very helpful.'

As they hurried off, it was noticeable how loudly her colleague's footsteps sounded on the hard institutional floor compared to hers. No killer heels for Faith.

I whiled away the time deciding which books mattered most, and soon regretted that I hadn't brought a pencil. My frequent changes of mind were leaving messy ink-marks on what had been impressively clean copy. Maslow had it easy by comparison. The task must have taken up considerable mental slack since I hardly noticed the forty minutes which passed before she returned.

'That took longer than I thought but, really, you wouldn't believe it.'

People say things like that without considering what they mean. Not Faith.

'What am I saying? Of course you would, you're a psychologist.'

She was in apologetic mode. Since it was nearly lunchtime I suggested we would suffer less interruption if we ate out. A light snack, nothing fancy. Though she agreed, I could imagine her regret at the neatly packed snack with her name on it somewhere in the building. We met in the library foyer five minutes later and hit the street talking. I liked the way we walked in step, never feeling the need to adjust my pace since we never got out of synch. A small thing, maybe, but small things soon add up.

There was a long queue at my usual watering hole, trunk to tail, so we headed for a café across the road. It seemed the stream of traffic would never end, but when we finally stepped off the pavement she took my arm. She may have felt there was greater safety in numbers, but this simple gesture had a strong effect on me. I was overcome by a feeling of fellowship, as if no longer journeying through this vale of tears on my own.

She told me what had happened over soup - spicy parsnip for the lady, tomato and basil for me. An older man had been seen tampering with a biography of Goya in the fine art library. The staff called security, who detained him as he was leaving. Inspection of his bag revealed a plastic craft knife with retractable blade and a plate of La Maja Desnuda, cut from the book and neatly protected by card. The offender had come prepared. I could see Faith found the incident upsetting, so I started thinking out loud about the man's motivation.

'Perhaps he was offended by the artist's frank portrayal of nudity.'

This explanation didn't reassure her one bit. Given the number of books in the fine art library containing illustrations of nudes, I could see why.

'Did he also make off with La Maja Vestida?'

'No.'

'Then he was only interested in the woman naked.'

We agreed that the man had probably been using the library as a free alternative to top shelf magazines featuring scantily clad women (Hot Stuff Monthly, Killer Babes), but the more we talked the more troubled Faith became, because this might not have been the first time he'd done it and, worse, he might not be the only one resorting to this practice. How many of their books had been vandalised in this way? Only a thorough check could tell, and that was a time-consuming business.

'But surely,' I ventured, 'readers draw missing pages to your attention?'

Sometimes, but not always. In any case, what I was suggesting was hardly a methodical approach to the problem. And as I discovered over the next few months, Faith Gordon was nothing if not methodical.

The incident had ended when the police arrived, taking the culprit with them when they left. But mention of the Force reminded Faith of something she had seen.

'I couldn't help noticing you were looking at law books.'

'Ah, yes, and thereby hangs a tale.'

She gave me a quizzical look, with just the hint of a smile.

'Tell me.'

I don't always do what I'm told, but on this occasion I did, because the injustice of it all was troubling me greatly and a sympathetic ear might make me feel better, even if nothing else changed.

As I explained the events of the day before, she listened so intently her parsnip soup, spicy though it was, cooled rapidly in the bowl. Half way through my account, she reached into the shoulder-bag hanging on the back of her chair and took out a spiral notebook, asking me to go through the main points of the interview again. She referred to them as the 'main heads'. As I did so, she asked for clarification as required. Her glasses slid down her nose a little as she wrote, and when they did she pushed them back onto the bridge, rather daintily I thought, with the middle finger of her left hand.

'But this is outrageous!'

'Isn't it just.'

Having established the facts, she started writing on a fresh page, almost as if I wasn't there, but when she finished she had covered the angles wonderfully well. Firstly, the fact that Mr Brown had taken LSD did not show I had supplied it. Secondly, there was no evidence whatsoever that I had bought drugs from Charlie or anyone else. Thirdly, there was no evidence that Charlie had drugs he could have supplied me with. Fourthly, there was no evidence that Charlie's bill was large for any reason other profiting from his work as a mechanic. Fifthly, and following on from the previous point, there was no evidence that Charlie had a lot of money in his bank account for any reason other than profiting from his work as a mechanic.

'In fact,' she concluded, 'the only thing they can prove is that you have complied with the law as it concerns the roadworthiness of a motor vehicle.'

She looked up and paused.

'How am I doing so far?'

'Very well.'

'They have no evidence against you. Their case is entirely circumstantial.'

She laid a hand on mine in a gesture of sympathy, and although she wasn't a lawyer I was reassured.

'How do you deal with something so distressing, it must be difficult?'

My main reaction was one of anger at the unfairness of it. I had noted this tendency when watching films and television dramas: nothing got me more involved than someone being treated unfairly. Now it was affecting me directly, which made it even harder to tolerate. Apart from that, my mind kept returning to the subject whether I wanted it to or not. I couldn't stop scratching the itch.

'We have to remember you haven't been charged with anything.'

'Not yet.'

She removed her hand but the warmth remained, a feeling I liked.

'I hope you won't mind me saying this, but those law books you were looking at . . .'

'Completely beside the point. I don't know what I was thinking.'

'So we won't go down that blind alley again.'

I liked the word 'we'. She'd drawn a circle round herself and I was inside it too.

When the waitress removed our soup plates she asked if we wanted anything else, by her expression expecting a negative reply - we hadn't exactly polished off the bread and soup – but talking and eating at the same time doesn't come easy. We ordered coffee and it arrived with dinky little biscuits on the saucer.

'I've read your flier, as you know, and had a look at your website.'

My site was basic, one of those where a technical innocent like me chooses a template and adds his own text and graphics.

'I was considering,' she suddenly seemed hesitant, 'I don't know how best to put this – of consulting you on another matter.'

Although the interior of the café could have been better lit, I could see signs of tension in her face which hadn't been there before.

'I think I may have an issue.'

11

I had just arrived at the studio when Janice came in to remind me of the meeting which, she correctly guessed, I'd forgotten. What did it have to do with me? I was a paid-up member of the Collective when it came to rent and sundry other incidental expenses, but an artist I was not. In any case, my mind was elsewhere: my problem with the police on the one hand, and on the other my growing involvement with Faith. However, Janice told me, skirting the walls in a vain search for additional landscapes by that well-known photographer Maxwell Frei, my presence was expected. By which she meant required. In her studio. Ten o'clock sharp.

'You still have time to brew up.'

What a motley crew they were, the art world writ small. But the turnout was so good I met George for the first time. How he made a living painting portraits in this photographic age was a mystery to me, but judging by his silver Mercedes in the courtyard he knew what he was doing.

'You have to understand, Max, there's a question of status here. Anyone can point a camera at anyone else and shoot, but how many people have a genuine oil on canvas over their mantelpiece? Precious few. And you have to remember my sideline.'

He wanted me to ask, so I did. Yes, he told me with grin, he was into pet portraits too. He made more from them than painting people. They were very popular.

'Hard to believe but it's true,' Ceramick confirmed. 'Horses, dogs, cats. You've even done a parrot, haven't you, George?'

George looked immensely pleased with himself. Yes, he had done a parrot. From what I later saw of his work he had probably done it very well.

Janice called the meeting to order and, rather surprisingly, they all shut up. The sooner it started the sooner it would end. First on the agenda (entirely in her head) was matters arising from the visit of Lyndsay Craig. The meeting agreed that Miss Craig had been helpful. Unlike her predecessor, she did not live and die by the regulations. Ceramick begged to differ, but was swiftly silenced. She'd been right about his cables: the sooner he sorted them out the better. Next up was the suggestion from Antonia and Vicky that we collaborate to publicise our work by holding an open day cum exhibition at The Warehouse.

'I mean,' Antonia pointed out, 'we're paying for the place already. Might as well make full use of it.'

'And,' Vicky added, 'if we're quick off the mark we'll benefit from the run-up to Christmas.'

This proposal had so much to commend it that those present (all of us) adopted it by acclamation. A selling opportunity was not to be missed. Why had no one thought of it before? I listened with amazement as Janice spoke.

'Carried nem con.'

The woman was a polymath.

The meeting went on to consider matters relating to the exhibition – date, time, publicity campaign – but my mind was wandering by then. I wouldn't be involved. How could I be when I wasn't the real deal? I was idly examining a knitting machine (1,200 stitches per minute) when Colin came over.

'First Saturday in November. That doesn't leave us much time.'

Since his show at the Art Centre would be over by then, I couldn't see what the problem was. Surely that was the whole point of prints, if you sold some you ran off more. The open day was a second chance to sell what he'd sold already.

'Max, wake up! If this comes off, which it will with Janice at the helm, they'll be crawling all over this place. We can't take any chances. We'll have to replace the borrowed shots on your wall with genuine Max Freis.'

Which sounded like a tall order for someone with little time and even less talent.

'I don't have any.'

'You will.'

Shortly after one I was visited by Mr Blake, persuaded by his wife to come along. He had complied under protest, as was clear from his aggressive attitude. I'd heard her side of the story but now I wanted his perspective.

'Why? Do you think she was lying?'

Time to Talk

I had recently acquired, at a knock-down price, an art deco figure of a lady with elegantly arched back, arms raised supporting a lamp. As the days got darker I would buy a suitable shade.

I removed her from the window ledge and placed her carefully in the middle of my desk. Mr Blake watched me intently as if I was springing a trap – which, in a way, I was. I pulled my chair well to the side and sat down.

'Tell me, Mr Blake, do you see her right ear?'

'No.'

'I can.'

'Bully for you!'

I rose to vacate my chair and let him see for himself.

'OK, you can see her right ear. So bloody what?' I was about to reply but he forestalled me. 'Wait, no, don't answer that. We're both looking at the same thing but we're not seeing the same thing. No, hold on a bit, that's not quite right,' (one must be pedantic to be accurate) 'we are in fact seeing the same thing, but not in the same way.'

'You are evidently following my moves.'

'Not very difficult, I would have thought.'

'So if we added what you can see to what I can see . . .'

'We'd have the whole picture.'

'Worth a try, wouldn't you say?'

By the end of the session the only thing I had achieved was a commitment from the husband to see his book-buying habit from his wife's point of view. And Colin arrived so soon after he left, he must have been hanging around in the corridor waiting his chance.

'Right,' he said, 'I've got it all worked out.'

He slapped a sheet of paper on the desk, on which he'd drawn a rough map. On Sunday we would go to Holyrood Park where I would attack the following targets with my DSLR: St Margaret's Loch, Dunsapie Loch, the Duddingston Loch bird sanctuary, the little that was left of St Anthony's Chapel, Arthur's Seat, and the Salisbury Crags. He would take a few shots for me where the exposure might be difficult – light reflecting off water, shooting into the sun. The trick of it was to take as many as poss-ible. He would make a selection when we got back and sharpen them up with Photoshop.

'It might be raining.'
'Sorry, Max, I've checked the forecast. We're good.'

When the day of rest came, everything went as planned. Colin was suitably fetching in his North Face jacket and I kept the cold at bay with a lumberjack shirt and an old Shetland gansie. Each to his own. We parked near St Margaret's Loch and, as they say in the films, I shot first and asked questions afterwards. Like why were we taking so many? Provided I took enough pictures, Colin replied, a few would be good by mistake.

I don't consider myself lazy. I could cope with the circular trek he had planned, but taking photographs the Kirkpatrick way was something else again. For heaven's sake, he would shout against the wind, get down for that shot. According to him, standing with the camera at eye height all the time was not the best approach. The fact the grass was wet didn't matter. He wouldn't rest till I was lying in it looking up, or climbing a heathery knoll looking down. After two hours of this friendly encouragement, I began to think fondly of my counselling sessions with jobbing gardeners and overzealous sociologists. Anything was better than a five mile hike led by a photographic sergeant major.

We spotted a grey heron on the far side of Dunsapie Loch and Colin replaced the standard lens with my latest acquisition, a telephoto from the Cash Machine. The bird was so utterly motionless I began to suspect it was a stolen garden ornament left there by a whimsical wit the worse for wear. You had to admire a creature which could stand on one leg, motionless, for minutes on end in the teeth of a headwind. I took several shots of it but, as ever, the best I could come up with was a standard image of the bird and its reflection in the water – though I thought I had captured the plumage well, and the trademark yellow eye and yellow beak. Colin reviewed my efforts and nodded.

'You might consider the rule of thirds – remember we spoke about that? Our feathered friend is smack in the middle of the picture every time.'

I have been accused of many things, but breaking the visual mould has not been one.

By the time we reached Duddingston Loch the sight-seers were out in force, feeding the ducks and swans and chatting with the geese which, close up, were larger than I had realised.

Had geese been spotted on radar flying at twenty thousand feet? I could believe it. But the best I could hope for was the DSLR equivalent of holiday snaps. Not much mileage in that. When a bench was vacated by an elderly couple we moved in quickly and, to my delight, Colin produced a bar of high quality chocolate straight from the Côte d'Ivoire.

'I always come prepared.'

Knowing him, he probably had a compass, sextant or astrolabe in one of those big pockets, but what we could really have done with was a hip flask.

'Sorry to disappoint you, Max.'

He was still disappointing me when we were joined by a girl.

'Any for me?'

His girlfriend, Catherine, accountant to the stars.

12

The following Monday, having recovered from multiple exposure on the blasted heath, I spent the first hour junking the worst of my pictures, then those that were merely passable. Colin left with the best seventeen, four of which had been taken by him, and I returned to my work.

All of the cases still on my books called for background reading: whether I revealed it to the client or not, I had to be sure of my ground. Not to the level of certainty of a broken leg or an outbreak of measles, but as near as could ever be expected with information mined from between the ears.

Thanks to his accident, Mr Brown wasn't a problem any more, which was just as well since I had no idea why his dream-life had withered and died. Perhaps he should have asked Eva at the garden centre. Mr Robertson wasn't a problem either. All he really wanted was to chew the scriptural fat. He was certainly not afflicted by religious melancholia, like poor Robert Ferguson: in fact, as far as I could gather, he rather enjoyed backing prelates into a corner and tying them in knots.

He had noticed certain omissions and, much more thought-provoking, certain inconsistencies in holy writ. Sometimes he came over as a crossword enthusiast having trouble with thirteen down. He couldn't wait for the answers in next morning's paper, which was too bad considering they never appeared anywhere, not even in Biblica or The Tablet. I told him several times he needed neither therapy nor a therapist, but he preferred to come anyway. It did no good, but did no harm either and kept him off the streets.

'I don't know if you've noticed, Mr Frei (I hadn't), there's a bit of a problem with the chronology of Our Lord's life in the gospels.'

I must have looked stumped, which I was. He then explained that the gospel of St John placed the attack on the money lenders in the Temple at the beginning of His ministry, whereas the other three gospels had it at the end. My memory failing me on this point, I took his word for it and agreed there was prima facie evidence of a discrepancy – exactly what he wanted me to say.

'But that's just it, Mr Frei, if the Bible is the word of God, there would be no discrepancy whatever! You see my problem here?'

Since it was three to one in favour of the incident occurring at the end, I suggested that's where it had been. He put on a show of outrage.

'This isn't a question of simple arithmetic, Mr Frei, it's a question of divine truth!'

At that time, Mr Blake was by far my simplest case. He was insecure. Since he had a degree and was close to completing his thesis (Structuralism and Post-structuralism: Research Trends in Contemporary Sociology) that should not have been the case, and I began to suspect the problem lay within his department. A recent appointment, he did not have tenure and, in the current economic climate, had little prospect of achieving it. The fact that he was on a permanent contract failed to reassure him: they could let him go with one month's notice. Not so permanent, then, yet more so than countless others. Much more so than me. To all intents and purposes he was secure (salary and pension scheme) and should have felt it.

Mr Blake was circumspect in his references to other members of his department, yet I began to discern, through the fog of words, a competitive group of individuals complete with changing allegiances and a poisonous atmosphere to match. The fact that people have letters after their name is no guarantee of civilised behaviour. It couldn't have been easy for a thin-skinned person like him. But his way of dealing with it – happing himself about with learned texts – was not a solution. As for his wife, I detected no sign of tension there except when it came to a haemorrhage of money the couple could ill afford. She had his best interests at heart. The starting point for this one was agreeing an analysis of the problem with the client, though sometimes I had to resist an anarchic desire to noise the man up. *Security, Mr Blake? The fact that you want something doesn't mean you can have it. Relax and have a bad time like the rest of us!*

Then there was Jean Ritchie. Despite her best efforts, she had so far failed to persuade her daughter to come, but having

Time to Talk

made an appointment attended again in her place. She supplied additional background: descriptions of Zoe's erratic behaviour, episodes of self harm, dead-beat boyfriends with problems of their own. But when it came to her suicide threats I was in two minds. Many people who commit suicide make no mention of their intention beforehand. For those left behind it comes out of the blue. But we cannot afford to assume that because someone has threatened suicide many times the day will never come. It might, and if we have dismissed the numerous warning signs as mere talk where would we be then?

It was sheer coincidence that I was thinking about suicide when Ceramick knocked on the door and came in, beaming from ear to ear.

'It's Fate.'

I was quite prepared to believe it, but I had no idea what he was talking about so he said it again at higher volume.

'It's Fate!'

'What is?'

'She's here.'

I didn't figure it out till Faith appeared in the doorway behind him. Ceramick came from an area in the southwest of Ireland where 'th' was habitually rendered as 't'.

I don't know what had got into him, but having shown the lady in he bowed himself out in the exaggerated manner of a liveried flunkey and left us to it.

She walked up to me and offered me her hand as I rose. Making physical contact was good anyway, and even better when accompanied by a smile. She sat in the chair farther from the desk and laid her shoulder bag on the floor at her feet. She hoped she wasn't too early but she'd managed to arrange an extended lunch break. She'd been thinking. If I wanted to follow up on the law, the best place to do it was the National Library across the road: unlike the Central, they had access to the library of the Faculty of Advocates. Maybe I'd used the National when working on my degree? Perhaps I was still a member.

All this was very logical, yet without a working knowledge of the law resorting to legal tomes was time wasted on a grand scale. So under the guise of giving me information, she was seeking it. Had I studied in Edinburgh and, if so, did I make use of the

National Library while researching a dissertation or thesis? And she had to ask because my promotional material made no reference to the subject of my degree. With good reason, since it was not in my chosen field.

'I went to Edinburgh but I didn't use the National, I'm afraid.'

'Nor the Central, I imagine.'

'No offence meant.'

'None taken. We both know our stock of psychology books has room for improvement.'

She was fishing again. Either I told her now or not at all.

'The truth is, my degree is in Ancient and Mediaeval History.'

'Ah, really, how interesting.'

This response was unexpected. I have crossed swords with too many people who consider ancient history of no possible relevance to psychology, Aeschylus and Sophocles notwithstanding. As for the Middle Ages, when the subject comes up I scarcely know where to begin. The naysayers refer to 'The Dark Ages', which they take to mean 'unenlightened'. Yet sticking strictly with the psychological, and giving only one example, how subtle was the medieval church to recognise as sin confessing to a crime which one had not committed? Yet now, in many jurisdictions, when the defendant pleads guilty the court takes him at his word and proceeds to sentence. How shallow is that?

'But you didn't come here to talk about me.'

She contested this at once. Communication was a two-way process. For her it would only work if we talked with each other about each other. How could she evaluate what I said without knowing who I was? She went farther still. There are things she would never tell me unless she trusted me, and how could she trust me if she didn't know me?

'These sound like conditions.'

'They are.'

I had never come across anyone like this, who appeared complete with a reasoned, relationship-centred view of the therapeutic process. And though it made sense it also raised questions, particularly for me, as will later become clear. But there we were, sitting together in the here and now. I didn't have time to think these questions through and made my decision on instinct, as we make so many. I had trusted her from the start without knowing why.

'OK. But in that case we drop this Mr Frei, Miss Gordon stuff. My name is Max.'

'Mine is Faith, as you know.'

'What seems to be the problem, Faith?'

I asked this in a mock role-play tone, as if we weren't totally serious – which can make being serious come a little bit more easily.

She responded with a wry smile and told me. Right from the start, she followed my moves. It concerned her work. Increasingly she was taking exception to the fact that however hard she and her colleagues tried, the public undermined their efforts. They took books from the shelves, read them at desks and didn't put them back. Worse still, they put them back but in the wrong places. Then there were those who failed to return them on time (a nice little earner, I would have thought) or failed to return them at all. Not to mention people, as in the recent case of the man and the nude, who defaced or vandalised stock. All this, she conceded, was in the nature of the service they provided, but she was coming to resent it because she saw it stretching to infinity.

I could understand how irritating this must be, but surely it was just one of many things in life which conformed to the same analysis? I clean my flat this week and behold, lo, I have to clean it again the next. I wash my clothes, wear them again and, guess what? – I have to wash them yet again. I eat today, I eat again tomorrow. Repetition could not be avoided.

She accepted what I was saying but I was missing the point, which was that to the repetitions I had mentioned at home she had to add those she experienced at work. So there was no escape, and her resentment was increasing by the day.

'But Faith, there are many people in the same position – waitresses, shelf-stackers, bricklayers, bus drivers. There's no escape for them either. Think about maths teachers, or language teachers going through the same grammatical points from one year's end to the next for the whole of their lives. Don't they tire of that?'

'You're right. It's not my situation that's the problem, well it is, but what really concerns me is the way I'm reacting to it. That's why I'm here.'

She was sure she'd put that reference book back, but had she really? She had to check, and often more than once. Multiply that by the number of books she dealt with every day . . . She gave me other instances to do with cataloguing and record keeping. In every case she was adding to the repetitions which already beset her, and these were not confined to the library.

'It's past a joke, Max. It's becoming compulsive. I lock my car, walk off, and then have to go back and try the door. Hardly a day passes.'

'That's not uncommon. I see it all the time in the street, in supermarket car parks. As you lock the car you're already thinking ahead to other things. You do it automatically, without thinking about it, so later you can't remember having done it.'

I could see she was unhappy with my response, which placed her behaviour within the acceptable range and, by implication, not to be concerned about. So I offered her a tea or a coffee. When I rose to go and make it she followed me past the screen into the kitchenette. As it turned out, my mugs were in the basin waiting to be washed.

'Repetition,' she said as I washed them.

She took the dishtowel from the counter and dried them.

We were tending towards the domestic, a new experience for me, but I liked it.

She seemed more relaxed (the less formal location, something to do with her hands) and started describing the fantasies which troubled her. They hadn't involved machine guns, hand grenades, machetes or scimitars, but thoughts of anthrax and ricin had crossed her mind, lightly dusted between the pages. A quiet solution. No violence. No blood. No readers left and everything in its place. She also reported a dream in which the library began to fill with water from the floor up till no air was left. Did she see objects floating in the water — sheets of paper, pencils, hats, scarves? Not that she could remember.

A strange one that. The damage to the books would have been severe, a possible interpretation being that her resentment extended not just to the public but to the library itself. When I put this to her she wasn't convinced.

'You think you have OCD.'

'It's crossed my mind.'

We stood there leaning against the sink and the counter, mugs in hand, talking freely. When she looked at her watch and realised she had to go, she suddenly leaned forward and kissed me on the cheek. Maybe Ceramick had been right, when it came to Miss Gordon perhaps it really was fate.

13

My feeling of elation persisted long after Faith had left, reminding me of a room with a fire I had sat in once when everyone else had gone. From the small pile of logs nearby, I kept it going as the night wore on, the only source of warmth.

By the time I got home the feeling hadn't faded one bit. I stepped over mail (it could wait) shut the door behind me, hung the key on the hook and went straight to the living room. It was tidier than before. I could sit at the computer without moving books from the chair, but catching up on the day's news couldn't compete with my thoughts. The kiss had been an act of female politesse. A man wouldn't have done it, but Faith had, coming so close I could smell her: fresh, wholesome and totally un-influenced, as far as I could tell, by artificial fragrance of any sort.

As I put it all together – reassembled as it were, the whole package – I realised she had got to me big time. When she'd taken her jacket off and hung it on the chair (I had yet to acquire clothes hooks or a stand) she was trim as they come in her slacks and simple white blouse. I sometimes detected a hint of laughter in her voice, a note of self-deprecation which seemed to include me too. And her hair was still up. Did she sleep with it that way? Maybe one day I'd find out.

I was scrolling through the headlines and taking nothing in. Client-centred therapy was well known, but relationship-centred therapy? Not in the way it had visited me today. But when I thought of my code of practice I realised something had to give. I also knew what it was. I wanted the relationship to continue, to develop, so Faith could not be a client. No money had changed hands. No money ever would. She could never be on the books. When we met it would be as equals, as friends. Yet the more I thought about it the more evident it was our relationship was sexual in nature, at least in part. Not because of the kiss, a first move at best, but because I knew full well I wouldn't have entered into it with a man.

Though I was then thirty-four my experience with women was limited. I had been a romantic once, but learned the hard way how dangerous that was. If we depend on another to make sense of the world, what happens when that other leaves? The world becomes meaningless? We are suddenly deprived of all motive? I would sit in the dentist's waiting room reading articles about improving your sex life with spoons or ways to find Mr Right and wonder where we were headed. (He had several women's magazines plus assorted other titles ranging from Performance Car to Total Carp.) Did people really believe that out of the billions of souls inhabiting the earth one, and only one, was meant for them? Meet that person and their life would be complete?

It seemed to me then, and still does, that just as the cosmos may be thought of as a multiverse (a concept from a psychologist, believe it or not) so it is open to most of us to make one of several marriages each of which would be different in quality and work in a different way. (To be clear, I don't believe that all these possible marriages actually take place, each in a parallel universe.) So in my case it might be that, Bernard and Creative Scotland notwithstanding, I could marry Janice and her filing cabinet, our relationship would flourish and I would be more stylishly attired. Or I might marry Lyndsay Craig, and we would happily tramp the West Highland Way, wind in our face, cromach in hand. Or I might continue on the course I had set myself for years, holding to open sea to avoid the rocks. Then again, I might marry Faith. Or given her strength of character, Faith might marry me. Or, to express it correctly, we might marry each other.

What I am describing is not a romantic understanding but a classical one, these words being stick-on labels for opposing views of the world deriving, for example, from the romantic poet whose most important subject is himself - not the wonders of nature but his reaction to them. To put it another way, imagine a window: the romantic prefers to look in, projecting what he sees on the beloved. So in his love there is love of self. The classic, looking out, will tend to see the beloved more as she is, though he might, through no fault of his own, miss her right ear. If you were the beloved, which would you prefer?

In offering these modest thoughts, I don't pretend to be advancing the analysis of this subject one bit, though what I have read by others has not impressed me much. For example, it is clear that Stendahl would not have written De l'Amour had he ever matured beyond the romantic. Constantly regretting his unattainable true love for decades didn't get him very far: what did it matter that his book on love was published when the woman stayed forever out of reach? The mere existence of the book, for all its engrossing asides, attests to failure in the personal side of his life. The only reason for this brief digression is to document my frame of mind as it was at the time, and still is.

My train of thought was derailed by a ping. Colin had edited the photographs and wanted me to look them over. We didn't have much time. (He said that so often I was starting to think his biological clock was faster than Catherine's.) He'd collected them in a folder which I was invited to join by clicking the link. Once in, I noticed each picture was available as before and after versions for ease of comparison – and also so that I'd appreciate how expert an editor he was. All the scenes were well known: in that sense, there could be nothing new. So he had gone for ways of presenting, often cropping the original, adjusting the contrast and getting creative with colour curves, whatever they might be. All told, I was impressed with the results. I also agreed with his choices of those most worth printing.

I was halfway through an effusive reply when it struck me: how was I going to print them? My home printer was perfect for my purposes, but monochrome wouldn't do. The last thing I needed was another trip to the Cash Machine. A photo-quality colour printer would cost, as would the paper. I chewed all this over for a while, checking prices online. Surely there was nothing to get hung up about here? Colin was a printer, he had the technology. Yet I couldn't remember seeing a photo printer in his studio. His favoured techniques were lithography and etching, though he had recently been experimenting with batik. And as usual, when branching out into pastures new, his enthusiasm knew no bounds.

I deserted the email and phoned him. Catherine answered, so that was still back on track. I apologised for disturbing him, but he didn't mind. In the background now, Catherine reminded him that food would ready in five minutes, so I kept it short. I was delighted, he had turned the competent, the run-of-the mill into the interesting and eye-catching. But what about printing? Nothing to it, he assured me. A trip to Kodak Express or some such outlet, tomorrow or the day after.

'All we need to do, Max, is synchronise our diaries.'

14

Tuesday was a quiet day, the lull before the storm. On Wednesday morning Colin and I went to Kodak Express and did the business. Left to myself I'd have been there all morning, assistant or not. As it was we completed the job in under an hour and went for a coffee in Kilimanjaro. As usual it was full of students, some of them noisy with it. Apart from a hardened smoker, the tables outside were deserted thanks to persistent drizzle.

When the waitress brought our coffees to our table, complete with the now obligatory leaf pattern on the froth, I was prepared to relax in the glow of a good job well done. Colin was not.

'Right,' he said, in purposeful tones, 'now there's the question of framing.'

I had noticed frames in Kodak Express but Colin had other ideas.

'The thing is, Max, we want people to concentrate on the pictures – it's not as if we're dealing with portraits of the aristocracy here. The last thing we need is distracting frames. And then there's your finances to consider.'

He suggested we use frameless mounts. We could pick them up at the art shop on Nicolson Street a short walk away. I liked the idea, especially if it cut the bill.

'But what if they don't fit the pictures?'

Colin smiled. He'd gone for print sizes corresponding to the frames. Even if he'd got one wrong he could always trim a picture.

'Leave it to me, we'll hang them tomorrow. On the subject of priceless art works,' he asked with a twinkle, 'what are you charging?'

'I didn't have you down as a comic.'

'You have to know the answer if you're asked.'

As a newcomer to the scene I should be modest. After I'd bought the frames, I should add the cost of the prints, divide by the number of pictures (reduced to fourteen) and add fifty percent. This didn't seem modest to me.

'Fifty percent!'

'I know it's perverse,' he explained, 'but charging too little puts them off as badly as charging too much. If it's cheap it can't be good.'

Back at The Warehouse I dropped in on Janice, admired her latest work and retrieved some files from her cabinet. She was pleased to see me, very glad I'd dropped by. It had been decided (she used the passive voice on occasions like this) that the open day eats would be in my studio. For the others, peddling their wares was a serious business, for me it was not. In any case, anything of mine would be displayed on the walls, leaving the floor free for drinks and nibbles. Her logic was impeccable. I agreed at once, not that I had any choice.

I sat at my desk eating a sandwich and reviewing my notes from the day before. Mr Armitage, by his own account, was suffering some distress. He had always taken an interest in astronomy and believed he knew the score. In four billion years (give or take) the sun, running low on fuel, would expand to burn up Mercury, Venus and the Earth. Whatever was left of life would be well and truly boiled off leaving not a trace of all our puny efforts, which included the complete works of anyone you cared to mention: Botticelli, Shakespeare, Beethoven, H Rider Haggard.

'But surely, Mr Armitage,' I suggested, 'in that event we move farther out, colonise Mars or one of the moons of Jupiter or Saturn?'

He found this suggestion ridiculous. In his view, with which I privately agreed, space travel was not a practicable proposition.

'In any case,' he added, 'even if we could do it, what would it solve?'

Having hit me with the first barrel he finished me off with the second. According to him, the universe itself was slowly dying as the finite material available for the formation of new stars was used up. It was inevitable, he said. Over a period of time, albeit a long one, the stars would die and, with them, all activity. The universe would still be there, but dead. So what was the point of trying? The problem – life was pointless. The solution – end it.

'Would you say you were depressed, Mr Armitage?'

'No, I would not. I just don't see the point of continued existence. Effort expended is effort wasted when failure is inevitable.'

Time to Talk

If computers could talk they would sound like Mr Armitage. What he was saying was logical, as was the conclusion he had drawn. Yet if he took any joy in life, any pleasure at all, his argument surely fell. Only if this man was all thought and no feeling did his so-called solution stand up. But if someone likes cake you don't offer him cabbage, so I tried to connect with him on his own terms.

'If life is pointless there's no point living it.'

'Exactly.'

'So if life is pointless there's no point ending it either.'

Mr Armitage wasn't impressed.

'You're being Jesuitical now, Mr Frei. I'm sorry, but that won't do at all.'

I didn't see that it way and told him so. We agreed to differ. We would lock horns again another day.

In some ways, Mr Armitage should have been the easiest of cases to crack. He was led entirely by logic therefore, you would think, could be reached by logic. But that was not the way it was. He could hit me with his reasoning, but if I hit him back with mine he called me a casuist or accused me of sophistry. So beneath his logical veneer there was evidence of an emotional attachment to his conclusions. It could well be that these conclusions, so called, were actually the starting point from which he'd worked his way back looking for justifications. I had just made a note to this effect when DC Hunter darkened my door.

Several days had passed since my meeting with DS MacNeil and I'd assumed, having heard nothing more, that it had all died down. It probably had. Since MacNeil hadn't come herself and sent her underling it would be something less important, some minor detail.

'It's about the car,' he said, going over to the window and looking out.

It had passed its MOT (just), it was insured, the road tax was current and displayed, as per regulations, on the windscreen. How could it possibly be about the car?

'Go on.'

'We were checking through our surveillance photographs, the ones we told you about. Routine, you understand. We have to be methodical.'

'I'm sure you do.'

'According to our records you are not the registered owner.'

This came as news to me. I had the log book at home somewhere.

'The registered owner is one Maxwell Anderson.'

Of course it was, how could I have forgotten!

'I see.'

'Correct me if I'm wrong, sir, but your name is Frei.'

He was now standing with his back to the window leaning against the sill, the light behind him. He may have considered using available light a cheap form of the third degree, but it was well into October, four o'clock in the afternoon and raining. I wasn't exactly blinded when I looked in his direction.

'You have to understand that in my line of work there has been a long history of practitioners with German names: Freud, Jung, Adler, Reich, Klein, Spielrein, Fromm, to name but a few.'

'So you thought you'd join the club.'

'Think of it more as a trade name.'

'And just to be clear, you've done this through New Register House?'

'Why would I do that? For all purposes other than my work as a psychotherapist, I continue to be Maxwell Anderson.'

'Which is why your car is registered in that name.'

'Exactly.'

There was a brief pause while DC Hunter gathered his thoughts, which helped me to gather mine.

'You do realise, sir, that it's against the law to use a change of name for fraudulent purposes?'

Though I could honestly say that there was no fraud whatsoever in my use of the name, DC Hunter was moving onto difficult ground so I sought to direct him down another path.

'I see where you're going with this, but let me set your mind at rest. If I were a fish and chip shop, I might operate under the trade name Deep Frei. Deep Frei would be emblazoned above the shop door, hopefully in lights, and would be prominent on all my stationery, invoices and the like. But I would continue to file my self-assessment tax return under the name Maxwell Anderson.'

'Very witty, sir, if I may say so.'

'I thought so.'

'What you're really saying is that using the name Frei makes you sound a bit more like the genuine article.'

I was on point of protesting that I was the genuine article, but thought better of it.

'That's exactly what I'm saying.'

As he was leaving, apparently satisfied with my answers, DC Hunter revealed that they had yet to track down the source of the LSD supplied to my unfortunate ex-client, Mr Brown. So, technically, I was still under suspicion. But he thought I'd like to know that, as yet, there was no evidence against me. I thanked him for making this clear. Now I could free up my mind for other, more useful things, such as my meeting with Faith. I was expecting her within the hour, and was thinking ahead to how I would handle the several tricky issues involved in my dealings with her when my phone rang. She'd been delayed at work. Any chance of me coming to her, perhaps around six o'clock? Instead of meeting at the library she suggested a restaurant on Lothian Street. There was parking in South College Street.

I arrived early and waited in a doorway nearby, though it didn't provide much shelter. When Faith arrived she kissed me lightly on the cheek (blessed, then doubly blessed) and we went in out of the rain. What with the weather ruling out the tables on the pavement, the popularity of the hour, and the free wi-fi so attractive to students, we had to hang around for a while till a table became available. This was a peak time for Negociants so we should have known what to expect. Faith took her coat off and laid it on an empty chair. I put my cap in the same place. For obvious reasons service was slow, which gave us time to talk.

'I'm sorry about this. Something came up.'

I didn't ask what but she told me anyway - food that one of the librarians had eaten not long before. Faith had taken her place till the end of her shift.

'I hope she didn't buy it here.'

'I didn't think to ask.'

'So,' she said, opening the door to whatever it was I wanted to discuss.

I took a folded flier from my jacket pocket and watched as she read it.

'Open day at The Warehouse, November 3rd. Recent work in a variety of media by well-known local artists. Wide range of artwork and crafts not available on the high street. Tea, coffee and cakes.'

She laid the flier on the table.

'All welcome, it says. Does that include me?'

'Of course.'

'About the photography, Max . . .'

I didn't want to get into that and quickly wrote it off.

'A sideline, nothing more. The others are genuine artists, some better than others. All I do is rent a studio which would otherwise be empty.'

'So you won't have anything on display.'

'If you must know, I'll be hosting the food and drink.'

'Can't see you in an apron.'

'Neither can I.'

We paused for a moment as a waitress arrived with water. She'd take our food orders when she came back with the coffee.

'How's it going with the police?'

As questions go, this is always a good conversational gambit. She was relieved to hear that they were no further forward in pinning anything on me. Which left the other matter DC Hunter had brought up. There was no future with this woman if I didn't tell her now what she might later find out for herself, so I gave her a full account.

'Your name isn't Frei?'

'My name is Maxwell Anderson.'

'And they found this out by following up on your car?'

She suddenly looked thoughtful.

'Checking up on people isn't so difficult, Max.'

'I don't suppose it is.'

'It certainly isn't for me.'

Well no, it wouldn't be. She was a librarian. She knew the ropes.

'When people graduate their names are published.'

Of course they were, and this time I saw it coming.

'No one named Maxwell Frei graduated MA in Ancient and Medieval history, ever. But you did, Max. As yourself. Under your own name.'

By now I was exceptionally nervous. If I hadn't just admitted it, that would have been the end. Perhaps it still was. And it was interesting, was it not, that she had chosen to check. Why had she done that? Was I the sort of person who naturally attracted suspicion, or was she simply following her instincts? She wasn't a librarian by accident. Faith was methodical by nature.

'Anything else I should know?'

There was, of course, but I couldn't risk telling her yet.

'Wife and children, perhaps? Your gate swings the other way?'

I smiled, relieved.

'Neither of the above. But we do need to talk about us.'

Her idea of equality in the counsellor/client relationship didn't fall within any code of practice I'd ever seen, and certainly not within mine. Already, in just one meeting, she had confided in me, but I had also confided in her, which was not what a session was for. It couldn't go on like that.

'Yes, but Max, my problem is psychological, yours isn't. There's a difference.'

'True, but not one recognised by the code of practice.'

'So what are you saying – this is as far as it goes, this is it?'

She was upset and making no attempt to conceal it.

'No, that's not what I'm saying at all.'

'So what do you suggest? It isn't easy finding someone I can talk to about this. Or anything else, for that matter.'

That was something we had in common. For though there were people with whom I got on reasonably well, there were rooms in the house they didn't know were there. But Faith was different. She didn't know what lay behind them, but already she'd sensed the doors. We had to find a solution.

'We continue to meet, but as friends. Then we can say what we like, when we like. Completely off the record and off the books.'

She took a sip from her glass. She was thinking.

'Off the books?'

'Yes.'

'I pay you, but you don't record it.'

'Faith, come on. All I meant by that was writing nothing down.'

'Sorry, Max, but I'm looking for clarity here and there's only one way to find it.'

When the waitress came with our coffees we ordered carelessly, after minimal thought – if we let her go, there was no telling when she'd come back.

'I've been going over what you told me.'

'As a friend.'

'There's no harm in hoping.'

She took her cup in her hands as if she was cold, but I don't believe she was.

'And your opinion?'

'For what it's worth, and we've only discussed it once, I don't think you have OCD. I do think, though, that you show signs of OCD traits.'

'The art of the fine distinction.'

'I don't think it is.'

As she raised her cup to drink, vapour from the coffee condensed on her glasses. She took them off to dry them with a napkin, which confirmed my impression that though her vision was poor, Faith had lovely eyes.

'From what I've read, there isn't a cure.'

'It's not a disease.'

'So what would you call it?'

'A condition. One that can be managed.'

'By the patient or the counsellor?'

'By both working together.'

The food when it arrived seemed strangely appropriate. My peppers were stuffed and her chicken was skewered. If she wanted to stab me, this was her chance.

Neither of us cared for talking and eating at the same time, so we didn't say much for a while and I became aware of piped music above the din of people talking. Why did restaurants do that? I'd read that in the old juke box days you could choose a recording of silence to give yourself a break. Things had regressed since then – now you could pay for everything else but you couldn't pay for peace.

When Faith spoke again she went for it. She needed to know.

'A counsellor can't have a sexual relationship with a client, am I right?'

'Yes.'

'So a counsellor that way inclined might clear the ground by bumping the client in question off his list.'

'That's true. He might.'

'So tell me, Max, is that what's happening here?'

I had already given this question some thought, so although it went directly to the heart of the matter I was able to answer it. Which was fortunate, since evasion was never a viable option with Faith. I don't believe I expressed myself well and her summary made me sound like an idiot, but there wasn't (and isn't) an ounce of malice in her. All she was doing was trying to understand and making sure she did. It may have been uncomfortable for me, but it worked.

'Let's see if I've got this right. You find me attractive; you like the way we walk together in synch; you think I smell good; you find me intelligent, more than a match for you; your feelings for me are sexual in nature, but go somewhat deeper than that; you think about me when I'm not there – oh, and you like me, which is very important. Have I missed anything?'

Liking is something over which we have little or no control. We like someone long before we know much about them. It's an instinct. An instinct can be wrong, but you can't make it up. That's why it matters.

She hadn't missed anything out, but I had.

'I can be open with you.'

'And that's unusual?'

Clearly it was.

I'd known Colin for several years, we got on well, but I already knew that there were things I could talk about with Faith which I would never discuss with him.

'Very.'

15

On the Friday before the big day, Janice sent each of us a text and an email: she didn't believe in taking chances. We were to appear by 8.30 at the latest the following morning. Since I wanted to live longer, I arrived at 8.20.

I knew that Vicky and Antonia had gone to a cash and carry the previous day and returned with bulk supplies (crisps, peanuts, Battenberg cake, sausage rolls, teabags, instant coffee, milk, sugar, and various soft drinks) so I assumed that before the arrival of the hoped-for crowds, I would spend my time fighting trestle tables into an upright position, spreading creased table cloths and filling borrowed urns. But it didn't work out that way. Catherine and her friend Sally, a dental technician, had volunteered to handle the hospitality so my services in the studio were surplus to requirements till the doors opened.

I was making a tour of my prints, admiring the neat little labels Colin had fixed beside each one identifying the location and boldly stating the purchase price, when Catherine pinned me to the wall: was I aware there were no knives or teaspoons? What were the punters supposed to do? Oh, and napkins might be a good idea. Think of the grease in a sausage roll! So before I knew it I was setting off in my car in search of plastic cutlery and other sundries, which I duly obtained in a large supermarket.

I was uneasy about the Open Day, not because I couldn't handle it but because, for me, only the arrival of Faith would make it worthwhile. Did we understand each other now? I believed we did, but it remained to be seen.

The Warehouse was busy when I returned, mostly with my colleagues and their friends, though an orderly queue of three had formed at the entrance two of whom, I was told, were well known on the jumble sale circuit, their method being to get in quick, pick up what bargains they could at a knock-down price and sell them on later. The third was a gentleman who specialised in left-handed golf clubs, so what he expected to find was one of those mysteries no one cared to solve.

The table in the entrance was staffed by Friends of the Warehouse, not a large group but tireless with it, whose benefits included a member's discount on selected purchases and occasional workshops in arts and crafts. Janice had supplied The Friends with a cashbox and float, purchases to be paid for on the way out against a bill issued in the studio concerned. She had come with Bernard in tow and set him up in the ground-floor office with a spreadsheet for running totals, separate columns for each artist - according to some, the first useful thing he'd done for the arts.

We couldn't handle plastic but could process cheques through The Warehouse general account. If a cheque bounced that would be something else but, as Ceramick pointed out, if most people weren't honest crime wouldn't pay. Albert wanted to know what was to prevent a light-fingered individual secreting objects about his person and just walking out? Many of his toys were small and easily concealed. We'll just have to keep our eyes peeled, then, won't we, Ceramick said. Fine, replied Albert, but wanted to know if 'we' included Ceramick himself. I'll be in my studio, Ceramick replied. And everyone else would be in theirs. Albert had a point.

Walking round The Warehouse that morning, I was impressed myself. Albert, Ceramick, Colin and Janice were well set up on the ground floor, but I was more struck by the first. The eats would do a roaring trade, they always did, and Steve had come prepared with something he hadn't made himself, an electric fiddle, which punters could play wearing headphones – to get the feel of a stringed instrument without embarrassment since no one else would hear them play. But it was George, leading with his bow tie, who was going for the jackpot – charcoal sketches he could dash off in minutes for a modest charge with a view to future commissions. He was still banging on about portraits above the mantelpiece, but he didn't need many takers to be, as he put it, quids in.

We opened the doors at ten. Business was quiet at first, but by half past the place was buzzing. By eleven, Catherine needed a comfort break and I found myself up to the elbows in teabags and small change. It turned out that my arithmetic left a lot to be desired, as was pointed out to me with some asperity by an older lady in tweeds.

'Did you never play cribbage, young man?'

If I had, I'd forgotten. Apparently the game was wonderful for improving one's mental arithmetic.

'I don't believe I did.'

Rather than wait for me, she sorted her change for herself and wandered off to check Vicky's handiwork. I'd overheard several people praising it, though being silver it didn't come cheap. It left cheap, though, as we found near close of play when she checked her stock.

'Well, well, Mr Frei, if it isn't yourself.'

Lyndsay Craig had arrived, full of the joys. If anything, she was even more tanned than before and looked the picture of health. By comparison Faith looked anaemic, though I'm sure she was perfectly healthy. But health is one thing, rude health another.

'Who else would it be?'

'Have you a minute?'

I did, when Catherine came back. There was something Lyndsay wanted to ask me, so we headed for the window with our teas.

'I've been looking at your photographs, Max. Some of them are excellent.'

'Glad you like them.'

'I don't know if you've seen our adult education programme.'

I hadn't, but she had a copy with her. Their photography teacher had run off with a married physiotherapist and they were seeking a replacement for the following term, starting in January.

'Well the thing is, Lyndsay, January must the worst month of the year for an evening class in photography. Next to no light.'

I considered this a wonderful side-step till she pointed out that the class ran during the day.

'Think about it, Max. Another string to your bow can't be bad in these straitened times.'

Knowing the official perspective never does any harm, I asked her what she thought of the open day. Ceramick had a large banner in his studio. THE GREATEST LIVING IRISHMAN. Had I seen it?

'You're having me on.'

'I may have to advise him about the Trades Descriptions Act.'

'He wouldn't pay any attention.'

And then there was George. When she'd entered his studio he'd pounced at once. The charcoal sketch was a good likeness. She'd left it with him for later collection but really, the man had been all over her. Positively salivating. He'd extolled the virtues of her profile, her complexion, and was about to move down her body to fields and pastures new when she recruited other visitors as insurance.

'How do you put up with the man?'

'Easy for me, I'm male.'

Lyndsay left me with a copy of her adult education programme, which I put in a desk drawer for safe keeping. But by that time the girls we were running low on sausage rolls and I, as the least useful member of the crew, was sent out for more. Several visitors had asked for Earl Grey tea, so that was added to my list as well. When I returned the place was still busy, but as I approached the studio I heard a voice I recognised.

'Takes them himself, does he?'

'Of course he does. That's what it says.'

'Doesn't have much of a track-record.'

'Everyone has to start somewhere.'

Looking through the open door I saw them both, DS MacNeil and DC Hunter. They were talking to Catherine as they checked out the photographs.

'Sold any yet?'

'The ones with the red dots.'

This was news to me. Colin had come up while I was out, mostly to cuddle Catherine but also to add a red dot or two – as he put it, to encourage the others. People bought what was selling, it validated their choices.

When I walked in, DC Hunter took it in his stride.

'We both live locally,' he lied, 'thought we'd take a peek.'

DS MacNeil, on the other hand, managed to make a compliment sound like a threat.

'It seems you are a man of many talents, Mr Anderson.'

Given where she said it, making no attempt to lower her voice, it was an act of obvious provocation. This officer had her knife into me for no other reason, as far as I could tell, than personal animus, yet I could hardly lodge a complaint that a police officer had addressed me by my own name.

By half past two and no sign of Faith I was beginning to lose heart. In fact she had arrived, but had been intercepted by Ceramick on the way in and gone on to look at Colin's prints, also on the ground floor. She wanted to meet this man I talked about so much. When she finally made it upstairs she was attracted to Steve's end of the building by the sound of someone trying out a cello. And then she wandered into the atelier of that much-admired portrait painter, George Abercrombie, RSA. (According to Ceramick, who knew a thing or two, when George was still an associate he had taken great exception whenever the final letter of his ARSA was replaced by a different vowel, the culprits being a coven of aggrieved ex-partners and models.)

And that was where I finally found Faith (as they say in religious circles) during a tour to see how things were going. Ignoring the many visitors admiring the sketches on his wall and the few portraits he'd been able to borrow back for the day from reluctant owners, the great man only had eyes for her. He realised at once what a striking subject she would be. Even by his standards he was remarkably forward, heaping fulsome praise on her bone structure (the usual stand-by) but also on her lustrous dark-brown hair and wonderfully light complexion - so pale, so white yet so aglow with oestrogen it would light up a darkened room! He could see the finished portrait in his mind's eye, one of a contrasting pair. (The other was probably Lyndsay whom he described, without naming her, as an energetic young lady, the very embodiment of the callisthenic physique.) The working title of his diptych was Light and Shade, but he hoped to improve on it later. To my great irritation he led her to the nearest window where he placed a plump hand on her chin and tilted her head to one side.

'Yes,' he said, 'beautiful. I can visualise it now as clear as day.'

I had seen George several times before, but never so worked up. His face was more florid than usual, no doubt caused by a rush of blood to the head – and a rush of blood somewhere else if I knew the signs. He was making a fool of himself, which I didn't mind at all, and embarrassing Faith, which I minded a lot. It couldn't go on. I was just stepping forward to rescue her when Faith, regaining possession of her head, turned away from the window into the room. She was clearly relieved when she saw me.

'Sorry about this,' I said in her ear, escorting her from the studio and leading her to the refreshments. 'The man's over the top.'

But he'd already joined a group of visitors admiring his portrait of an Irish setter which was, I have to admit, beautifully done. The coat shone, the eyes lived with light. Tiring as he was, the man had talent.

Faith left his studio with relief, and with an excellent charcoal sketch which is still in our possession. I was pouring her a tea when I caught up with the fact she really was standing beside me: Faith, the constant object of my thoughts. Was there anywhere she could store a sketch? I slipped it into the desk drawer, where it joined the Adult Education Programme. No doubt they'd get on well.

'You wouldn't have something stronger, by any chance?'

I could see she was unsettled, handed over to Catherine and Sally, and led her behind the screen, where she had the privacy to recover her composure. She had a theory.

'You know what the worst of it is? If you responded he'd run a mile. That man wouldn't know what to do with a woman if he actually got his hands on her.'

Either that, or he was concealing the fact that he was homosexual. But George was bold as they come. He wouldn't have concealed it, he'd have used it as a selling point. I could hear that mellow voice very clearly – *Michelangelo and I*. In any case, we had the string of ex-partners to contend with. The answer seemed clear. He painted more women than men and wanted to keep it that way.

'Here I am complaining, and I haven't even seen your photographs yet.'

'Maybe not, but I can tell you some people who have.'

We hadn't been in our little hideaway long when Catherine appeared, ostensibly on the hunt for more plastic teaspoons, though it was obvious she was following her nose, the end of which was almost visibly twitching. Colin had told her about Faith. I left them to talk for a while, joining Sally at the drinks. The table cloths, which had been pristine at ten, were heavily stained, and the available eats were dwindling fast. But so were the punters, as most had seen what they came for and were gradually making their way to the stairs.

The pair of them reappeared together, deep in conversation then, to my dismay, Catherine took Faith on a tour of the photographs. It lasted too long for my liking, and when they finally made it back to the tables Catherine left me to my fate.

'Well, Max, you are a dark horse. They aren't at all bad.'

Nothing like litotes to put a man down, reminiscent of report cards from earlier years: not without merit, not unworthy of encouragement.

'A sideline, I believe you said.'

Sally, looking at a sheet of paper behind the counter, chipped in with the news that I'd sold seven. I reminded her about Colin's scheme with red dots but, even allowing for that, I'd sold four. I could hardly believe it. Was there no end to people's gullibility?

'You'll have to keep records of your sales,' Catherine pointed out, 'if you don't, you'll sink without trace. And not in a shoe box!'

It was nearly three, an hour before we were due to shut up shop, when I heard a commotion farther along the corridor. Vicky had discovered that several items of jewellery were missing from her display and was letting everyone know it. When we reached her studio we were met by DC Hunter, Antonia and Janice, all trying to calm her and none of them succeeding. Vicky was explaining through her tears that though she had a table to display her wares, items of value were mounted on a board behind it and should have been safe. She had only left for minute to go to the toilet.

But Janice was looking on the bright side.

'If Bernard spots him leaving he won't stand a chance.'

'How do you make that out?'

'He plays for the first fifteen. Forward. Front row. Built like a tank.'

DC Hunter was less easily impressed.

'Right you are, Miss, and how would he know who to tackle?'

Vicky produced photographs of the stolen items and handed them to DC Hunter.

'These are excellent, but they probably won't do much good.'

Antonia, with her arm round Vicky, was offended by the suggestion.

'But officer, come on, theses pieces are amazingly distinctive. Really easy to identify.'

'Not when they're melted down.'

'But who would do a thing like that?' Vicky wailed, as if she was seeing the conquistadores reducing exquisite Inca art to bullion before her very eyes.

According to DC Hunter, silver was currently selling for twenty dollars per troy ounce. Perhaps we didn't realise that over the last five years it had almost tripled in value. He produced a smart phone with the latest must-have app – live spot prices for silver and gold. Yes, he confirmed, the price he'd quoted had hardly dropped off at all.

'So I'm sure you can see what's in it for them.'

There was nothing to be done. The chances of the thief being still in the building were vanishingly small. The roof had leaked, all we could do was mop up the water. I could see Faith sizing up DC Hunter and feared for a moment she was going to tackle him on my behalf. It wouldn't have been the best time to do it.

'Is he the one who's been harassing you?'

'One of them.'

'Seems very pleased with his technology.'

He also wanted to know if anything was missing from anyone else's studio. When Colin and Catherine appeared a plan was agreed. The artists would check their stock, while Catherineand Bernard would reconcile bills against receipts.

I could see at once that Colin didn't like the idea. He realised how long it would take and knew it would ruin the cosy foursome he had planned in a local restaurant. His hopes of a relaxing end to a long day had disappeared.

As well as silver artefacts, the thief had stolen time.

16

We stood in the courtyard, Faith and I, with decisions to make. Neither of us was skilled at saying one thing and meaning another, though I found it relatively easy to pick up these nuances as an observer when not directly involved. And both of us were poor at small-talk, even with each other.

It was growing dark rapidly and getting colder by the minute. What we needed was an apparent contradiction, a public place where we could talk in private. Neutral ground. This was more of an instinct on my part than a reasoned position. If we were going to talk about Faith's mental issues, or mine for that matter, then we should not contaminate either her place or mine with such a discussion. The home should be a haven, a refuge where, when you shut the door, your problems and anxieties are left outside on the mat like a pair of muddy boots. I was well aware that this can never be wholly achieved without leaving your head outside too, but I aspired towards that state of being. (If the Green Knight could do it, so could I.)

Acting on this principle, I suggested a suitable venue and told Faith where it was. Since I already knew it well she said she'd follow me, but we all know how easily that can go wrong, especially in the dark – a red light at the wrong time, vision obscured by a van on the road ahead, leaving too large a space and having it filled by a boy racer.

Despite such hazards we arrived safely and drove up the side-street near the venue. I stopped on my usual spot outside the builder's yard. Faith headed for the opposite side of the road, which was occupied by a large warehouse used by several firms of funeral undertakers. Aside from leaving large black limos there overnight I had no idea what it contained, but I could guess. I had often the seen their unmarked vans outside or, to use the favoured euphemism, their private ambulances.

The building was long and windowless but had five garage doors at intervals along its length. Faith decided to park between two of them, making sure to block neither, though no one used them at that time on a Saturday night. (Die when you like, but we reserve the right to conduct our business at designated hours.) We were walking down the road to the restaurant and had almost made it to the door when she stopped, turned on her heel, returned to her car and tried a handle. It was locked.

We made it at the second attempt. Two of the walls were lined with banquette-style bays, so the privacy angle was catered for. We selected one near a heater. When the waitress came (Hungarian and civilised with it) we ordered burgers and salad with a bowl of chips to share. Food was not what this was about. Nor drink, I thought, but Faith wanted wine so we ordered a glass of house merlot, which proved to be a good idea since both of us grew more forthcoming than usual. As Charlie so rightly put it, there is nothing like a bit of lubrication. Our talk turned to theft.

Vicky had asked DC Hunter where his boss had gone, since two officers had come to the open day. She also wanted to know why they hadn't warned us in advance. If Albert could do it, so could they. Hunter had replied that their intelligence, such as it was (I couldn't help agreeing with him there) was far too vague for that. They didn't have names or faces, just a tip-off from the retail sector via the Shop Watch scheme. Known shop-lifters were operating in the area.

'That's not why they were there, though, was it. They were turning the screw on you.'

She was showing signs of wanting to protect me from the massed ranks of my enemies, and I was grateful, but I knew I hadn't merited such a turn-out from the law. But for the shop-lifters, they wouldn't have been there at all.

'They were probably killing two birds with one stone.'

Faith raised the subject of photography. How seriously did I take it? Determined to be as open with her as possible, I admitted I was an amateur at best, but had to profess an art or craft to qualify for renting the studio. She appreciated that, but did I need to rent it at all? Surely I could set aside a room in my flat and keep the photography as a hobby?

If she'd ever set eyes on my flat she wouldn't have suggested it, so I risked a reference to a possible future.

'When you see my flat you'll realise why I can't do that.'

Time to Talk

Then I remembered Lyndsay's offer. Faith was amused.

'Adult education, what next?'

Her smile outshone the candle at our table.

'Still, your photographs are good enough to have some market value.'

'Because a few were stolen?'

'Tells you something, doesn't it?'

Yes it did, but what? My clients usually told me something too, but what they really meant was another matter.

'It tells me they hadn't a clue. They weren't worth stealing.'

I was reminded of my chemistry teacher, popularly known as TNT, and not because of his highly charged personality. He added one substance to another till something happened: the colour changed, noxious fumes were given off, or – his preferred result – they exploded. Then he would attempt to see if we were still there through his glasses and pose the question, *Is this significant?* Even in my innocent years I knew the answer could only be yes. At which point the real question followed: *So what does it signify?* And this was the question I'd been asking ever since.

It seemed that when Catherine had taken Faith on a guided tour of 'my recent work' they'd got on well. Catherine, of course, was sounding her out at a polite remove on the nature of her relationship with me – were we an item? – while Faith was doing her best to classify Catherine under a human version of the Dewey system in the hope of finding her a happy home on the correct shelf. But she had failed and it troubled her.

'From what you've told me they've run out of options – she wants children, he doesn't – yet there they were together again as if it wasn't a problem.'

'I don't get it either.'

'But you know Colin really well, haven't you asked?'

I hadn't liked to. In any case, I thought I knew. Colin had no interest in anyone but her and Catherine had nowhere else to turn. But if she met someone else (and if she was classic rather than a romantic) Colin's days were numbered.

Living with an accountant everything is numbered. Living with a librarian everything is filed. One function of the stereotype is to reduce the need for thought, thus saving time and energy, features it shares with the routine. Both are dangerous. With the stereotype our gaze stops at the surface which, unless that's all there is, will usually mislead. The routine is more insidious. You check certain things before you go to bed: the doors are locked, the radiator off, the clothes you will wear tomorrow lying on the chair. But when you feel the need to check that you have checked, that you really have covered all the bases, then the routine becomes an in-growing toenail of the mind, harming what it exists to protect.

A well-known OCD trait is the need to keep things in good order – a place for everything, everything in its place. There were clear signs of this in Faith's behaviour at work, but in her case it so happened that good order was a requisite of her profession. So which came first? Did working in the library give rise to her need for order, or did the prior existence of that need lead to her choice of profession? And even if we could figure it out, would it help? Probably not. We had to start from where we were, regardless of how we'd got there.

Eating and thinking, chewing things over – they go well together. Faith asked if I'd given the other matter any thought. She was clearly referring to her possible OCD. We'd been thinking about the same thing, which I took to be a sign.

'Isn't that amazing.'

'Telepathy,' she agreed, with a wry smile.

Well, yes, I had given the matter some thought, but before going any farther there were some questions.

'Fire away.'

I'd listed them the day before but left my briefcase in the car. When I returned, she was writing in a note-pad. Her hand, as they used to say, was small, neat and leaning slightly to the right. A graphologist might have made something of it, and no doubt her style of writing reflected her character to a limited extent, but not enough to tell us anything we didn't know already.

'I have questions too,' she said, as I sat down. 'Anyway . . .'

I started with what she'd told me before, scenes of borrowers lying dead on the floor, the library slowly filling with water. She evoked them well, but I began to wonder at her apparent calmness.

'So, Faith, don't you find it upsetting, the prospect of your beloved library filling with water and ruining your books?'

She'd given this thought enough some days since to have drafted an answer. Turning back a few pages she handed me her notebook open at the place. When the library was flooded no farther harm could come to it and the problem was at an end. She didn't need to worry any more since there was nothing she could do. (A consoling thought: when the cancer kills you, it also kills itself.) Likewise, customers taken out by ricin could do no harm either. Her analysis was logical, but that was a problem in itself. Worry isn't regulated by logic, nor is anxiety. The fact that there is nothing you can do about a problem doesn't make it go away, and if it doesn't go away why wouldn't you worry?

'Of these two scenarios which do you prefer?'

'The second.'

And she knew why. Although it was more radical it didn't damage the stock.

'I realise having no users defeats the purpose of having a library in the first place but Max, this isn't a solution I advocate. It just pops into my mind from time to time.'

My impression was that these thoughts were akin to waking dreams, her fears expressed as visual images including extreme solutions. But the fact remained that though she found them thought-provoking she didn't find them disturbing, so it seemed to me that they did not indicate full-blown OCD. On the other hand, Faith did report the following: a need to keep things in order or arranged in a specific way; a need to check lights, taps, radiators, windows and doors; a need to rewrite letters and reports which were already adequate; a tendency to open envelopes she had just sealed to ensure that the contents were complete, error-free and destined for the correct recipient.

We had just established all this when the waitress appeared to top up our coffees: a welcome diversion before we cut to the chase.

'Well?'

'In my opinion, you don't have OCD.'

'But I do have OCD traits.'

'I hope you're not disappointed.'

'Why would you say that?'

'Some people like to have a condition. It helps to define them. Lends them a certain status. Makes them special.'

Faith smiled. 'I'm special already.'

She wanted to know what to do and asked me the obvious question. What was the best approach to dealing with her problem? I reported the current thinking, but pointed out that I wasn't trained in cognitive behavioural therapy.

'But you could help.'

'We could manage it together.'

'How?'

'By talking with each other.'

'It can't be as simple as that.'

'Why not?'

A large group came in from the church nearby, joined three tables together and got to work sorting out the world. They seemed happy. Perhaps it was the security of the group, or maybe they knew they were chosen. (I could almost hear Mr Robertson quoting from Revelations Chapter 14.) But I was the one who had Faith, or so I thought.

'By the way,' she said, 'I nearly forgot. There's someone else.'

My shock must have shown in my face.

'What's wrong, Max? Are you alright?'

I was when she explained that the someone else was not a competitor but a friend who hoped to consult me. Hazel was married to an actor.

'Is that a problem?'

'It is for her.'

Half an hour later, with only twenty minutes to go till the restaurant closed, Faith invited me back to her flat. She didn't say 'for coffee', she simply invited me back. And what did he do, the man who believed that sex was more trouble than it was worth and in any case preferred a life uncomplicated by relationships? He accepted her invitation.

17

I was sitting at my desk on a cold November morning. My heater was on, but taking some time to make an impression on the studio, which would double as a consulting room when Hazel arrived for our first meeting. It had an hour to improve things, but I wasn't planning to grow tomatoes. I wasn't expecting Colin either, though I should have been since he often dropped by and this time had more reason than usual. He'd heard a rumour that my stolen prints had been spotted in a second-hand shop. It didn't surprise me. I hadn't expected them to surface at a fine art auction.

'That's the beauty of the digital age,' he mused, 'the thief can steal a copy of the image but not the image itself. The file's still there on your computer.'

'If only Vicky could say the same.'

It was clear that all this talk about thieves and images was a preamble to the subject he really wanted to talk about, which was strange because Colin usually came straight to the point. We had planned to meet for coffee the day before, but I had called off and Colin was sure he knew why. Faith and I had left together on that memorable Saturday night and he'd drawn his own conclusions.

'So how did it go?'

The fact that a question is simple doesn't mean the answer is too. I was reminded of word association tests. When a word is full of meaning, so many thoughts pass through the subject's mind that a rapid answer is impossible. So how had it gone? I fobbed him off with generalities (very well, better than expected, early days yet) and assured him I'd be seeing her again. He knew I was keeping him at a distance and probably put it down to my natural reticence in personal matters. If he did, he was right. My thoughts were interrupted by an outbreak of barking from the other end of the corridor. George had a new customer: a man wanting a likeness of himself posing with his basset hound. In baronial style, no doubt.

When Hazel arrived. She was wrapped in a black velvet cloak lined in red, her head protected by a hat, also black, with a wide, floppy brim. She swept to her chosen chair as if a fair wind had caught her and carried her before it. Once seated, she removed her gloves and laid them on the desk. Quite an entrance, by far the most dramatic I had yet experienced, but faintly ridiculous, since she was barely five feet tall. If you've got it, flaunt it. If you've not got much of it, flaunt it even more.

'Faith suggested I should come. She's told me a lot about you.'

Her voice was surprisingly sonorous for one so small. Apart from the fact that Hazel had married an actor, Faith had told me nothing about her.

'Are you in the profession as well?'

'Good morning to you too.'

I had forgotten the formalities.

'No, I'm not an actor. And before you ask, I don't usually go around in this get-up but,' she said, stroking the cloak, 'we have such things lying around the house and this is just terrific in the cold.'

They had been married for thirteen years following a whirlwind courtship. Everything had gone well, very well in fact, until she heard a rumour. I had to understand how difficult it was when the company was touring and she was home alone. What did they get up to after the show? What did they get up to when they returned to their hotel? They drank of course, they were actors, but after that, their inhibitions weakened by alcohol? Anyway, to cut a long story short, she was on the phone to him one night when she heard, and she was sure of this, a woman's voice in the background. He claimed the television was on, but he would, wouldn't he? And when she'd made enquiries the people she spoke to were strangely reticent – not something they could normally be accused of. Something was going on.

'Have you put this to him directly?'

'Of course. I have no intention of sitting on my hands. He denied it outright. Said he was shocked I would even think such a thing.'

'But you didn't believe him.'

Belief was at the heart of her problem. As far as I could tell from divorce statistics, lurid tales in the tabloids and even a few individuals I had known, many people out there were not to be trusted. Some were masters of duplicity, only being found out by accident after years of double-dealing. So deception was not only possible, it occurred on a large scale, and there was no reason to suppose that actors were any different in that respect. Yet they represented an added layer of complication. Your average cheat could be expected to lie, and anecdotal evidence suggested many of them were good at it. But the whole point of acting is to put across emotions the actor doesn't genuinely feel and, for the duration of the performance, to be believed. So when Hazel had faced her husband with his infidelity his denial had been convincing. Of course it was. To the talent of the natural liar he had added his professional skills. So Hazel was no longer sure she knew, when her husband spoke, what was true and what was false. Nothing seemed real to her anymore.

I asked her if she would like a tea or a coffee. I was being civil, I was also bearing in mind how cold it was, but mostly I was buying myself a little thinking time.

'Love the screen,' she said, as the kettle boiled, 'you can almost smell those blossoms.'

Some people followed me behind it to my little kitchenette. She did not.

When I came back with her coffee she frowned at the biscuits, patting a stomach I could barely detect as if weight was an issue, but quickly returned to the subject.

'You see my problem.'

I did, only too clearly.

'So what do you think?'

'I don't feel my thoughts will be helpful.'

'Tell me anyway. That's why I'm here.'

I was not a relationship counsellor and had always made that clear, but her husband, actor or not, could be understood like anyone else by comparing what he said with what he did: if she was right, there had to be a tension between the two. The more she could see him in action the better, perhaps by going with him on tour. Failing that, an external eye might be necessary. In theory, this could be provided by another member of the company, but only if one could be found who wouldn't lie for him through loyalty or friendship. Failing either of these alternatives, the services of a professional would be needed to resolve the question once and for all by keeping him under surveillance.

'You're probably right, Mr Frei, in terms of the practicalities, but I would take exception to your notion of once and for all. I am living with a lack of trust now. I can't spend the rest of my life checking up on a man who is, let's face it, a master of the plausible by profession. I'm not looking for the truth so much as help in managing my emotions in this cesspit of falsity.'

'It sounds as if you've marked his card already.'

Hazel told me that she lectured in English literature, had done for seven years. I didn't see where that got us but I knew there was more to come.

'The classics have a lot to teach us, Mr Frei.'

I perked up for a moment till I realised she was referring to authors as recent as Jane Austen and George Eliot, on whom the dust has barely settled.

'I wrote a little monograph on Austen, I don't know if Faith told you, with special reference to Mansfield Park.'

'I don't believe she mentioned it.'

'The question of acting comes up in the book.'

'Your monograph?'

'Mansfield Park. Austen makes the case that the essence of acting is pretence, deception, lies, fantasy – you name it. It's inevitable, really, when you have men and women on a stage pretending to be people they're not and saying things made up by someone else. They aren't who they claim to be and don't mean what they say.'

'The moral case against the theatre.'

'Exactly. Well all I can tell you is I'm beginning to feel like Fanny Price.'

Hazel could see I was trailing in her wake and patiently explained that young Fanny had refused to take part in a play on the grounds that she couldn't act. She didn't have it in her to do it. But according to Hazel's thesis, which I cannot confirm or deny, the fact that Fanny couldn't act also signified an inability to take action.

'It's what we might refer to as polysemous verity.'

I was beginning to wonder if I could cope with a woman who could use such a phrase with a straight face. 'Double meaning' would surely have done.

'Your husband is the actor and you are Fanny.'

'That's how it looks to me and I have no intention of being passive here. Oh, and by the way, this issue crops up in Daniel Deronda too.'

I pre-empted a tutorial on that book as well by summarising her position. She thought her husband was playing the field, but because of his acting skills she couldn't be sure. She expected him to continue playing the field, but she couldn't be sure of that either for the same reason.

It occurred to me then that marriage could be thought of as a play with starring roles for two and a variety walk-on parts for family and friends. But the fact is we all have roles. We are not the same person to everyone we meet, so becoming a husband or a wife does little more than put a label on the fact. But I kept my thoughts to myself.

'If I might play devil's advocate here, Hazel: since you feel totally undermined by the present situation and nothing's going to change on his side of the bed, your only recourse is to kick him out of it or get up and leave.'

She didn't like the sound of that at all.

'We've been married for thirteen years!'

Her cri de coeur was affecting, but irrelevant to our shared understanding of the facts. Yet I hoped it might stiffen her resolve. If her suspicion was correct, and she was adamant it was, Henry had been unfaithful, and possibly more than once. A man like that may become more careful but, as we know, the leopard will not change his spots nor the tiger his stripes. And if her thirteen years of marriage were considered an investment of human capital, what then? It had lost some value already. Was she going to sit by as more years passed and watch it depreciate further? The only way forward I could see was that the lady cut her losses. The truth hardly mattered any more. If she was right, it was time to sever the knot. If she was wrong, even if Henry was unblemished as the driven snow, what did it avail her if she didn't believe it.

'I take it there are no children involved.'

Fortunately not, unless we counted the cats. Two of them. Siamese. I was thinking how easy that was, one going to Henry, the other to Hazel.

'They have to stay together, of course. They'd be lost without each other.'

Unlike the loving couple, it would seem.

We agreed how important it was that Hazel kept talking during this difficult period, to iron out any fresh wrinkles which might arise but mostly to manage her anger. She wanted to consult me on a regular basis (eight for the price of ten) and that was fine by me. But it shouldn't have been for her. A friend could have met this need as well as I could, probably better, and certainly more cheaply. I was surprised by her resistance when I suggested it. Though she was less clear on this than she had been on Mansfield Park, it seemed a sense of failure was something she was reluctant to share with a friend, however close. Faith knew of her suspicions but she'd told no one else. She had her pride. She was going to behave as if things were better than they seemed, adopting a certain front with those who knew her. She intended to take up acting.

Rising to leave she lifted her gloves in her left hand and offered me her right. I wondered for a moment if I was expected to kiss it. I couldn't help noticing, as she walked out, that the top of her head maintained a constant distance from the floor, as if she were gliding on well-oiled hips. It was almost a cartoon moment, a clip from an animated film. And shortly after she left the ever alert Ceramick appeared. I could tell he was impressed.

'Who the hell was that and what's her number?'

'That, my friend, was Hazel. Out of your league.'

I withheld her number, of course. It occurred to me that a fling on her own account might help ease the pain, but a fling with Ceramick could only make matters worse. Emotional turmoil and bad jokes don't go well together, a point he underlined when he compared the vision of this long-suffering lady to an Orson Welles sherry ad which he remembered and I did not. After a moment or two of retrospective verbal ogling, Ceramick left me to my own devices. I intended to write up notes on the session just ended while it was fresh in my mind, aided by my voice recorder. But I made little progress. I kept returning to my weekend with Faith and was visited by an impulse to write that up instead in a vain attempt to explain me to myself. And it is to that impulse that I owe this account of these events and not, as has been suggested, from a desire to justify myself.

I had always liked an uncomplicated life, and nothing was more complicated than a relationship, yet I'd agreed to go home with Faith. I'd found her attractive from the day we met but had, as far as I was aware, no conscious designs on her body. This may seem odd, given the evident sexual attraction, but I was playing it by ear and in this department of life my hearing could have been better. So I was not, as some are, equipped with protection on the off-chance that an opportunity might arise whenever I hit the street, and the café, being a civilised place, had no machine. But Faith had a packet in her bathroom cabinet and pulled my leg for a while playing the femme fatale, till she finally told me more than I wanted to know about an STD awareness day at the library.

We were fastidious people, Faith and I, with vanishingly short back-catalogues of partners, but agreed afterwards that however clumsy we may have been we would surely improve with practice. In my case, over-excitement caused me, as they say in sporting circles, to peak too soon. A starving man offered food will bolt it down so quickly he will fail to savour it at all, but in subsequent meals he will savour the turmeric, basil and dill even if he can't put a name to them.

As far as this narrative goes there has to be a limit. It is not a work of fiction. If it were then graphic descriptions of sexual congress would be expected or even required, but the interest of such descriptions is in inverse proportion to the detail provided – because the real material lies not in extracts from the novelist's handbook of sexual plumbing but in the emotions of those involved. In real life, as here, these have to be protected to some extent from the scrutiny of others, since that is where we reside and deserve to be secure.

Late that first night, when we lay talking in bed, my overwhelming feeling was one of closeness and fellowship. I knew I could talk to Faith about anything, and she was so straight I could always believe what she said. And for the first time, and in more ways than one, she let her hair down in my presence.

I had never given much thought to death – what's the point, when there's nothing we can do about it – yet now I had the feeling, which I'd never had before, that I wouldn't die alone.

18

It is not always possible to define exactly when things begin to unravel. In my case, it may have been when the police discovered my real name since that, for no good reason, aroused their suspicion. Or it may have been the moment when DS MacNeil took a dislike to me. I don't know exactly when that moment was, but that was her instinct and she went with it. I would have done the same. Or it may have been the occasion when Mr Robertson came for the first time.

I thought then that there was no harm in his visits, but as the traffic increased, not only in person, but by increasingly frequent texts, my doubts grew. The man suffered from monomania. He knew the Bible much better than I did, which wasn't difficult, but even if I had known it inside out and back to front it would have done me no good. Since the Bible was the word of God all we could do was accept it. To query any part of it was close to sacrilege. So whenever he raised a contentious point of exegesis there was nothing I, nor anyone else, could say. He always had a take on it to which he was totally committed and would brook no dissent. (I can only assume he had a direct line to the executive suite on the top floor.) The result was that whenever he paid me a visit no genuine dialogue took place because none could. Talking with Mr Robertson was hard enough, talking with God was beyond me.

So there was nothing for it but to terminate our sessions which, after the usual pleasantries, I attempted to do as gently as possible. At the time he took it quite well, or so it appeared. On reflection I realised why. His apparent ability to think quickly was an illusion. He had studied his subject for so many years that his many opinions hung neatly laundered and ready to hand in his wardrobe or lay folded, equally neatly, in his drawer. Taking one out was easy. I remember the day was cold and Mr Robertson, by virtue of working outdoors was redder in the face than usual, though growing choler at my decision may have been a factor.

On this last, memorable occasion, he had come armed with the view that while the Bible was entirely the word of God, not all of God's words were to be found within it. For this sorry state of affairs he blamed a dark conspiracy by the fathers of the early church, who had deliberately chosen to exclude texts which did not accord with their views or which, if published, would have greatly complicated the theology they sought to defend. At first I assumed he was referring to the standard apocrypha such as the Book of Judith, but he had cast his net so widely it took in the Gospel of Mary Magdalene and the Nag Hammadi texts. Mr Robertson was coming to the view that God was not some exterior being viewing events from on high, but that He lived within us, where it behoved us all to seek him out. (Even in accounting for his views I find I am overtaken by his language.)

I heard him out, of course, but told him I was not a fit person to conduct such a discussion, which was no more than the truth. What did I know about the hypostasis of the archons? Absolutely nothing and, truth be told, I hoped to keep it that way. And that, I thought, would be the end of the matter. But just one day later the first of several querulous texts arrived. Mr Robertson was not a happy man. I had turned my back on a fellow human being in his hour of need: just as well the Good Samaritan hadn't done the same!

Unfortunately, Mr Robertson was one of those people who liked, as he put it himself, to take pen in hand, which he duly did, writing to the relevant professional association and accusing me of failing in my duty of care to a vulnerable client. Had I been a doctor he would have written to the BMA. Since I was a counsellor, he wrote to the BACP. In the light of the reply he received from that body, he phoned the police where, as luck would have it, his call was patched to DS MacNeil. But I did not know any of this till three days later, when DC Hunter called in at The Warehouse. Items had been found, believed to have been stolen from Vicky, Albert and myself. He would be grateful if we would call at Leith police station at our earliest convenience to identify the objects in question. It was a trap, of course, and all the more effective because DC Hunter was unaware of it himself.

Vicky's car was an old Peugeot built like a tank. She dismissed mine as a tin can on wheels. According to her, a minor collision in 'that thing' and our legs would be written off. She wasn't too keen on my driving either. Albert was nowhere to be found, so she drove us to the station at a sedate speed, keeping her eyes unswervingly on the road.

'Better to get there in one piece than not get there at all.'

When we arrived DC Hunter led us to a room so full of objects I thought he was going to open a shop.

'You have to realise this guy's a full time thief. We found all this stuff in his flat. Well, not his flat exactly, but where he was holed up.'

'Amazing.'

'What's even more amazing is he hadn't sold any of your silver yet, Miss Naismith. His father's a tax inspector back home in Nigeria so you could say thieving runs in the family.'

'How did you find him?'

'Tip off.' DC Hunter tapped the side of his nose. 'We have our sources.'

'I'm sure you do.'

'You know what's really funny?'

We didn't, though he appeared to find it diverting.

'We found a stash of money in the washing machine.'

It didn't take Vicky long to identify her work, though she was disappointed to hear that the police would be keeping it as evidence pending the trial.

'How long will that be?'

'We're talking months, I'm afraid. The legal process and all that. Sorry.'

He was, but not as sorry as she was. On the other hand, while she was reunited with her work, I saw no sign of my landscapes.

At that point, DS MacNeil popped her head round the door.

'I wonder if I could borrow you for a moment or two, Mr Frei. I have your photographs in another room.'

I followed her to the interview room we had used previously and there on the table were my prints.

'I heard they'd been spotted in a second-hand shop.'

She shook her head. 'They didn't make it that far.'

I checked them over: a bit grimy but the glass would clean up.

DS MacNeil was exactly as I remembered her, though her hair was, if anything, even more straggly and lank.

'I take it my colleague has run his money laundering joke past you.'

She invited me to take a seat. There was another matter. It wouldn't take long.

My suspicions were aroused when she asked if I minded our talk being taped. I told her I didn't, but when she started recording I told her I'd no objection to the interview being taped provided she gave me a copy. She wasn't amused.

'That can be arranged.'

'So, what's this about?'

A complaint had been received from a member of the public concerning my work as a counsellor. Not only had I failed in my duty of care towards a client, I was laying claim to accreditation to which I was not entitled. DS MacNeil had followed up on this last point and found it to be the case.

'So let's cut to the chase here, Mr Frei: as you put it so well yourself, it's time to talk.'

She was referring to a line in my publicity, quoting me against myself and loving it. Back to the wall, all I could do was deprive her of the pleasure of rising to it.

'You are not in fact accredited by the British Association for Counselling and Psychotherapy. They have confirmed this by phone with a letter to follow.'

'You're right. I'm not.'

She produced one of my fliers and put it down in front of me.

'But if we look at this flier which you have been using to promote your business, we see a reference to the BACP, do we not?'

'We do.'

'The same statement is to be found on your website – and before you go home and change it you ought to know we have taken several screenshots.'

'I see.'

'I have to tell you, Mr Frei, that this appears to be a clear case of fraud.'

I wasted some time explaining to DS MacNeil that I been nothing but courteous in my dealings with Mr Robertson, though at first she refused to admit, on grounds of confidentiality, that Mr Robertson was the complainant. I then pointed out to her that there was a difference between appearance and reality, and that her case might not be as clear as she thought. (This was the first and last time I tried to protect her from herself.)

'I have no interest in philosophical digressions, Mr Frei. The police budget won't run to it. I follow the evidence, and in this case the evidence is clear.'

'You don't like me, do you?'

She paused the recording.

'No, I don't. I've had the feeling from the start that you're nothing but a jumped-up charlatan, a fraud, a mountebank, a leech on the unfortunates of society. My intention is to put you away for as long as possible. Failing that, to make your life a misery. Do we understand each other?'

'No.'

'I beg your pardon? How much clearer do I need to be?'

'I understand you perfectly. You don't understand me.'

'Oh, I think I do, Mr Frei.'

She resumed the recording with a deliberately fake smile.

'Just to be clear, Mr Frei, I don't like you, but I don't dislike you either. I'm just doing my job.'

DC Hunter knocked, DS MacNeil excused herself for a moment and joined him in the corridor. She should have shut the door. Apart from the expected loss of upper frequencies, my hearing is excellent.

'It's definitely her stuff.'

'Is she willing to testify to that in court?'

'Willing and eager.'

'Good.'

'What about him?'

'I haven't asked him yet. His photographs were hardly worth stealing.'

'Maybe not, boss, but they were.'

'OK, Douglas, I'll ask him, but it goes against the grain. The man's a total wanker.'

As she came back in, MacNeil flashed me another of her wonderfully fake smiles and sat down.

'We'd prefer to give your photographs back to you, but we can't till after the trial.'

'Fair enough. I can always print replacements.'

'Would you be willing to testify in court?'

'His case or mine?'

This time her smile was genuine. She was beginning to enjoy herself.

'His.'

'What would that entail?'

'Identifying your photographs, stating that you gave them to no one, and confirming that you gave no one permission to sell or pledge them.'

'Sounds OK to me.'

'But to do that you'd have to identify yourself – a bit tricky in your case, wouldn't you say, since you don't seem to know who you really are?'

Another example of the woman's dead-pan humour, though she had been so keen to get one over on me she'd forgotten her insult had been recorded. But my joy at this thought was short-lived: there was more to come.

'For example, we now know that the biographical details supplied on your flier are wrong. Leaving aside your name, we find that your age, place of birth and university attended are all incorrect. Now why would that be, Mr Frei?'

I told her about my fear of identity theft and the steps I had taken to prevent it, all on the advice of an expert on the subject in a national newspaper. And after all, I had been to university, admittedly not the one mentioned in my flier, and left with an honours degree in ancient and medieval history.

'It doesn't get more relevant than that,' she said, with an unattractive curl of the lip.

That was a battle best avoided with her, so I let it pass.

'Am I under arrest?'

'Of course not. You haven't been charged with anything yet.'

'So I'm free to go.'

Vicky was restive on the way back. She couldn't see any reason why her artwork had to be kept. They had photographs, they'd caught the thief red-handed so he was hardly likely to plead not guilty, and she was more than happy to sign an affidavit. The festive period, for her the most profitable time of year, would pass her by. I could only sympathise, which I did.

When we drew up in The Warehouse courtyard she was still looking thoughtful.

'You don't have a hundred pounds to spare, I suppose?'

'No. Why?'

'If you did, you could buy a ticket for the Creative Scotland Awards.'

'Why would I want to do that?'

'You wouldn't, not when all the judges are male.'

I considered asking her why that mattered but I knew what she'd say.

'Are you going?'

'Can't afford it. Janice is, though – with a megaphone and a placard.'

'Bernard will love that.'

'By the way, I meant to ask, is that awful woman still trying to pin the drugs thing on you?'

Not this time, no. Her hand had progressed from the groin to the throat.

19

Sitting at Faith's kitchen table that evening, I told her about the arrest of Mr Olatunde and the retrieval of the items stolen at the open day in a flat off the Royal Mile. I could tell she was listening with half an ear but she was pleased, particularly for Vicky who had most to lose. She had something else on her mind.

'I'm thinking about Christmas.'

I groaned inwardly. It had been Christmas since late August in some of the shops and several TV ads.

'I'll have to buy some presents and send them off.'

We had a lot in common or, to put it another way, very few relatives still above ground. Faith's dad had done a runner, probably when he realised how brainy she was. Her mother had died several years before, suddenly: an aneurism which the consultant, in a tired but appropriate image, compared to a ticking timebomb. Faith and her brother inherited the family home, where we were now sitting on opposite sides of a beech table comparing notes. In search of a better life (sun, sand, beer and endless sport) Alan and his wife had emigrated to Australia. At which point Faith had bought him out.

She was now an aunt and showed me photographs of her nephew to prove it. I have never warmed to children, nor to the images of children (I'm not a landscape photographer for nothing) but I could tolerate the boy as long as he stayed in Adelaide.

'I have to sort this out soon, in time for the last posting day.'

'Or,' I suggested, trying to make her life easier, 'you could buy something online from an Aussie outlet and have them deliver it. Then you won't need to worry about last posting dates.'

'Doesn't seem the same, somehow.'

After another pause for thought, she told me more.

'Alan wants me to get a webcam so we can see each other as we talk.'

'Sounds good to me. Better than going there.'

It was then she revealed for the first time just how stubborn she could be, a trait which helped me a great deal in the months to come.

'Oh, no way, I wouldn't dream of it. It's well over ten thousand miles!'

'Not even to see your family?'

'Alan chose to emigrate. He didn't have to. If he wants to see me, he knows where I am.'

At the time he left, heating and ventilation engineers were in high demand. They probably still are.

I wasn't so different. My father had been a serial philanderer so the marriage ended in divorce. Never content with making a mistake once, he married again. As far as I knew, I had a half-sister out there. Somewhere.

'As far as you know! Don't you keep in touch?'

'I don't even know if the man's still alive.'

I hadn't seen or heard from him for years. Faith was amazed, she wouldn't let it lie, pursuing me into every nook and cranny with forensic skill.

'You overheard his new wife lying about you to your half-sister!'

'She was only four years old. I could hardly take her to one side and set the record straight.'

'So you gave up?'

'The antelope never returns to the poisoned well.'

She gave me a withering look.

'You're mistaking yourself for Confucius.'

'I don't believe he said that.'

'Neither do I.'

Initially, Faith was critical of what she saw as my fatalistic attitude, but as the weeks passed I noticed an increasingly acid tone when she referred to my father and his wife, a resentment she felt on my behalf since I hadn't the sense to feel it for myself. She didn't tell me at the time, but in spare moments at work she was on the case, hunting them down in their lair in the west. (Since one of them at least is still alive I will be no more explicit than that.)

Our conversation was interrupted by the sound of the door bell in the bread bin. The original front door bell, Victorian by the look of it, needed an electricity supply it no longer had so Faith had bought a wireless device from a DIY shop. She had glued the bell-push to the wood of the doorframe but had yet to find a home for the receiver, which she sometimes took with her from room to room, forgetting where she'd last set it down.

'Who could it be at this time of night?'

It was only eight thirty, but Faith didn't get out much.

Hazel had arrived. She was in a state of some agitation and Faith had her join us at the kitchen table. She sat down rather heavily where Faith had been sitting. I took her coat to a chair in the hall (no cloak this time) and laid her hat on top of it, a genuine fur ushanka sporting a Red Army badge. It was cold outside and a sensible choice of headwear, but I couldn't help feeling an air of theatricality about it as if the inner Hazel had just stepped off the set of Doctor Zhivago, trailing into our kitchen cold arctic air made visible.

'It's Henry,' she wailed, moving Faith's laptop to the middle of the table to make way for her gloves. Then she turned to me, her eyes tearful with emotion, though it may have been meibomian gland dysfunction brought on by the cold weather.

'I'm really glad you're here, Max.'

Furnished with a coffee she broke the news. A close friend, Harriet, had seen Henry on two separate occasions with a woman, name unknown, in the Botanic Gardens. They had obviously met for lunch and 'canoodling' was seen to take place. Hazel was upset, but also relieved that her suspicions had been justified. She had come to talk it over with Faith, but was delighted to see me too because I figured in her plans. This came as no surprise since I was her therapist but, not for the first time, I had totally misread someone's intent.

'You don't understand.'

Hazel wanted to make use of my services not as a therapist but as a photographer. I was to follow the errant husband on his next trip to the Botanics and document his infidelity with my long lens, the existence of which she inferred through my close-up shots of the heron, a bird I was beginning to resent. All at my usual hourly rate, of course. There was a dangerous attraction to this: Max in the undergrowth, Max as the private glass eye.

'Don't worry about it, Max. Just bill me. Henry will be paying.'

I was sure he would, for the rest of his life.

'But Hazel,' I asked, still trying to wriggle out of it, 'how could I possibly know when their next assignation will be?'

'Simple. I've checked the dates. It's always on a Friday. Whenever they meet he spins the same old story - he's going to his chiropodist in Stockbridge. Handy for the Botanics, wouldn't you say? Anyway, the next time he comes out with it I'll text you at once.'

Hazel spoke as if I'd already agreed, which is what I ended up doing.

We sat for a while in silence after she had gone, then Faith asked me what I hoped was a rhetorical question.

'We're not going to end up like that, are we?'

Apart from the fact that we were both unusually fastidious by the standards of the times, Faith was the most steadfast person I had ever come across. As for me, conventional wisdom had it that men were more likely to stray than women, as my father had often done. But having been drawn into his deceit more than once (*there's no need to tell your mother about this*) I had developed an aversion to such behaviour. Some people model themselves on their parents, others react against them.

Faith opened her laptop. It wasn't the latest model but did all that she asked of it. If she wanted one, a webcam could be attached by USB. An obvious idea for a present crossed my mind, but I couldn't help feeling her brother wanted it more than she did. Then a wonderful way out of my quandary occurred to me.

'Wait a minute.'

'What?'

'I have no idea what Henry looks like. How am I supposed to follow him?'

She collected her mobile from the kitchen counter and joined me again at the table.

'Hazel, hi. Max has never seen Henry. He hasn't the faintest idea what he looks like . . . right . . . . OK . . . . so it's one of the two but you can't remember which . . . . don't worry, we'll handle it. Get back to you. Bye for now.'

'It turns out,' Faith explained, 'that Henry is featured on one of two websites, Lip Service or Global Artists. All we need to do is look him up.'

Her fingers rattled across the keyboard but she couldn't track him down. No Henry Harrison on either site. Another call to Hazel. When Henry had registered with Equity many years before they already had a Henry Harrison on their books (vaudeville artist, music hall a speciality, basic ukulele, valid driving licence) so he had been obliged to work under another name, his chosen moniker being Henry Harriman. According to Hazel it had really rankled at the time that anyone could prevent him working under the name which was his by law, the name on his birth certificate, the person he thought of as himself. Identity is a difficult subject. Some of us choose to work under another name while others are compelled to do it: what would DS MacNeil make of that?

His profile contained what Faith assured me was a flattering shot but an excellent likeness which, to my dismay, she saved and forwarded to me as an attachment. There was no escape from Henry. Looking over her shoulder, I was struck by how much more effective the monochrome portraits were: better lit, stronger contrast. And most people must have thought the same, since relatively few were in colour.

Faith was still thinking.
'It's Friday tomorrow.'
'So if I'm really unlucky . . .'
'You'll be heading to the Botanics.'
She typed some more.
'You're not going to believe this.'
'What?'
'Olatunde has a meaning.'
I waited patiently till she stopped laughing.
'Wealth has come again!'

20

I didn't plan to, but spent the night at Faith's. Slowly, by degrees, I was losing control of my life, though in this case I was comfortable with it. I knew that for sure as I lay in her bed, half awake, hearing her quietly make her breakfast, slip on her clothes and clean her teeth in the bathroom. She liked to breakfast alone in total silence (no radio) which was easy to understand – a working girl preparing for the day ahead. I heard her lock the front door behind her as she left and open it again a moment later. Something she'd forgotten in the kitchen, something she had to check.

But acting on impulse has it down sides: it left me without a clean shirt, socks and underwear for the day ahead. For these I had to take a detour home. The moment I let myself in the contrast was clear. Even though I'd imposed a modest order on the books and magazines, my flat was a mess compared to hers. For years I'd extolled the benefits of creative disorder without knowing what it meant. I still had much to learn. Had that not been the case I'd have picked up the mail behind the door, not used it as a doormat. I would also have tracked down the things I needed much faster. Compared to mine, her flat was uncluttered, lucid, a physical extension of the woman herself. An impression reinforced by an accident of location resulting in more light. Her street was wide, the buildings opposite several yards farther away. Her rear windows faced due south.

But for the moment I was stuck with what I had. I stood in my bedroom in a mild state of panic, wondering if the shirt I wanted was clean or still in the laundry basket, if the only socks in the drawer were really those light-weight cotton numbers. Surely I'd washed something warmer than that? I'd have to sort myself out, be more methodical in my domestic arrangements.

And then there was the toothbrush. I stood in front of the bathroom mirror applying it to my teeth and gums, splattering the sink-surround with toothpaste and pondering my reluctance of the night before to use hers. Where was the logic? What was the problem with using the toothbrush of a woman I regularly kissed? It made no sense. I began to suspect an area of confusion, a troublesome overlap between the opposing realms sex and hygiene. Maybe I should draw myself a Venn diagram or raise the issue with a sex therapist. Pamela, perhaps?

Knowing I might get the call, I prepared for a possible hour or three in the Botanics by tracking down one of the lumberjack shirts I kept for arctic weather, hauled a Shetland gansie over it and completed my survival kit with an old waterproof jacket. I threw a notepad and couple of pens into my briefcase and clattered down the stairs to the street, pulling in to The Warehouse an hour later than usual. Only to be met by Mr Robertson, the last person I expected to darken my door, hand-delivering a letter of apology.

'I have to admit,' he began (which wasn't true, he could have kept it to himself) 'I have to admit to second thoughts. On mature consideration, I may have acted hastily.'

Against my better judgement I invited him in. Translating what he said into underlying motive, he had found no one else to belabour with his insights and hoped to revert to me. To make matters worse, he now believed his action had fallen short of his Christian principles.

'It wasn't the charitable thing to do, Mr Frei. There's no getting away from it.'

There was no getting away from him either, but he was holding out an olive branch (he was, after all, a gardener) by offering to withdraw his complaint. On one level, it was a meaningless gesture. He had given MacNeil the ball and she wasn't going to give it back. On the contrary, she'd kick it as far as she could towards the nearest court of law. On the other hand, and in the unlikely event of a court case, it might help if the original complainant appeared for the defence rather than the prosecution. I could imagine Mr Robertson, having done a hand-stand on the oath, grinding the court into submission with an elaborate character reference supported by quotations from Habakkuk and Nehemiah. So I told him I was expecting an urgent message but was happy to converse with him for ten minutes. And hearing this he relaxed enough to lay out his case.

Did I watch sport? Because, if I did, I must have noticed certain athletes giving thanks to God when they won their events.

I admitted that had passed me by.

'Two things trouble me here, Mr Frei. Do we really think God takes an interest in sprinting, middle-distance running, putting the shot and throwing the javelin? And even if He does, do we really believe He cares who wins?'

He had a point. It seemed unlikely to say the least.

'And the other thing? You said there were two.'

'Right enough, yes. I don't know if you've noticed that del Potro chap.'

I hadn't. He played tennis and whenever he won, which happened quite a lot, he crossed himself and cast his gaze heavenwards, yet when he lost he did neither of these things.

'So you see, Mr Frei, here we have a man who thinks God is on his side when he wins. But when he loses it doesn't occur to him that God might intend him to lose and that fulfilling His intention might also be a cause for gratitude. Don't you find that strange?'

Going on the assumption that the Good Book had little to say concerning Olympic Games and Grand Slam tennis tournaments, I felt able to engage with him on this subject. And since he was no longer a client, I also applied a quantity of soap or, as they say in the trade, provided him with validation.

'You've pin-pointed a contradiction, alright. You're definitely on to something here, Mr Robertson.'

After he had gone, my thoughts turned to Faith. I had told her about my visit to the police station concerning the stolen items and what little I had heard about the nefarious Mr Olatunde. But I had yet to tell her about the accusation of fraud. This might prove a costly omission, but the time to tell her, I felt, was when I was charged. Until then, all there was to report was MacNeil's breath on the air. Nothing definite, nothing significant. And to lay it before her when nothing might transpire, what would be the point of that?

And so I justified it to myself without putting paid to my unease. But nothing dispels analysis more than action, as I found when the call came through. For Hazel couldn't settle for sending the promised text, she had to know I had got the message and was acting on it.

'Of course. I haven't forgotten. I'm on my way.'

She was reassured, but she wouldn't have been if she'd seen me looking for my camera. In my panic at the flat I'd left it on the bed. A clean shirt is all very well, but not so good for documenting actors in delicto. I did, however, have the camera I used before I took up residence at The Warehouse, a compact little number with ten times optical zoom. In the absence of the real thing it would have to do, and I consoled myself with the thought that it was so easily concealed the guilty party was unlikely to spot it.

I set off at speed, till it occurred to me that the last thing I needed was more trouble with the law. And what with traffic and the road works it was twenty-five minutes before I made it to Arboretum Road, and another five till I found a place to park the metal. And there the time of year helped a lot: the number of visitors had always fallen sharply by mid November.

I walked up the path towards the Terrace Café, where Hazel's source thought the loving couple met, but when I entered I saw no sign of anyone resembling Henry Harriman, star of stage and screen. Assuming I'd got there before him, I ordered a hot chocolate and sat at a window table giving a good view both inside and out. The café was a popular meeting place for young mothers, au pairs and nannies, who took over large parts of it with their pushchairs and chattered noisily among themselves as they fed babies, cuddled babies, burped babies, talked about babies and regressed to baby noises in an attempt to make contact. As far as I could see, it didn't work. And how, exactly, did a diet of meaningless noises aid infant development? One for the child psychologists.

My mobile rang. It was Hazel. Where was I? She'd followed her husband at a discreet distance. He was now in the grounds. He wasn't with his fancy woman so she might already be there. I should keep my eyes peeled. That's exactly what I was doing, I assured her, and pointed out with some asperity that if Henry caught sight of her our plan would be ruined. She accepted this point under protest, but agreed to depart the scene on the understanding that I kept her appraised of developments.

Henry arrived shortly afterwards, protected from the cold by a dark, double-breasted overcoat and a black gaucho hat. He didn't look in good shape to me, somewhat gaunt about the face as if under attack from a wasting disease yet to be diagnosed, though the probable cause was the stress of duplicity. It was also possible that the portrait on Global Artists had been taken some years before and he was now advertising his talents on an out-of-date prospectus. Whatever the explanation, he strode over to a woman I had barely noticed, took off his hat and kissed her. I heard him ask if she wanted anything else, and he returned from the counter shortly afterwards with two coffees and a large slice of carrot cake.

They talked for some time, obviously very much at ease in each other's company, but nothing out of the ordinary. They might have been lovers but could just as easily have been close friends. After half an hour or so, the woman stood up and I realised she couldn't have been more than five feet tall, the same height as the aggrieved wife. When she returned from the toilet they left the building, the lady linking her arm in his. They were behaving like a couple who'd been married for years, though they may have kept their wilder moments out of the public eye. They disappeared into the Gallery for a while (When Dinosaurs Become Modernists) and when they left, headed downhill towards the Chinese garden. I followed at a discreet distance, just another visitor on a cold autumn day.

When they began their slow descent down the winding path, surely a metaphor for our downward spiral through life, I took my camera out hoping for action. In the summer months this area would have been busy, but now it was pleasantly people-free. My targets lingered for a while on the one of the bridges over the cascade leading down to the pond. Using an oriental bush for cover, I zoomed in as far as I could and lined up a shot. I was shooting from the side with the woman nearer to the camera. Had it been the other way round, Henry's bulk would have hidden her from view. With any luck, Hazel might know who she was. But this time the luck was theirs – I'd forgotten the automatic flash.

The woman reacted instantly, looking round to pinpoint the source. I crouched beside the nearest shrub, pointing my camera at it, an amateur botanist, a plant enthusiast gone mad. If she saw me, she wasn't concerned. Five minutes later, having fought my way through several menus and sub-menus, I finally found a way to turn the flash off, but by that time the couple had disappeared. Since they'd been heading downhill, I guessed they'd arrive at the pond, and that's where I found them – inside the T'ing, looking out over the water surrounded by hopeful ducks. The lady obliged from a brown paper bag. I doubt Henry was so easily satisfied.

Using undergrowth on the other side of the pond as cover, I waited with increasing impatience, one knee on the ground to make myself less visible. At first this seemed a complete waste of time, and a wet one at that. And then it happened. After a quick look round to ensure they were alone, the couple embraced and kissed and I, amateur photographer and sleuth, took a series of shots documenting their display of passion.

I checked the pictures on the camera's display. The resolution wasn't in the heron league, but what they were up to was clear. As I was checking the images I noticed a small red button. A record button! I'd forgotten that this little device recorded video as well, so I added a live action scene to my library. It wasn't in line for the Penthouse Porn Awards of the Year, but it was steamy enough to get by. A gripping encounter.

I was starting to feel pleased with myself when my mobile alerted me to an incoming text. I should have switched it off, but since I hadn't I threw myself flat on the ground. I couldn't afford to be spotted twice. When I finally risked looking up, they had gone. It wasn't a ringtone, they probably hadn't heard it or, if they had, the sound was lost among the birdsong. Hazel was anxious. She wanted to know if there was any news? Well yes, Hazel, there was: your private eye has done the business but he is wet, bedraggled and cold.

And strangely uneasy for one who had successfully completed his task. As I walked to the car, images from film noir came into my head, set-ups where the private eye bursts into the bedroom with a camera, etching the erring couple into the wall in a blinding flash of light. As they sit up in bed, we see that the man is naked from the waist up and the woman is partially draped in tasteful lingerie, probably silk. Apart from the couple, no one is shocked because this is the way adults behave, the very model of adultery, the base material for films with 'adult' content. But private eyes cost. Wouldn't it be better if the warring parties got round a table and talked? Of course it would, which is why they don't. It's too much like work. Giving way to emotions is the easy way to go, and so the child dictates to the man and neither sees trouble farther down the road.

21

Hazel insisted on reviewing the evidence as soon as possible so we agreed to meet that evening. Faith obliged by making a wholesome meal of turbot, sautéed potatoes and spinach. My role was restricted to peeling the potatoes and washing up. I noticed Faith making sure, when she thought I was occupied laying the table, that I'd cleared all the peelings from the sink.

Our visitor arrived wrapped in a rough-textured shawl which resembled a superior carpet underlay and felt like it too as she gave it to me to dispose of. So now I was reduced to the doorman dealing with a glamorous arrival at the hotel, though I looked in vain for the under-arm pooch or the tip. I put her condescending manner down to her distraction, though since she had retained me in two capacities at least she probably regarded me as a suitable candidate for the tradesman's entrance.

Faith wouldn't hear a word spoken or a damaging image viewed till we had eaten, and though I was happy with this Hazel was not and ate too quickly. She had brought a bottle of red wine to drown her sorrows, and though conventional wisdom would have indicated white her need was great and she made quick in-roads into it.

As we sat together at the kitchen table I was struck by the difference lighting can make to appearance. Whatever the natural colour of Hazel's complexion, it was overlaid by make-up strong enough to neutralise the overhead light. The contrast with Faith was stark. The lustre of her hair was unaffected, but she wore no make-up and the light reflecting from the pale skin of her face made her look just a little unwell. The fluorescent tubes, apparently white, contained a high level of green.

When we had finished the main course, Faith suggested a dessert (lemon mousse, I believe) but Hazel wouldn't hear of it. That was absolutely lovely, she assured the cook, but she was stuffed to the gunwales. And assuming we must feel the same way, our visitor leapt to her feet, piled the plates up and took them to the sink. I knew this troubled Faith, who always laid them separately on the counter. The top of the plate was dirty already: she didn't see any reason to dirty the bottom as well.

She had a point. What she didn't have was a dishwasher, and she had no intention of buying one on the grounds that they wasted metal, electricity and water. Another unnecessary appliance with the potential to fail. When the table was cleared and we all had coffee, Hazel couldn't wait any longer.

'Right, let's have it. Spill!'

She spoke with such force I began to fear for Henry. Here was a woman who could pack a punch when provoked, and provoked she was about to be.

Faith brought her laptop to the table.

'We transferred the photographs so you could see them better.'

'Very thoughtful.'

She played them through as a slide show, then went back and studied the errant couple at the T'ing very closely.

'These could be clearer.'

This was true, but considering the adverse circumstances and the camera I'd used . . . though I couldn't very well admit to that.

'I take it we can zoom.'

Faith showed her how.

'I don't believe it!'

We waited to find out what she didn't believe.

'You know who that is, don't you Faith?'

'I'm afraid I don't. Should I?'

'It's Lizzie Smith, you met her at the Brunton a few years back. Their Christmas show. Surely you remember? Mother Goose!'

'I'm afraid I don't.'

'Understandable, I suppose. The woman's totally forgettable, a bland, mouse-like creature not worth crossing the road for.'

Lizzie was a set-designer, prop maker, and occasional colleague of Henry. They'd been on tour together several times – Pitlochry, Inverness and, for all Hazel knew, Ecclefechan as well.

'She isn't married, of course. I mean, no self-respecting man would take her in a lucky bag!'

And so it went on for several minutes until Faith, in an attempt to stop the flow, asked me if there wasn't a video as well. It worked, but only for a moment.

We watched Hazel glaring at Henry and Lizzie in close embrace and, what was less evident in the stills, Henry's roaming hands, which didn't get everywhere but made a good stab at it. Faith mouthed the word 'sorry'. She knew she'd made a mistake. Hazel wasn't happy.

'For fuck's sake!'

She had that right.

On Saturday morning Faith insisted on Christmas shopping. I reluctantly agreed, thinking we could go to the German market, but it wasn't due to open for a couple of weeks so we ended up in John Lewis, partners to the nation, which was full of desperate people sweating and breathing out. Their cosmetics counters were doing a roaring trade, but Faith led me past them on our way to the toys, where we spent a tedious hour checking out such wonders as electronic Daleks and Lego digital cameras.

Our choice was constrained by Faith's desire to inflict something educational on her nephew or, as she put it, something improving. We ended up buying several smaller items, all I can remember being a dinosaur adventure set from the Natural History Museum. And the ordeal wasn't made easier by parents who'd made the mistake of bringing their children. Alright, so they got a steer on what would go down well on the big day, but at the cost of serious harassment, much of it at high pitch and even higher volume. I longed for a remote control to turn the little perishers off or, failing that, a spray. If this wasn't a market niche I didn't know what was.

But Faith seemed unconcerned. She moved among the parents and children almost as if they weren't there, as if there were no impediments and no noise. Her motion was fluid and elegant. As for children, it was hard to tell what her attitude was. Would she be one of those women who only felt fulfilled by having one of her own, or would she be the natural aunt, wonderful with children as long as they weren't hers. I suspected the latter. I thought of Colin and Catherine. Unlike them, we might not have this problem – as Catherine would say, 'going forward'. Looking for clues I asked her a question and was reassured by the answer.

'Have you ever worked in the children's library?'

'No, Max. Not my scene.'

We headed for the restaurant with a feeling of relief, which didn't last when we saw how busy it was. Queuing at one counter, then queuing at another before queuing at a third to pay was not an attractive prospect, so we left the mall and made for the Café Camino. I'd been there once before, Faith several times. It would have been busy anyway, but Christmas shoppers left only a small table by the partition dividing the café from the Cathedral – as near to the Nativity as we were likely to get and very draughty.

It was clear at once that the staff were mostly Polish, and if you couldn't tell by hearing them talk to each other there was always the Polish sign at the entrance to the kitchen – WASH YOUR HANDS. I began to anticipate the return of King Casimir the Great. Faith ordered a sandwich, I ordered another and we split them half and half. Variety may not be the spice of life, but it helps. In a departure from our usual routine, we both ordered tea. We think we understand events as they happen. We can analyse, after all. But it doesn't seem to work like that. Often the message takes time to arrive. I couldn't get Hazel out of my head.

'Why is she so worked up about Lizzie? She really has it in for her.'

'Hazel has a certain image of herself – attractive, alluring, irresistible. To find herself supplanted by a woman who's none of these things – to her, it's like a slap in the face. Why does she bother with all her routines? Propped up on her pillow with her cleanser and night cream. Spending half an hour at least in front of the mirror before leaving the house. What's the point, when a drab creature like Lizzie, who plainly doesn't bother, can steal her husband from under her nose?'

'Maybe it was the other way about. Maybe Henry made the move on Lizzie.'

'Maybe. Either way, her effort's been wasted.'

'Maybe Lizzie has a bubbly personality.'

'There are too many maybes here, Max, but you may be right.'

Time to Talk

Questions remained. Why had Hazel spent so much emotional energy inveighing against Lizzie and so little attacking Henry? After all, it was Henry who was in breach of contract, not Lizzie who, according to Hazel, had never married because no one had wanted her. It was Henry, not Lizzie, who had done the dirty. It was almost as if his treachery, bad enough anyway, was made ten times worse by his woefully bad taste. So she was to blame more than he was, hence Hazel's rage. I couldn't begin to imagine how relationship counsellors coped. People are irrational enough to start with, but when sex is added to the mix the result can be catastrophic.

These thoughts were interrupted by an incoming call from Hazel. She'd had it with the two-timing bastard. She hadn't waited for him to pack, she' done the job for him and left his cases in the garden. They'd already been filleted by an urban fox, though it might have been a badger. He was out on his ear. She should have done it years ago. Now she had the house to herself. Now she could do what she liked when she liked. And if that included taking in a toy-boy, so much the better. The world was her oyster.

When she could get a word in edgeways, Faith asked where Henry was going. Hazel didn't know. He could join the dossers in the Grassmarket for all she cared. Henry was history. The phrase had a nice ring to it, but Henry was nowhere near as interesting as history and had much less to tell us.

22

If we can speak of turning-points in our lives the following Monday was one, the day going from the deeply serious to the utterly ridiculous in the course of eight hours. At ten o'clock, I was visited by Jean Ritchie, who brought her sister along for added support. It was almost as if they considered I was the impediment to Zoe receiving the help she required, as if they were confusing me with the Health Service. They were both so upset, and falling over themselves to express it, that they refused tea or coffee. There would be no beating about the bush.

'So Mr Frei, what do you think of this?'

She showed me a letter from the NHS. Although the word-count was high, its sole purpose was to deliver a short, blunt statement: *Zoe has been discharged from this service.* I read it carefully, conscious of two pairs of eyes monitoring my progress, checking my face for any expression which might betray my reaction.

'Hard to believe, wouldn't you say?'

'If she went to the hospital with a broken leg,' Edith asked, 'would they discharge her from this service before they'd fixed it? I don't think so somehow, do you?'

The letter didn't say why she had been discharged, didn't even hint at it.

'Oh, we both know why that is: they keep accusing her of failure to engage.'

Zoe had failed to attend the clinic on a number of occasions. She had refused to see me too. So what was the difference, if any, between non-attendance and failure to engage? From what Jean had told me, her daughter's non-attendance was the result, not of a failure to engage but of an inability to do so. Zoe was trapped in her head, which was trapped in her room, knowing she should make the appointment, wanting to, but feeling incapable of doing it. Irrational, yes, but no more so than the official response: the Team was refusing to treat a condition because the patient was displaying a symptom of that condition. Plainly, this put the patient in an impossible position. Joseph Heller himself would have been impressed, and maybe Franz Kafka too.

'Where do we go from here, Mr Frei? I'm at my wit's end.'

I suggested they complain to the Mental Welfare Commission and gave them the address. But before they did they should refer to a copy of the relevant ICP, since it would probably appear from this document that, in Zoe's case, the integrated care pathway had not been followed. If that could be demonstrated, their chance of a successful complaint would be greatly increased. A contact had offered to provide me with a copy. My guests were hostile to the jargon but, as they might with a medicine, swallowed it whole in the hope of improvement.

'This process may take several weeks.'

'There's a surprise!'

'And in the meantime,' I pointed out, 'we have to consider what to do about Zoe.'

For the time being, the only possible therapy would be private, but even that wasn't an option if Zoe continued to say no. As those who had discharged her were well aware, the problem was intractable. No doubt they were subject to performance indicators, in which case, concentrating their effort on the problems most easily solved would be an attractive option. And the corollary? The equally attractive prospect of removing from their books those cases which took time and effort yet held out little prospect of a positive outcome.

'Couldn't you help her, Mr Frei?'

This was an understandable cry from the heart, I knew only too well the effect her daughter's condition had had on her mother over the years.

'I'm afraid my options are limited.'

'Oh yes?' Edith had an acid streak absent from her sister. 'And why might that be?'

'As you well know, Zoe is none too keen to come.'

'We've noticed, believe you me. But what's stopping you going to her?'

In theory, nothing. But even if I did, there was no guarantee she would talk to me or cooperate in any way. But still, the idea was an interesting one. Why didn't therapists visit their clients?

Because to do so would entail cutting down on their lists with a consequent reduction in throughput. You can't be dealing with a client when you're travelling to meet another, nor when you're travelling back. My second problem was equally serious.

'And as I'm sure you realize, BPD is very difficult to treat. My review of the literature suggests that the most effective treatment is dialectical behaviour therapy, but I am not qualified in that technique.'

'Why not?'

'There are many therapies, Edith. No one therapist could possibly offer them all. I can't sit here and pretend to a competence I don't have.'

'I don't see why not. Everyone else does.'

This was the by far the most serious case with which I had to deal, and it was having a marked effect on those involved. Zoe was living in a permanently distressed condition, her aunt Edith was turning into a dragon of righteous indignation, breathing fire at all who crossed her path, and her mother had been worn out by years of struggle with nothing to show for it.

'I blame myself, Mr Frei.'

'Why would you do that? You're plainly a caring person doing her best for her daughter.'

'I must have done something wrong or she wouldn't have turned out this way.'

Unusually, Edith didn't chip in. Perhaps she agreed. If she did, she shouldn't have.

'I know a mother of five. She's done her best over the years. Four of her children have turned out well but the fifth is a junkie who steals to fund her habit.'

'What are you saying?'

'We can't blame the way this lady brought the girl up, because her other children were brought up in the same household, in the same way, and they've turned out well. It's just too easy to blame yourself because Zoe, your only child, has serious problems. If you had more children, the others would be fine.'

There was a downside to this scenario which I kept to myself. They might not have been so fine growing up with Zoe, and for Jean protecting her other children from the permanent black cloud that was her daughter would have been time-consuming and stressful.

'So Jean should have had more children.'

'I'm sure that if she had, she'd realize what an excellent parent she is that and Zoe's condition is not her fault.'

'So it must be genetic, then.'

'I'm sure that's part of it, yes.'

On their way out, to my great surprise, Edith leant forward and whispered in my ear.

'You made that family up, didn't you?'

'Yes, but the point still stands.'

'A parable.'

I had no wish to assume such an exalted position nor to be reminded of Mr Robertson.

'More of a cautionary tale.'

'You're not so bad, doc. A girl could warm to you.'

She squeezed my arm and ran out after her sister.

The building had been quieter than usual for a few days. Ceramick, who made most of the noise, was at home dealing with an attack of gout. Usually subjecting others to jokes, he had been on the receiving end of quite a few, mostly relating to his consumption of port and misplaced references to the madness of George III. In fact, Cermick never drank port but did indulge in beer and spirits, both of which were thought to be implicated. Before retiring temporarily from the field he had grandly declared that if gout was good enough for Karl Marx it was good enough for him.

George had gone relatively quiet too, the word on the street being that he had taken up with a comely matron whose beagle he was painting. The two had been observed strolling along the riverside in Haddington and were rumoured to disport themselves on a waterbed in the master bedroom of her detached house on Somnerfield Crescent. How anyone could have known all this was a mystery to me.

Noise still emanated from Steve's workshop as people tried out his instruments. He occasionally played the fiddle himself when no customers were present, mostly reels, jigs and airs. He was particularly fond of Afton Water, which always struck me as rather intense. But in my own studio noise, as a manifestation of life, was produced by Colin and Janice, who met there to engage in robust exchanges about Creative Scotland and Bernard's role

Time to Talk

in the organisation. These conversations went above or below my head (delete as appropriate) but since Janice had now added a power horn to her loud-hailer she was a force to be reckoned with. She occasionally reinforced the stereotype that red-heads could be irascible, though I'm sure the colour of her hair had nothing to do with it.

Janice paid me a brief visit after Jean and her sister left. Was I any further forward in getting a filing cabinet of my own? She could do with her drawer back. (Which I mis-heard as drawback, and wondered for a moment what she was talking about.) Then Colin arrived, mug in hand, with the joyful news that Catherine – yes, they were still on speaking terms – had agreed to take on my accounts if, and only if, I could furnish the necessary invoices, receipts and other relevant documents. The saying that 'if' is a small word with a large meaning has never been so true.

'For a nominal fee. That's what she said, and I'm quoting.'

As a joke I suggested he'd bought all his Christmas presents. He had.

When DS MacNeil arrived and addressed me as 'sir' I knew things were getting serious. She walked in unannounced, without knocking. It was early afternoon. She meant business.

'I have reason to believe you are perpetrating a fraud.'

'Do come in.'

She ignored the sarcasm and continued.

'I'll need the names and addresses of your clients, past and present.'

'That might constitute an invasion of privacy. They may wish no one to know they're attending.'

'I'm not asking you for any information regarding what has passed between you and your clients, merely their names.'

'But officer, that would be confidential.'

'It would be if you were a bona fide counsellor, but we both know you're not.'

Her gaze raked my desk.

'You have a desktop diary.'

I took it from the desk, gave it to her and watched as she leafed through it with growing impatience.

'There are no names here, just initials.'

'No one but me needs to know who these people are.'

'I could easily obtain a warrant to seize any paper files and digital media which might have a bearing on the case.'

I indicated my empire with a wave of the arm.

'Be my guest.'

Her search of my desktop and drawers was thorough but yielded nothing. It didn't occur to her then or later that my client files were located elsewhere in the building or, as Ceramick would have it, in Janice's drawers. She did, however, find my digital recorder.

'Is this thing on?'

'No.'

'I may need it.'

'I take it you've heard of the Data Protection Act?'

It soon became apparent that she intended to interview me at the station and expected me to attend voluntarily. She would prefer not to arrest me but would if she had to.

'Much less embarrassing for you.'

'No cuffs, then.'

She smiled. The idea that a puny individual such as myself, weakened by thought, might need restraining – well, it was too ridiculous. Steve was playing again. We walked along the corridor towards the stairs to the sound of Niel Gow's Lament for James Moray of Abercarney, a sad tune which would have to do for me as well.

She insisted on driving me to the station, in silence, mindful that in my own car I could make an escape bid but with no thought whatsoever as how I would get back. As we entered the building, I was struck momentarily by a vision of the four grand columns as prison bars, though I soon pulled myself together. Even then, I was confident I was a match for this woman, whose hostility meant that she was on my side without knowing it, such did it warp her judgment.

She parked me in an interview room while she collected her paperwork, which didn't take long. She proposed to record the interview and I was happy with that. I was entitled to a lawyer but chose not to have one. Predictably, she had some fun at the outset establishing who I was.

'So how shall I address you, sir? You operate under two different names at least.'

'At least?'
'As far as we know.'
'Why don't we just use the name I work under.'
'Maxwell Frei.'
'Exactly.'
'So, Mr Frei, as you know, a complaint has been received from a Mr Hector Robertson.'
'The complaint has since been withdrawn.'
'That does not alter the fact that the complaint had substance. We can find no evidence of professional accreditation. In fact, the bodies concerned have no record of a Maxwell Frei ever having been accredited. We did, of course, check the registers under your given name as well.'
'Of course.'
'A therapist would require certain qualifications to apply for accreditation. They don't take every Tom, Dick and Harry who drops them a note. They wouldn't take me, for example.'
'I think we can safely say that.'
'In which case, Mr Frei, I have to tell you, I can find no evidence of you having an appropriate qualification under either of your names.'
'There's a reason for that.'
'What is it?'
'Such evidence does not exist.'
'Which would explain why you're not accredited.'
'It would.'
DS MacNeil paused the recording.
'I don't get it. Why are you sitting there admitting everything? If I accused you of stealing the Forth Bridge you'd probably admit that as well! I thought you were smarter than that. I'm must say I'm a little disappointed.'
'You were expecting more fun.'
She smiled. I had her on the hip. At the same time, and though I don't usually react to such things, I couldn't help wishing she'd do something about her hair. It was lank by nature, but surely there was some superior shampoo out there which could put some life into it: Molton Brown, Sainsburys, Boots? I felt sorry for her, which wasn't such a good idea considering our respective roles in the great play of life.

'So what are you going to do, plead guilty?'

I hadn't been charged with anything yet, but I answered the question anyway.

'No, definitely not.'

'But Mr Frei, come on, get real here, you don't have a leg to stand on.'

'You're probably right, but I do I have a case to make.'

'I can't see it.'

After I explained my position, she requested my attendance at a second interview, not at the police station but conducted by a professional at an agreed location. I had no objection. She excused herself and talked for a moment in the corridor on her mobile phone.

'Sorry about that. Had to make sure.'

'You have someone in mind.'

'Anthony Dwyer, Edinburgh University.'

'Professor, Division of Psychiatry.'

'That's the one.'

'Wednesday afternoon, two o'clock, his office?'

'Fine by me.'

She already had her expert lined up and I had to wonder why: she couldn't have known in advance how I'd react to her accusations. But short of revealing her hand, which wasn't likely, meeting the man was the next best way to find out.

23

It is easy to believe that we go through the motions of life largely unobserved. I had walked out of The Warehouse with DS MacNeil, no fuss, no noise, and got into her car. Perhaps that's all it took, the fact that we left together. Janice happened to observe us as we walked past the office door and Colin saw us in the courtyard through his window. They put their heads together, came to the conclusion that something was amiss and contacted Faith.

So when I left the police station there she was, well wrapped up, on the other side of the road. In addition to her coat and scarf, she was wearing dinky earmuffs which made her even more attractive than she was already, but I knew she'd take them off when she started asking questions. There was no getting anything past her, and even though I was yet to be charged it was just a matter of time. The game was up. I had to tell her now.

We went to a cavernous establishment at the foot of Leith Walk and, as was our custom, held off with the chat till we had eaten.

'OK.'

'You want me to tell you what happened.'

'All of it. Leave nothing out.'

I told her about MacNeil's visit to the studio and the interview at the station, including every detail I could remember. She listened intently, saying nothing till I had finished, at which point there was an uncomfortably long silence. I knew the most likely outcome: she would dump me on the spot and that would be the end of the only genuine relationship I had ever had.

'You realise what this means, don't you?'

I waited for the axe to fall, for Faith to end it and leave.

'I'll have to remove your flier from the board.'

Although this was true, and she duly removed it the next morning, she was also telling me something else: I would have to negotiate but there might still be a chance.

'You haven't been charged.'

'No.'

'That's good.'

It wasn't, but neither of us knew that at the time. Faith assumed that MacNeil was waiting for feedback from Dwyer: was I certifiable, or simply subtle in the way I took forward my deception? That she might have been up to something more devious didn't occur to either of us, who might then have been characterised as a pair of innocents against the world, something which, in the hard light of experience, we can't be accused of now.

'So run it past me again, your rationale.'

When I did, she subjected me to a series of searching questions, a few about psychology but most calling into question the honesty of my dealings with my clients and with her. I found them challenging, as anyone would when his motives are called into question. I have never felt so drained, and certainly not by my later appearance in court. I dealt with her as openly as I could, but she was far from happy.

'So, what do you think?'

I was expecting a reasoned evaluation of my position, but that's not what I got.

'You'll have to stop seeing your clients.'

This came as a complete surprise, and the fact that it did showed how far my feet were still off the ground. If I continued to see my clients, I could be accused of persisting in fraudulent activity following a warning from the police. If it came to the bit, that would be held against me. I could always explain the situation to the people on my books, and some might chose to remain, but they came for help with their problems, not to help me with mine. Alternatively, I could continue to see them without charge.

'I think it's time to get real here, Max, don't you?'

The ghost of TNT whispered in my ear, *Women keep telling you to get real: is this significant?*

'In the first case your income will drop, in the second it will dry up altogether. You couldn't keep paying the rent.'

I assumed she was referring to my studio in The Warehouse, but she soon set me straight: my flat was at stake as well.

A family appeared at the next table, alive with talk of who wanted what. They seemed nice enough: with any luck they'd quieten down when the food arrived. Then MacNeil confirmed a time and place by text: the Kennedy Tower, Wednesday, two o'clock. Faith didn't know – why would she? – that the Tower was in the grounds of the Royal Edinburgh, our local psychiatric hospital.

'If I go in there they might not let me out.'

'That's not funny.'

'Everything's funny looked at clearly.'

This was something I firmly believed, confirmed in that view by Horace Walpole who had written, in a fit of blinding light, *The world is a comedy to those that think, a tragedy to those who feel*. It had long been my opinion that those who embraced the tragic sense of life took themselves too seriously. Human life was cheap: you only had to look at wars, famines, natural disasters and fires in third-world sweatshops where all the exits were barred.

'So our relationship is funny.'

I would have to take Horace aside for an earnest chat: his maxim required some qualification. As far as I was concerned, our relationship was one thing that wasn't.

'Not to me.'

The signs, both verbal and physical, couldn't have been clearer: I was on probation. She was already working on a plan, but for the time being let me in on only part of it while she started the lengthy process of sorting me out. If we can speak of the balance of power within a relationship, it had shifted in Faith's favour and was set to stay that way for several years. If she had been tempted to abuse it, this was the beginning of the end. But control for its own sake was not in her nature.

She said she would check out the learned professor and brief me before the meeting. I had to know who I was dealing with, his background, his interests and, if possible, his take on psychotherapy. And it can't be denied that she did her best, but some of his published work was as far beyond her as it was beyond me. We have examples of it still, including an instructive paper on white matter tractography and another on the neurofilament antibody RT97. It soon became clear to us both that the leaning Tower inclined towards research. As far as we could see, there wasn't a practising therapist in the building. The interview, when it came, would be interesting.

Meanwhile, though, I needed to work on my case, sharpen it up. There was something in what I was saying – not a lot, but a kernel of truth – and if Faith needed more convincing so would everyone else. And that wasn't all.

'Dwyer will report to DS MacNeil.'

'I know.'

'So if this ends up in court he'll be an expert witness for the prosecution.'

'It won't go that far. The sums involved are trivial.'

'So they are, but they might act on a point of principle. You must avoid giving this man anything that could be used against you later.'

As Faith saw it Dwyer, the fully qualified professional, was licensed to hold a gun, and though I worked behind the counter in the hunting, shooting and fishing shop, the one thing I couldn't give him was ammunition. Game bags, Barbour jackets, shooting sticks, fine: bullets, out of the question. Which was all very well in theory, but how could I make my case and avoid it?

'That,' she said, 'is what you're going home to figure out.'

And she told me how to do it. On one sheet of paper I should list the main heads of my argument, on another the admissions I couldn't safely make. I should then compare the two. Any points from page one also on page two should either be reworded till they were safe or, if that couldn't be done, removed entirely. This was my homework for tonight, she would go over it with her red pen in the library at lunch-time tomorrow. I knew it made sense but I didn't like this plan at all. I had the sinking feeling that after I'd carried it out my reasoning would be shot full of holes. The professor, who would be hostile anyway, would conclude he was dealing with a fool. And the worst thing was I wouldn't be spending the night with Faith, something I yearned to do, not for sex but for comfort. The heat pad I put in the microwave wasn't the same.

Our meeting next day at the library was short but useful. Faith checked my notes and, with a few neat annotations, gave me the all-clear. I left with a thick folder of information about the professor, which I was to bone up on that afternoon. As I left, with the customary peck on the cheek (all I ever got in public) she promised to make a meal to remember that night. It might, she said with a smile, be my last as a free man. She was joking, of course, but I felt uneasy all the same. What is a joke but a trap for the unwary, as Henryson's fox discovered to his cost?

Professor Dwyer's room was on the fourth floor of a utilitarian rectangular block of recent construction. Awaiting my arrival, he'd left his door open and invited me in when I knocked with a smile and a shake of the hand. He offered me tea or coffee but I declined, fearing that an urge to relieve myself at a critical moment might weaken my performance. (Though it might have been more accurate to say that the weakness of my performance would lead to an urge to relieve myself.) The man seemed pleasant enough and informal with it: cable-knit cardigan with faux leather buttons, beige. White shirt, no tie.

'Do take a seat, Mr Frei, we have much to discuss.'

He produced a voice recorder: did I mind, his memory wasn't what it was? I produced mine, which I had recharged that morning.

'By all means.'

MacNeil had given him the gist of my case and that had piqued his interest. He invited me to state it in my own words since, as he delicately put it, she might have given it a negative slant. Keeping Faith's strictures in mind, I made heavy weather of my task but got there in the end.

'So if I understand you aright, Mr Frei, you believe that, ultimately, the patient cures him or herself regardless, or in spite of, any intervention by a professional.'

'I believe that is often the case, though some interventions will be beneficial.'

'And how have you arrived at this conclusion?'

'By listening to my clients and collating publicly available information.'

I noted a solitary plant on his window ledge, a Christmas cactus in full bloom. If the cactus had it right, the princes of the church might have to move Jesus' birthday forward a month – a new topic for Mr Robertson. On his desk, photographs of his family: an intelligent-looking woman and two less intelligent-looking children (regression to the mean) smiling coyly at the camera. Another picture included the man himself, though he had more hair when it was taken than he did now.

'The first by its nature is anecdotal, wouldn't you say?'

'I would. People are real, not tables of statistics.'

'You set great store by that?'

'Don't you? The first thing the therapist has to deal with is the patient's narrative.'

'Which may be suspect, in whole or in part.'

'And that in itself will tell him something.'

'Only if he knows it for what it is.'

'In saying that, you're describing his job.'

'It might be said,' the professor remarked, 'that you rather incline to the subjective.'

'I wouldn't argue with that.'

'Could you perhaps expand on this subject a bit?'

'Well, yes. OK. Have you read The Amateur Immigrant?'

'I'm afraid not, no.'

'A passage in the book deals with economics. Stevenson says, and he is quite right, that where economics are concerned there is too little mention of pies.'

'Pies?'

'It is through their mundane details that we understand the lives of real people, people of flesh and blood. Without those details the exercise is anaemic. Those who incline to the objective - who, if I may say so, are often to be found in academic redoubts such as this - concentrate their effort on endless reams of figures, graphs, statistics and charts.'

'Information in its various forms.'

'But then they disagree about what it means.'

'The problem is not the data but its interpretation.'

Conscious that I was becoming somewhat strident, I remained with economics, that alien discipline where neither of us had anything at stake.

'Take the present economic downturn. Both sides accept the figures but there the argument starts. One lot says we must persevere with austerity, we can't keep spending money we don't have. The other says we must borrow for growth. If we don't, we'll plunge the economy into recession. Their views are diametrically opposed yet they're based on the same figures.'

'So it all boils down to a matter of opinion.'

'Exactly.'

I was conscious that I'd just subjected the professor to a brief rant but also that he was slyly oiling the wheels, encouraging me to continue and offering little resistance. An obvious ruse. I'd have to keep an eye on the man, he was winning on points.

'So you would claim that objective truth might not exist?'

'I would.'

'A rather extreme position, wouldn't you say?'

'Not at all.'

I took him through both doors of the well-known experiment which showed that whether a photon passing through them was a particle or a wave depended on how it was measured. The act of observation altered what was observed.

'I take your point, Mr Frei, but really, you can't be suggesting that we extrapolate from the behaviour of photons what happens in the world as a whole. Quantum physics is all very well, it has its place, but you would surely concede that place is not the consulting room. Let us say a patient presents with paranoia – reference to wave-particle duality won't help him one bit.'

'Of course not, no. But I would contend that observation of the patient by the therapist is likely to modify the patient's behaviour. And you would surely concede as a general principle that if there is no objectivity at the quantum level there is even less in the labyrinthine workings of the human brain as we observe it day to day.'

The professor did not concede that, though he didn't deny it either.

'I presume you checked me out online before coming.'

'My girlfriend did it for me.'

'Ah.'

He was surprised by something: either that I hadn't done it for myself or that I had a girlfriend at all. Probably the latter. I was still surprised by that myself.

'So you will know that my own modest efforts concentrate on the objective.'

He proceeded to run past me his current project, the use of brain-scan technology to better understand the workings of the schizophrenic mind. It might be that in this, as in some other areas, a mental condition had a physical basis. If that proved to be the case, implications for treatment would follow.

'I'm simplifying. Nonetheless, I consider my approach objective.'

'So do I.'

'I also consider it valid.'

'It is.'

'So you might have some truck with the objective after all?'

Like tragedy and comedy, the objective and the subjective are on a linear scale but at opposite ends. Some incline more to one than the other. Some of us are farther out. But except in cases of extreme psychosis, the ends can never be reached. So, yes, I had some truck with the objective. I had no choice. But having said all that, the professor's work, despite its psychiatric implications, was a branch of medical research. And medical research could not be compared to what went on when a client was in therapy. There the process was entirely different, depending as it did on the ability of the therapist to penetrate through the client's words to their underlying meaning, a process which was essentially subjective.

'All well and good, Mr Frei, but you have just conceded, have you not, that we cannot be wholly subjective. What is missing from your account thus far is the frame of reference against which the therapist understands the client. I would submit that the therapist's intuition is underpinned by knowledge. I would go further. Without that underpinning knowledge the therapist's intuition could be totally misconceived and therefore dangerous.'

I was about to point out that the therapist's intuition could be wrong regardless, I had cases to prove it, but at that point the professor showed a rare ability to talk without stopping for breath.

'So my question to you is simple: what is the source of your knowledge? Since it doesn't come from the acquiring of relevant qualifications, we are surely entitled to ask from whence it derives?'

Like the professor's question, my answer was simple. Study. I had read the literature. Starting with the classics – Freud, Jung, Adler – I had worked my up to the present day. The professor was impressed. He wasn't sure he would have attempted such a thing himself – a ridiculous pose to adopt since we both knew he had done exactly that.

'In the course of your study, were there areas on which you placed less emphasis?'

'Of course. If we are to remain motivated we must follow where our interests lead.'

The professor was taking notes now, though I couldn't imagine why since he was recording the whole discussion.

'Could you give an example of such an area?'

'Child psychology. I have never related to children or dogs.'

'So you don't propose a parallel career as a veterinarian?'

Good one, professor. Very clever, very smart indeed.

'Certainly not.'

'As for children, Mr Frei, you will concede that they grow up to be adults. Childhood experience informs the adult mind.'

'I don't deny that for a moment.'

'Apart from child psychology, is there any other area . . .?'

'Sex.'

'You're not into that.'

'Not where therapy is concerned.'

The professor spent the next half hour attempting to verify my knowledge of the main trends in psychology, the major figures, the various lines of argument. For the most part I coped reasonably well, though he caught me out several times, which was only to be expected. My knowledge of Wilhelm Reich left a lot to be desired.

'Well I must say, Mr Frei, you've attended to your reading.'

'Thank you.'

'Though some would say the weakness in your approach lies in the area of testing. How can you be sure of the extent of your knowledge? How can you be sure, working on your own, what you know and what you don't? Had you attended a formal course of study your knowledge would have been assessed by examination. Just as important, from my point of view, would have been the cut and thrust of discussion – putting your opinions to the test not only in tutorials but also in informal gatherings of fellow students.'

'The sword forged in the heat of the blacksmith's fire.'

For a moment I thought I'd over-reached myself, that the professor would pick up on the other denotation of the word 'forge', which the MacNeils of this world would welcome as more appropriate. But the moment passed.

'I wouldn't have put it that way myself, but yes. And not having a formal qualification does expose you to criticism should things go wrong.'

'But professor, things go wrong as it is.'

Without mentioning her name, I gave him the low-down on what had happened to Zoe over the last few years.

'And all of the people who failed her, every last one had formal qualifications.'

'And you will doubtless have gathered evidence of other such cases.'

'I have.'

'Well they are all to be regretted, but I have to ask you this – have you also gathered evidence of those which went well? I rather suspect you have not.'

'But professor, really, that's a question I should be asking you. Of all the research projects carried on is this building, has any one of them ever attempted to measure the work of psychotherapists with respect to outcomes?'

He didn't know, not off the top of his head, but he doubted it. Psychotherapy could not be compared to hip replacement surgery, where success was easy to measure. A patient in therapy might improve a little, a lot, or not at all, but how would one measure the improvement? By X-ray? By clinical examination?

The answer to this question was staring him in the face.

'This will sound a bit extreme, but we could always ask the patient.'

At that point, though he'd requested that no calls be put through, his phone rang, so if he had an answer I didn't get to hear it. You could say he was saved by the bell. According to his secretary the matter was urgent, something to do with a grant application. (In academic circles, nothing is more urgent than that.) He assured her he'd deal with the matter within the hour so, for me, the end was in sight.

'Sorry about that.' He looked down at his notes. 'Two more areas of concern.'

The first followed on from the one before. Not having been on a recognised course I'd had no opportunity for supervised practical experience, for example, on a ward. Though I had volunteered from time to time, there was no contesting this. I knew it wasn't the same. He was right. And so to his final point.

'Of the therapies currently available, which do you consider the most effective?'

'You want me to sink my spoon in the alphabet soup?'
'If you would.'

This was a question I should have anticipated. When I asked him if he wouldn't mind giving me a minute to frame my response he jumped at the chance. Since I hadn't brought blank paper he passed me a couple of sheets with a sympathetic smile.

'Pen and paper - I find it helps to crystallise the thoughts.'

As I tried to figure out a reply, I saw him working with great concentration at his computer on what I suspected was a spreadsheet concerning his grant. He would need it. According to Faith's notes there were thirty-eight academics in the building plus a sizeable admin and janitorial staff, to say nothing of the contract cleaners. A resource like this did not come cheap.

After a decent interval, five minutes or so, when I could see he had made inroads into his problem and was starting to relax, I cleared my throat by way of a hint.

'Ah, yes,' he said, 'the vexed question of therapies.'

'Well I've looked at several – CBT, EFT, FAP, RETB. TA, MBSR, EMDR, DBT, SFT.'

'Looked at?'

'Studied.'

'In varying degrees of depth.'

'Yes.'

'And what did you conclude?'

He probably regretted asking in the light of my reply, which he had kindly given me time to rough out.

'It seems to me that any therapy, by definition, is a closed system, and closure can only be achieved by disregarding certain evidence. In this a therapy has something in common with an ideology, religious or political, and I have little trust in either.'

'Yes, but Mr Frei, really, we can none of us start talking with a client in the absence of any conceptual framework whatsoever.'

It sounded plausible alright, but it was an assertion I couldn't accept.

'On the contrary, Professor Dwyer, the best way to approach a client is to listen to what he has to say with an open mind free of preconceptions. When you come right down to it, each case is unique. So what are we supposed to do with a thousand cases, have a thousand therapies at our disposal? I don't think so, somehow.'

I could see that the professor was amazed or bemused, one of the two.

'Dear me, what a radical fellow you are! So from your perspective none of the available therapies is of any use at all?'

If I agreed to that proposition I was dead in the water.

'When dealing with a given patient it may well be that progress is improved by reference to one therapy or another, but it doesn't follow from that that we should confine ourselves within its limits.'

'I see.'

'And how would you decide which parts of the various therapies to employ?'

That was simple.

'Instinct.'

As the professor stood up and I prepared to leave, I had a question for him.

'This report you're writing, do I get a copy?'

I could see he was tempted, but had to turn me down.

'I'm afraid not, Mr Frei. You're not the one who's paying for it.'

Not now, perhaps, but I couldn't shake the feeling I'd be paying for it further down the line.

24

Hazel was in crisis, she needed Faith's support. Though she never took it when she asked for it, she also needed her advice. So Faith was sorry, there was nothing she could do. She couldn't see me that night. She was responding to an urgent call for help. Henry had left the marital bed but refused to leave the marital home as well on the grounds that he had nowhere else to go, a weak argument since he could always move in with his fancy woman. Her flat wasn't large but it would do, having no inconvenience such as a husband taking up space.

Listening to Hazel, Faith found it hard to separate fact from fiction. Henry was the actor of the household, but when it came to drama he couldn't hold a candle to his wife who remembered, or claimed to, every remark, gesture, sneer and withering look long after an argument was over. Faith believed that Hazel deliberately worked herself up to a frenzy, her language becoming steadily more colourful as she did so. And after some effort on her part, she usually achieved the levels of anger, spite and resentment she laid claim to at the outset. At such times, Faith's cool head was an advantage.

Henry had to go. Saving him the trouble of packing his own bags hadn't been enough, nor giving away his prized LPs to charity – Art Blakey, John Coltrane, Herbie Hancock and other hallowed names from the past. Henry had taken a taxi to the Oxfam Music Shop, explained the situation to the manager, and threatened him with legal action if his vinyl was not returned. When the manager asked him for evidence that the recordings were really his, Henry began to declaim the contents of his discs one after the other, projecting his voice, as actors can, to all corners of the shop and the street outside to the great consternation of the lieges. The manager had crumbled and returned from the back shop with two large boxes. Fearing that if he went home with them his wife would dispose of his discs a second time, he'd taken them to 'his paramour' and stayed there overnight. Not a good move. In his absence, Hazel's joiner changed the lock on their front door.

Faith suspected this was not the best thing to do, since the flat was jointly owned. But it was done now, and when Henry had threatened to call the police she told him what her story would be when they arrived – her husband had subjected her to vile and unspeakable practices and she had to protect herself as best she could. There was no other way. And then she turned the screw. His phone wasn't ringing so often these days anyway: what would happen when news of his perverted behaviour got about? The calls would dry up altogether. His answer to that had been short: he'd run out of money to pay the mortgage. They'd both be out on their ears. Was that really what she wanted? It was a classic stand-off with no end in sight. It wasn't obvious to me that Faith, civilised woman that she was, could intervene in this dispute to any good effect, but she had agreed to try.

'Love you,' she said as she rang off.

I liked the sound of that. And so, a lifetime ago, had Henry and Hazel.

The next morning at The Warehouse I was met by a delegation of Colin and Janice. Colin was more concerned than he might have been since I hadn't called him the night before or answered his calls. I claimed to have been out, though in fact I'd spent the night at home, going over in my head the events of the afternoon, replaying my recording of the interview and trying to figure out what the professor would conclude in his report.

'That MacNeil woman,' Colin said, 'don't like the cut of her jib. What did she want?'

'The fact is, guys, she's got it in for me. A client has complained that I failed in my duty of care. She's following it up.'

'My God!'

Given it was Mr Robertson, Colin was closer to the mark than he realised.

'Yes, but the man's since withdrawn his complaint. Not only that, he's still coming!'

'So what's her problem,' Janice asked, 'no real crime out there?'

Time to Talk

'According to her, complaints are withdrawn for all sorts of reasons – bribery, threats – so they always follow them up.'

'Sounds like she's mistaking you for the mafia.'

I had just brewed up when a lady knocked at the door. She was plainly distressed, so I made her a cup of tea and sat her down. Agnes Brownlee. Her dog had just died and she wasn't sure she would get over it. She was one of many who double-checked that the first consultation would be free. Since it would be the last as well I had no trouble setting her mind at rest. She spoke lovingly of the creature, a border collie taken out by cancer. Her collection of photographs suggested an excellent animal, but all animals die, including dogs and their owners. She must have known the average life-span of a dog and that, other things being equal, she would outlive it. Obvious as all this was, I kept it to myself since it wouldn't help her to hear it. But sometimes, with the over-emotional, I found myself wishing they could take the longer view, acquire a little detachment. Their lives would be so much easier.

'I don't know what I'm going to do without Ben, I really don't.'

'You're going to keep him alive and well in your thoughts, Mrs. Brownlee. Your memories of the good times you shared with Ben will help to sustain you over this difficult period.'

When she had calmed down a bit, I ran a well known theory past her, usually applied to people but no doubt applicable to dogs as well: that a person only dies when the last person who knew him dies too.

'In a very real sense, Ben is still with us now.'

I felt uncomfortably like a minister of religion saying this, but the balm was consoling and the lady left a lot happier than when she arrived, kindly bequeathing me one of her many photographs. (I see you're a photographer yourself.) Ben was sitting by a river bank, one ear up the other down, his amazingly long tongue hanging out as he lapped up the good country air.

Mrs. Brownlee had not long gone when DC Hunter arrived bearing my photographs.

'We have so many stolen items and so many witnesses we've decided to give you these back.'

'So I won't be called to testify.'

'Not on this occasion, no.'

There was something about the way he said it that aroused my suspicion.

'What are you saying – I might be on other occasions.'

'If DS MacNeil has anything to do with it.'

He looked unhappy, something was troubling him.

'Mind if I sit down?'

'Not at all.'

DC Hunter wanted to establish, before going any farther, that anything he might say would be in the strictest confidence. He laid so much stress on this that I began to wonder if he wanted to sign up as client, though his real motive soon became clear.

'I can't afford any of this to get back to the boss.'

I reassured him on that point. He had something to divulge and I wanted to know what it was.

'I know this bloke Robertson complained and all that, but it seems to me she's going over the top. Even if everything she says is right, as fraud goes this small beer. Not worth bothering about. A caution. A rap over the knuckles. Cut it out and we'll forget all about it. Low-level stuff.'

All well and good, but as reassurance went this was something of a put-down.

'I see.'

'I can tell you this right now, she's determined to charge you. She's just waiting for a report from that professor chap at the Royal Ed, practically camping on his lawn to screw it out of him as soon as possible.'

'Right.'

'But there's always the chance the Fiscal won't wear it and she knows that, she's not daft. So she's coming at you from other angles as well, drawing you to the attention of the social security and the revenue. But you didn't hear this from me.'

'Hear what?'

'Very good, Mr. Frei, still got your wits about you, I see.'

Though dealing with both these arms of the state might prove fatiguing, other than that I had little to fear. I had never applied for or received a social security payment in my life. A glance at their records would tell them that. As for the revenue, that wasn't so simple. I had always submitted an annual return and, so far as I knew, owed not in a penny in tax. But my records were untidy to

Time to Talk

say the least and there was nothing for it but to accept Catherine's kind offer as soon as possible. Then, if the taxman came calling, I could always refer him to my accountant. They spoke the same impenetrable language.

'What the hell are you wanting now? Can't you give the man a moment's peace?'

Colin had seen DC Hunter arrive and burst into the room assuming the worst. His nose was redder than usual. He had the cold.

'Steady on, sir, let's just calm down a bit, shall we?'

I pointed to the stolen photographs on my desk.

'DC Hunter has just brought them back. They've got so much on this Olatunde guy they won't need me as a witness.'

I felt like passing on Hunter's news about MacNeil's doubtful tactics, but he'd spoken in confidence and, in this pantomime season of ours, I couldn't afford anything getting back to the Wicked Witch of the North. If it did, his life wouldn't be worth living. Colin was mortified.

'Sorry, stupid misunderstanding. Max has been under a lot of pressure lately.'

I could tell from Hunter's expression that Colin's outburst scarcely registered on his Richter scale of incidents. It was over already.

'Like it, by the way.'

Hunter was referring to the little Christmas tree with fibre optic lights I had perched on the window sill beside the plants. As far as I could tell, he meant what he said.

Later, on my way out, I met up with Colin in his studio. He apologised again and I told him to forget it. Hunter had and so should he. I did want to know something though: was Catherine's offer still open. If so I'd like to take her up on it. Of course it was. All I needed to do was give her a bell and sort out the shoebox under my bed. He knew where I kept my receipts.

'Oh, I almost forgot.'

He led me to the back of his studio and handed me a long, thin cardboard container just over five feet in length.

'What you've always wanted.'

'What is it?'

'A fluorescent tube. Check the colour temperature, Max: 6,500 K!'

I have to assume I looked blank.

'Wake up, man! It's daylight equivalent output, less green more blue. A full spectrum light. The love of your life will look herself again.'

I stood in the doorway for a moment looking out at the courtyard. Behind me I could hear the generalized hum of artists at work and ahead of me stretched the rest of life. It was just nearing the end of November and even at noon, with the sky overcast, everything seemed dull and drear. Add in the cold and it was positively bleak.

There were several cars in the courtyard. I noticed two people in one of them as I went to mine. A man got out when he saw me.

'Good afternoon, Mr. Frei.'

It wasn't designer stubble, he looked as if he'd slept in his raincoat overnight.

'Just wondered if you could spare me a minute or two.'

'I have a couple of slots after two.'

'Do I look like I need therapy?'

If it was possible to tell by looking, the answer was 'yes'. He was the most crumpled individual I'd set eyes on for some time. A good night's sleep would have done him no harm.

'The things is, we've heard you're conning people out of their hard-earned cash, claiming to be a therapist when you're not. Anything to say?'

He was joined by his colleague, who started taking pictures with an amazingly large camera, making sure he had The Warehouse in the background. When I realised what was happening I was tempted to run for the car and take off, but I knew how damaging the images would be.

'Any questions you may have will be answered in due course.'

'Right you are, doc. But maybe our readers want the answers now, they don't want to wait till the trial. Ever thought of that?'

I walked past him at a steady pace and opened the car door. More photographs. No doubt he'd offer me the opportunity to put my side of the story, the usual way in. But he didn't want to know, he had all the answers already.

25

Faith held the step-ladder steady as I climbed to the ceiling, removed the cover from the light and handed it down. Two dead flies fell out and I could see it needed a clean.

'Disgusting!'

I thought she meant the flies, but what really upset her was the grease that came off on her fingers. It could only have got there as a result of cooking. If we looked closely, we'd find it on other surfaces as well: the tops of the wall cabinets, the blind on the kitchen window. Cleaning it slat by slat was not a pleasant thought.

I made to hand her down the tube but Faith was already at the sink with her rubber gloves, attacking the cover with a sponge and a non-abrasive cream cleaner. With the cover so long and the sink so small, there was soon water all over the floor, which she would mop up unless I got to it first. She looked exhausted. After a stressful but inconclusive session with Hazel the previous night followed by a hard day at work she was now faced with me, her errant partner, bringing home a problem of his own.

Later that evening, when we'd eaten and tidied up, we switched off our phones and sat down to talk. It soon became clear that Faith was into multi-tasking. During her cleaning and cooking, she'd further refined her thoughts.

'It's not just the social security and the taxman that woman's tipped off. It has to be her who leaked the story to the press. I'm sure it's not legal.'

'That hardly matters if we can't prove it.'

'It does to me and it should to you.'

She opened her laptop and started searching. I watched and admired. Her face looked so much better in the light of day, however artificially produced. The bilious wash was gone, the patina removed, the artist's model and lover restored to her fresh, unspoiled condition without any need of painstaking restoration.

'Right, so two things here,' she said, after a good ten minutes. 'If the journalist paid MacNeil for the low-down on you she's broken the law. We could have her for that.'

I thought this unlikely: her motive wasn't money but hostility.

'And the other thing?'

'As far as I can see, papers can print what they like about people, subject to the usual laws covering libel and defamation, except where court proceedings are underway. The minute you've been charged, all they can report till the trial is who you are and what you've been charged with. They can research you all they like, but they can't print a word of it till the trial's over.'

'I haven't been charged with anything.'

'Exactly. She's waiting for Prof Dwyer's report, so in the meantime she's going to inflict the maximum damage she can.'

Faith starting mousing again at remarkable speed.

'It's not in today's Evening News.'

'Pleased to hear it.'

'And there's no sign of it here on their website.'

'So what does that signify?'

'It signifies, Max, that you won't like the Sunday papers.'

It had crossed my mind before, but now it occurred to me to ask. Why was it that whenever anything serious came up we discussed it at the kitchen table – never in the living room, never in the bedroom, and never in the bath?

Faith looked up from her screen with a delightfully abstracted expression. Why had I brought this up, why had I brought it up now?

'Well, Max,' she sighed, 'the heavy stuff's too much like work, wouldn't you say? I associate the kitchen with work, so that's okay, but the living room is a place to relax and I intend to keep it that way. As for the bedroom, well, that's where we sleep, and I like my sleep untroubled by anxiety of any kind. And yes, I know there's a bit more than sleep involved in there right now, but if you put a stopwatch on us most of our time is still spent sleeping. They say couples sleep together for a reason, you know. It sounds like a euphemism but it's not. Sleeping together is really what it's about.' She looked back to her screen. 'I believe I've answered your question.'

I had seldom heard her use so many consecutive words. It was close to a speech. Where I preferred to deal with the heavy issues of life on neutral ground, outside the home entirely, Faith restricted them to a particular location inside it: the same goal by slightly differing means. But we had this in common: both of us quarantined the bad stuff to avoid contamination.

After another minute checking the web, she closed her laptop and looked me in the eye.

'So what's your plan?'

'I'm not sure I have one. I'll just have to ride it out.'

'By *it* I take it you mean the approaching storm.'

'I suppose.'

I was about to back-track, to claim that the metaphor wasn't appropriate, that I wasn't at sea at all, but that's exactly where I was.

'I want you listen carefully, Max. I have a plan, but you don't have to like it and you certainly don't have to accept it.'

It was now Thursday evening. In Faith's opinion I had a two day interlude before things went pear-shaped. In that time there were certain angles I should cover. She rose from the table, walked out to the hall and came back with a note-pad. (Her briefcase lived in the hall, a visual reminder to pick up it on her way to work.) The first was to keep my friends onside. They knew about the complaint but not about the rest of it. Awkward as it might be, I had to tell them everything tomorrow. If the first they knew was from the tabloids I wouldn't be at sea, I'd be dead in the water.

'In any case, they're your friends. You have to show them some consideration.'

I glanced up at Colin's fluorescent tube, I recalled Catherine's offer to handle my accounts, I thought of Janice and her filing cabinet, and my mind went back to the meeting where they accepted me as one of their own.

'You're right. I'll do it tomorrow morning.'

Her gaze travelled down the sheet to her next point. If they could, the press would contact my clients. How did they feel being at the business end of a con? What did they think of me now? They'd be looking for shock and horror, sensational quotes from scandalised punters.

'But Faith, they don't know who my clients are. MacNeil herself doesn't know!'

'And you're reassured by that?'

'Of course. Why wouldn't I be?'

'Let's face it, Max, we're just starting to learn what these people are capable of. Have the current proceedings passed you by?'

She was referring to the recent inquiry into the practices of the press, much of which had been televised. The coverage hadn't been pretty.

'You do realise they can hack into phones and computers.'

I had heard about that but it didn't concern me much.

'Do you really think they'd break the law to nail me? I'm not a big enough target.'

'Better safe than sorry. Cover the bases here, Max, or you might live to regret it.'

Faith's plan was simple but demanding: get my friends onside first and then as many of my clients as possible. I had all of Friday, a working day, and Saturday too if I needed it.

'I can deal with Hazel. In any case, she owes you.'

She owed me alright. I was still to be paid for my photo-session in the soggy undergrowth at the Botanics – though, in fairness, I hadn't billed her for it yet.

Which brought Faith to her most important point. If I'd gone home today I might have found myself door-stepped by the gentlemen of the press. They'd want shots of me entering and leaving my lair. They'd want a statement, anything they could use. If I denied it they'd portray me as a man without conscience, a monster preying on the vulnerable. If I admitted it, they'd done their job bringing a miscreant to the attention of public. Either way they were made.

'MacNeil tipped them off about you and she knows where you live.'

There was no getting away from that – not unless I moved in with her. MacNeil didn't know where she lived, didn't yet know she existed. I would have the run of the front bedroom, keep all my clothes there and anything else I liked. She knew I was untidy, so keeping on top of the room would be down to me. Another example of quarantine. There might be something to this OCD thing after all, but that was the least of my worries.

'There's a bed in there too.'

I thought I saw her suppress a smile but I couldn't be sure.

'Don't worry, Max, our sleeping arrangement won't change.'

I was reassured, delighted, but still missing the point.

'And this would be till it all dies down.'

'We've been over this before, Max. When the story gets out your income will plummet. How will you pay the rent? You're just scraping by at the moment. There's only one solution: give up your flat and move in here. My pay covers the mortgage already. The other bills we'll split as best we can. And then,' she added, raising her strategy to the next level, 'you can work on the qualifications you should have and don't.'

Either that, I thought, or get a job as waiter, a dishwasher, anything other than wading my way through the many texts I'd nearly drowned in already. I wasn't into video games, but if Sorrow Acre 2 didn't exist it was about to be invented. Forgotten lines of verse entered my head, written by a man who feared that by dint of abstruse research he would steal from his own nature all the natural man. Not an attractive prospect. Yet here was Faith proposing to support me through a degree, a thoughtful response to my situation and something I would have to face up to.

'That would take years.'

'Yes, Max, but don't you see – by the time you've done it this whole episode will be yesterday's news. You could start again with a clean sheet.'

I have to admit I wondered at the time whether Faith was planning to shut me down as an independent operation. It was a generous offer, but was it all or nothing? I had to know.

'Couldn't we carry on as we are?'

Her answer was short and to the point: she could, very easily, and I was welcome to try.

'And I could still sleep over.'

'Of course.'

No pressure, then. She wasn't forcing the pace because I was backed into a corner. But if she was prepared to do this for me and I accepted, there was something she expected in return. She was looking for evidence of commitment. I wondered what that might be: an agreement to wash the dishes in perpetuity, to do the housework, the ironing?

'If you move in we should get married.'

Not in my wildest dreams had it occurred to me that she would consider this. The thought had crossed my mind from time to time, but I knew I wouldn't have the nerve to bring the subject up. Now she was suggesting it herself. I could hardly believe it. I was stunned, so taken aback that words failed me altogether.

'I can see you don't like the idea.'

Faith had misinterpreted my silence.

'I do,' I said, before she came to her senses and changed her mind, 'I like it a lot.'

She smiled and took my hand, the only way to do it. You can see a person, fine, but such is the power of the brain to generate dreams and hallucinations that at some deep level you can't be sure she's really there till you touch her. So holding hands is good. Holding hands makes sensation, sensation makes sense.

Our marital moment was broken by singing on the landing outside as a group of students made their way upstairs to their flat. It may have felt like it for the last half hour, but we weren't alone in the world. Others lived and breathed – like us, celebrating the marriage of flesh and air. Faith shook her head in pretended disapproval.

'Young people nowadays.'

Her view was simple: if we were living as man and wife we should be man and wife. We should not, she said, giving me a meaningful look, we should not pretend to be what we were not. And that was the closest Faith ever came to a direct critique of my behaviour. As Frank said of apples, women like that don't grow on trees.

By this time I felt sure we'd covered the ground: what issue could possibly remain after marriage? I made us a couple of coffees and returned to the table feeling more relaxed, more hopeful, bathed in the light of a new dawn. But as I sat down, I could tell Faith had been visited by an afterthought. There was one last thing it was best to deal with now.

'When you're talking with clients you expect them to con-confide in you.'

'Not much point if they don't.'

'Yet you keep things to yourself. You only confide inpeople when you have to.'

There was some truth in that, but comparing me to my clients didn't help. They came to me for a reason, each and every one had a problem.

'And you don't?'

Why were we sitting there, at her kitchen table, working out how to cope with the mess I was in if I didn't have a problem? I considered pointing out that any problem I might have, though real enough, was not of the psyche. But maybe it was. Why had I chosen this singular path: was it solely to make a point through living it or was something deeper at work? Was I meeting a need I was unaware of myself?

'You can be as tight as you like with other people, Max, that's up to you. But you'll have to be open with me or it won't work.'

26

The following morning was the last day of November, not especially cold for the time of year, but overcast and dark when I made it in. I arrived at The Warehouse an hour earlier than usual, thinking that in so doing I would not have to fight my way through an unruly throng of reporters and photographers. I had overestimated my importance and their diligence: apart from one bicycle, the courtyard was empty. In any case, they already had their story and photographs of the culprit at the scene of the crime. Why would they waste their time coming back?

The only person there before me was Janice, doing admin work in the office. She saw me coming in and was glad of an excuse to put her papers to one side and chat.

'Well, Max,' she said, with her usual vigorous good cheer, 'what brings you here so early?'

I offered to tell her after I'd brewed up. Not wanting to see me disappear upstairs, she made me a cup of herbal tea and trapped me in the office by shutting the door.

I told her everything. As she listened her expression changed from warmth to concern.

'So let me get this straight, you've been working here as a therapist without the proper qualifications?'

'Technically, yes.'

'Cut the crap, Max.'

'OK, if you put it that way the answer is yes.'

The phone rang, she listened for a few seconds, barked *Not now, Bernard* and hung up.

'Why?'

Given my years of study, I believed I had as good a handle on the subject as most, and being in the hands of a professional was no guarantee of effective treatment, far from it.

'Qualified surgeons make mistakes too. Do we see you nipping into the Royal Infirmary with retractors and saws? No we don't. The fact remains you're not qualified.'

Her analogy was somewhat strained, but I let it go and tried another tack.

'You sell knitwear patterns.'

'I didn't realise that Max.' Sarcasm didn't become her. 'Your point?'

'As often as not, you told me this yourself, you sell them to other people who pretend the work is theirs. So you're committing a fraud against the people who buy them. I rest my case.'

'You don't have a bloody case! I'm the knitting equivalent of a ghost writer. Perfectly legal. You've been taking money from clients under false pretences and, what's worse, doing it in this building!'

Why doing it in the building made it worse wasn't clear, but it didn't seem wise to challenge her on the point. Her agitprop loudhailer was perched on some box files in the corner of the room, reminding me that I was no match for this woman.

'For fuck's sake, Max!'

There was a brief silence during which the cogs whirred and the steam rose, then she calmed down a bit.

'Are they going to charge you?'

I hoped so, but I couldn't tell her that. Nor could I explain the grounds of my defence to her or anyone else who might be questioned by the police as a witness, or by a journalist fleshing out the bones of a story. I had to reserve it for the day.

'What about your files? You realise I could be implicated here. They might turn up with a warrant!'

'I'll take them home.'

I assured Janice that I had not been acting with criminal intent: I had done everything I could to help my various clients. If the purpose of fraud was to clean out my clients, the law would look in vain for off-shore accounts, properties on the Algarve or shell companies in the Bahamas. I made ends meet on the most marginal of profits.

'How much do you charge?'

'Thirty pounds an hour, well below the going rate.'

The discounted price reflected the fact that I lacked a formal qualification, something else I could point to in my defence.

'Who else knows what's been going on?'

'Well, the press have got hold of it for a start.'

'For God's sake, Max, they'll be turning up here next!'
'And I told Faith last night.'
'She didn't show you the door?'
'No.'

According to Janice I'd been lucky. Women liked to know where they were with a man and Faith had her reputation to consider. She wouldn't want it tarnished by association with a common criminal like me.

'What are you planning to do?'
'Explain the situation to people as and when they appear.'
'And Colin, what about him? He's not going to like it.'

That was putting it mildly. Neither would Steve. Janice offered to let them down gently, but it had to come from me. Ceramick remained out of circulation and as for George, still very much in evidence, when he heard what I'd been up to he'd probably be impressed. I would achieve a new and unlooked-for status: a bit of a lad, a card.

A car door banged outside. Shortly afterwards, Colin walked in, beaming from ear to ear, with a large pile of Christmas cards. His woollen scarf was so bulky it functioned as a neck-brace supporting his head.

'Thought I'd get in quick before things tailed off.'
'The girls have just left for two weeks in Morocco.'

Whatever they might say about African art and culture, Antonia and Vicky liked their winter weeks in the sun.

'No stopping them, is there.'

Then Colin noticed that Janice and I were in sombre mood and wondered why. He didn't like what he heard.

'Well, I must say Max, I'm disappointed.'
'And Colin doesn't like to be disappointed,' Janice said helpfully.
'No, he doesn't. I really don't know, Max. I'm not sure I get it. I'll have to think about this, but it doesn't look good.'

He left to deliver his cards and Janice shrugged.

'You'll just have to wait and see. He'll get over it, but it may not be the same.'

I headed for her studio and started removing my files, sorting them to decide what to keep and what to shred. Since I didn't have to make these decisions there and then, this was doubtless a displacement activity – putting off the evil hour when I started to contact my clients with the good news.

I put the files I was keeping on the back seat of the car, under an old jacket to hide them from prying eyes. The rest I fed through the shredder in the office. Janice was working, but keeping an eye on me at the same time. I was on my way out when something occurred to her.

'Max, I'm sure you've thought of this, but what if they don't run the story after all and you've told everyone by then? You could lose your clients for nothing.'

Her question stopped me in my tracks. Why hadn't it occurred to Faith and I the previous evening? But surely they would run it. Alright, I wasn't a celebrity, I didn't take part in reality TV shows, but I was worth a paragraph or two on page twenty-eight. Even if they didn't run it, I might be adding to the charge sheet if, after my interview with the police, I knowingly continued as I had before. I'd no idea what the legal term might be, but I'd probably be compounding something and, as with interest on a debt, compounding would soon add up.

Back in my studio I switched the heater on and pulled it on its wheels towards the desk. I had enough problems without going down with the cold. Was there anything I needed to take? I sat at the desk I might not have a use for any longer and gazed round my studio and sometime consulting room: the landscapes on the walls, the prints Colin had leant me, and the oriental screen Janice had helped me select. Even with the IKEA chairs it seemed a bit bare. The small Christmas tree on the ledge had a forlorn look to it (add projection to displacement) and the plants had seen better days, days of more sunshine and warmth.

Rifling through the desk drawers I came upon my voice recorder: a useful device which should not fall into hostile hands. It occurred to me then, in what might have been a sign of incipient paranoia, that just because it was still there didn't mean that someone from GCHQ, Special Branch, MI5 or the Leith Police hadn't copied the entire contents onto another device. It frequently happened in films and television drama. It was time to be more careful both with the confidences of others and my own limited prospects.

In the next drawer down I noticed Lyndsay Craig's adult education leaflet, which I hadn't given another thought to since I'd put it there. Yet now, with one source of income about to dry up, it might be worth considering photography. But I'd be learning on the job – not an easy thing to do, keeping one step ahead of the class – and if my name was blackened in the press they wouldn't want me anyway. I might even reach the point where I didn't want me either.

I was becoming aware of a whimsical streak, perhaps a sign of panic, which I had not before detected in myself, and then I noticed, beneath the leaflet, George's charcoal sketch of Faith. Seeing her likeness I felt better at once. I was no longer alone, she was with me in the room. I took it out with care and laid it on the desk, so absorbed in her image I didn't notice Colin coming in.

'A penny for your thoughts,' he said, 'assuming they're worth that much.'

I had always believed that relationships complicated life and not always for the best. I had seen it often enough, most recently with Hazel and Henry. But they, by all accounts, had been happy for many years, so who was to say it hadn't been good while it lasted? There is always a balance to be struck between risk and reward. Many problems, real or imagined, arise from the fact that we don't always know where that balance lies. And some would add that a problem imagined – and mark this, Professor Dwyer, a problem with no 'objective basis' – is nonetheless real to the sufferer. Perhaps the poet had it right when he referred to the imagination as the one reality in this imagined world. Worth a penny? Worth a pound? Short of setting up a stall to trade these simple notions I had no way of knowing. But Colin had seen me studying the sketch and believed that if he didn't know what I was thinking, he knew who I was thinking about.

'Anyway,' he said, 'it just occurred to me that you have fliers in various places you might be advised to remove. I pass two of them on my way home.'

Something else we hadn't thought of, Faith and I, but he was right: removing them from the public arena was a good idea, and his offer had a sensation of thaw about it. Colin had never been one to bear a grudge and was less judgemental than most, though we were never again as close as we had been before.

'If it wouldn't be too much trouble.'

'It might help clear things up.'

It would. And that, in turn, might help clear the air.

I checked the courtyard from the office window before going out to my car. No one was there that I could see, but to be on the safe side I drove home by a circuitous route, repeatedly checking my mirror. The last thing I needed was journalists knowing where I lived. How naive can a grown man be? As I was opening the door the lady opposite, Mrs Forsyth, who wouldn't see summer again, let alone spring, opened her door. She had plainly been on the lookout for my arrival. She wasn't happy, wasn't happy at all. Did I have any idea how many people had been up and down the stairs wanting to talk to me? Several had rung her doorbell hoping for information. One of them had the cheek to leave his card, asking her to give him a call if I returned. She hadn't told them a thing, of course, a disreputable looking lot, but what on earth was going on?

That was obvious: MacNeil had given her journalist friends my address, but since I couldn't tell her that I told her something else. I apologised to the lady, explaining that it was all a misunderstanding which would soon blow over. Until then, I would stay in my fiancée's spare room till things died down, that way I could reduce further trouble to a minimum. Somehow she got the impression that I was putting myself to this trouble entirely for her, and was so appreciative she offered me a cup of a tea and a large wedge of Selkirk bannock. I could always eat it while packing. Diplomacy pays, except in the Middle East, the South China Seas and the sundry other places where it really matters.

Back at last in the relative safety of my flat, I soon realised that I had more belongings than I thought: clothes, socks, underwear, shoes, toiletries, books, magazines, CDs, and a computer. Sitting on my bed surveying partially open drawers, the wardrobe with its doors hanging open, clothes dumped on chairs and the half-full laundry basket, I knew it would take me some time to work out which items to take. And even then I would have to wash some of them on the shortest effective programme before setting the machine to dry. I was looking at two hours at least, not counting the packing.

I heard a siren in the distance, an ambulance. Someone else at a junction in the road.

It occurred to me that though I had been in Faith's flat many times and spent several nights there, she had never set eyes on what I was seeing now and probably never would. And looking around me I was glad. The shade-less overhead light didn't help, but even so there was something drab about the room, and the kitchen wasn't much better. Why would she want to see this dreary place, what good would it do? I was glad she hadn't.

Was this just the way things had worked out or was something deeper at work? I remember considering various metaphors, one in particular, Faith as the planet and I as the moon held in orbit around her. Whatever might be said for the idea, the tone was completely lacking. Celestial bodies aren't known for their emotion. But the answer was yes, something deeper was at work. She was the centre of attraction, she still is, and I would always gravitate towards her. Putting it another way, she was the centre of power in our relationship, which would have been destructive if she had abused it or I had resented it. Since neither of these was the case, it worked very well.

Nearly three hours later, when I had completed the washing, eaten a cheese sandwich and wolfed down my neighbour's excellent bannock, I realised that I couldn't fit everything in the two dust-covered cases in the hall cupboard. Even with bin bags I was looking at two journeys at least. And this dismayed me, not because of the journeys but because I would now have to make a series of tiresome decisions – what to pack now and what to leave till later. Low level stuff like that can be mentally fatiguing, and so it proved.

By the time I made it to the car, I was in a demoralised state of mind, the most despondent condition I reached during this whole affair, then or later. The events of the last few weeks had finally caught up with me, so instead of driving straight to Faith's, I headed to the beach. A strange thing to do at eight o'clock on a November evening, and amused myself with the thought that since I couldn't risk leading my pursuers to my new pied-à-terre in Lauriston, driving to Portobello was as good a way as any of throwing them off the scent.

I followed a simple route, though there were doubtless shorter alternatives, driving down to the old Portobello Power Station, which I could still see though it hadn't been there for years, turning right along Portobello High Street and left into Brunstane Road, driving all the way down to the Promenade.

On a sunny summer's day, parking there could be difficult. That evening it was easy.

At first, I felt I was still down on my luck: the tide couldn't have been much farther out. But as I followed the sand in its descent towards the water I liked it more and more because, when I finally reached it, I was much farther from human habitation than I would have been otherwise. Apart from the occasional dog-walker I had the place to myself.

The longer I spent at the water's edge the better I felt. The moon disappeared behind clouds from time to time, and then I felt even more that I had the place to myself. The sea was calm, and the quiet incoming waves, hardly visible, could be inferred from the white of their incoming crests. But as always it was the sound of the sea that soothed the soul, as the waves broke producing, as they fell back, the eternal note of sadness, that melancholy, long, withdrawing roar.

In the midst of happiness there is sadness, without which happiness cannot be, and there is solace in that. Because any happiness not rooted in this reality is froth on the beer without the body to support it.

27

Faith preferred books. Her attitude to newspapers was dismissive, once referring to them as transient ephemera best left to rot, though I have to admit this comment came after my brief moment of fame. On this occasion, since she had to know the worst, she walked to the nearest newsagent and came back shortly afterwards with a selection of papers, all at the tabloid end of the market. She put them on the kitchen counter till we'd finished our toast, then transferred them to the table.

There was nothing in The People or the Sunday Post. But when we turned our attention to the Sunday Mail there it was, well into the paper and not very long. Under the headline THE MISSING SHRINK the reporter, one Vincent Cochrane, claimed that Edinburgh therapist Max Frei had *gone to ground* as a result of his investigation. He hit the expected targets, claiming that I had been *masquerading* under a false name but now he could *make public for the first time* what my closely guarded real name was. In a stab at wit, he suggested that the use of two names might indicate a schizophrenic tendency on my part. He went on to claim that I lacked the necessary qualifications for working as a psychotherapist and had therefore been perpetrating a fraud on unsuspecting and vulnerable members of the public, who had enough problems as it was without an unscrupulous con man like me adding to them. Possibly the most amusing part of the article was its opening: *This paper can reveal that noted landscape photographer Maxwell Frei has been leading a double life.*

We read it through a couple of times. Faith thought it wouldn't have much impact given the major stories it was up against: The Dandy going out of print after seventy-five years and Arbroath holding Celtic to a shock draw. And though the paper had selected what was no doubt the least flattering image of me leaving The Warehouse, it was small and lacking in impact compared to a bejewelled Heidi Klum dressed as Cleopatra or Meryl Streep using her iPhone to take a photo of herself and Hillary Clinton after a dinner at the State Department. But as it turned out, it was one of the few things I had said when confronted by the photographer that caused me the greatest trouble.

On the following Monday the story was taken up, also in a small way, by the Evening News, and over a period of days it provoked some response, all of it unexpected. Jean Ritchie wrote a letter in my defence, which the editor published. Mr Robertson also wrote a letter in my defence which, to his great irritation, the editor binned. When he showed me what he'd written I had to agree with the editor: too many references to the casting of stones and the turning of cheeks. As I put it to him, it was altogether too erudite for these dumbed-down times. So far so good. Then Henry's letter appeared. Henry was not a happy man.

By what right did I complain about my picture being taken by a press photographer, he asked, when I myself had recently taken clandestine pictures of him and a lady friend while concealed in the shrubbery at the Botanic Gardens? Readers might like to know that these pictures, for which I had been handsomely paid with money from his own bank account, had been instrumental in ending a long and happy marriage. Not only was Maxwell Frei a fake therapist, he also had a second career as a paid snoop on honest citizens – an occupation for which he was only too well qualified.

When this letter appeared I asked Faith how Henry knew I had taken the offending pictures: we had told Hazel on no account to mention me. When Faith phoned her, Hazel was profuse in her apologies. My name had slipped out in the course of a blazing row when her guard was down. She was sure we understood. We did, but it didn't help much. And that, as far as we could see, was the end of it as far as the press was concerned.

But this modest coverage had consequences. For several days my business mobile was flooded with calls, texts and voice-mails. Several were abusive, and two were from reporters hoping to coax me into defending my corner. Faith was my coach and her attitude was simple: whatever their game, they couldn't keep playing it if I didn't hit the ball back over the net, and in every case I took her advice. Yet there remained a few calls which were more difficult to classify, two being from would-be clients. Of these, one was particularly intriguing and we discussed it at some length. The caller wanted to meet me regarding his problem, believing, after what he had read in the papers, that no one could be better qualified to deal with it than I was.

'It makes no sense. He has to know I'm not qualified at all.'
'There's another possibility.'

Faith was suspicious, and who could blame her? She also considered me naive, a trait which she liked though alive to its dangers.

'He might be a journalist posing as a client in the hope of a follow-up story. Have you thought of that?'

In the end we decided that I should meet him in the Filmhouse café on Wednesday at lunch time and texted him with this suggestion, which he accepted.

His name was Ian Kellock. He'd recognise me from my picture in the paper, and so he did. The café was still reasonably quiet. I'd spread myself out on one of the bays along the left hand wall, my coat beside me on the sofa and a notebook and pen on the table. I was reluctant to leave them there unattended, but let them reserve my pitch while I went to the counter and ordered a coffee. Kellock arrived shortly afterwards. When I rose and asked if I could get him anything he put me on the spot straight away.

'Peace of mind. How does that sound?'

It sounded good. I could do with some myself.

I studied him as he waited to order. His coat, which he'd left beside mine, looked warm but somewhat worn. He was slightly below average height, with straight, brown hair cut short and clothes so boring they could have served as urban camouflage – which, as I was shortly to discover, was their purpose. He had only intended to buy a coffee and a slice of cake, but the cooking smells got to him and he went for a baked potato instead. By the time it had joined us at the table, with its portion of healthy greens, I gave in and ordered one too. I got on so well with the man I had to keep reminding myself that I didn't know him from Adam. For all I knew, he could have been a journalist, or a detective gathering evidence for a civil action brought by a disaffected client.

'So?' I said, after a decent interval.

He began by admitting that his name wasn't Kellock: he couldn't tell me what his real name was so it would have to do. He was on a witness protection programme which meant, in his case, a new identity, not just till the trial was over but for the rest of his life. It wasn't a question of protecting him till he testified, he'd taken the stand already. Certain threats had been made. There was a very real risk of revenge so he had to make sure his cover wasn't blown. As he put it rather starkly, his throat was ripe for the knife. I found this image alarming and began to wonder if I'd made a mistake: being drawn into the world of Ian Kellock was not an attractive prospect.

'So why are you admitting this to a total stranger?'

'I should have thought that was obvious: we can't discuss the issue unless you know what it is, and you have an identity problem too, so I can be reasonably confident you'll understand. As for the total stranger bit, the papers saved me the trouble of checking you out. Right now, Mr Frei, you're very much a known quantity.'

'My name's no more Frei than yours is Kellock.'

'How true, Mr Anderson, how true.'

At first I assumed that being a witness meant exactly that – Mr Kellock had seen something he shouldn't have, an armed robbery, a murder. I had to understand, he said, that if he went into too much detail I might be able to work out from past press reports who he really was or, more accurately, who he once had been. But he wanted me to know that while the word witness was perfectly accurate, he had also been involved. He probably saw an involuntary look of alarm and moved to reassure me.

'There was no violence of any kind.'

'Glad to hear it.'

'But don't get the wrong idea either. We may be talking white collar crime here, but the stakes were high. I have certain skills, Mr Frei. I was the inside man.'

Reading between the lines, I now believe Mr Kellock transferred large sums of other people's money to off-shore accounts. But as far as I could see, he could easily have done that by himself. No one else was required.

'You have to understand I wasn't at all keen to do it, not at first. I had to be persuaded.'

'Pressure was applied.'

'Certain threats were made, yes.'

I wondered what these might have been: kidnapping his dog, threats against his wife and children. (He had no children, but I didn't know that at the time.) Perhaps they had something on him which might have lost him his job.

'And of course there were certain rewards, the golden carrot was dangled. These people knew the ropes. They offered to set me up in the sun, false passport, driving licence, the lot. I could do none of that for myself.'

A life in the sun: idling away the hours on beaches, patios, balconies and verandas, and to what end? What a boring prospect it was.

'Wouldn't you miss your family?'

'Not a lot, certainly not my wife.'

'Friends?'

'Some of them, maybe. A few.'

I sensed a note of regret. Ian Kellock was leading a restricted life alone.

'Here's the thing, Mr Frei, this is what people don't understand. To them it has a certain glamour, having a new identity, pretending to be who you're not. With every breath you take you're pulling a fast one and getting away with it.'

'But it's not like that at all.'

'Of course not. The reality is quite different. When they offer you a new identity it sounds like the real deal, you feel important, a major player. But they don't explain the quid pro quo.'

'Which is?'

'They take away the old one and everything that goes with it. You expect to lose touch with family and friends, you can work that out for yourself. It's the other stuff that grinds you down. You lose your credit rating, so getting a loan is out. You lose your record of work, so when you apply for a job you can't cite previous experience – you don't have any. And here's the worst of it: despite years of toil, certificates, diplomas and degrees – suddenly you don't have a single qualification to your name.'

'And you're sitting there thinking I didn't let that stop me.'

'It had crossed my mind.'

In my opinion there was little similarity. Unlike him, I was still in possession of my qualifications. He asked what those were and

I told him the one that mattered. He was less than impressed by ancient and medieval history.

'Not the best qualification for psychotherapy, I would have thought.'

'Not the worst either.'

Majoring on Sophocles, I made an abbreviated version of my case and he seemed to listen with an open mind, but I could tell he wasn't interested. What concerned him was something we had in common: the constant strain of being what we were not, the energy it took. It was totally draining. Hadn't that been my experience? Hadn't I longed to throw aside the mask and just be me? Embarrassing as it must have been at the time, surely I was relieved the whole charade was over at last?

I sat for minute chewing it over and realised he was right. I'd been so busy coping with events as they unfolded all I'd been doing was running on the spot. But since 'coming out' had always been on the cards, almost part of the plan, I should have expected some measure of relief when it did.

'Yes, I believe I was.'

Kellock leaned forward to his coat and took a sheaf of papers from the inside pocket. Spreading them out on the table he told me he had researched several cases of bigamy, mostly male. What possessed these people? Keeping one wife happy was difficult enough (it was clear that he spoke from experience) keeping two on the go at once beggared belief. As for this guy, pointing at his newspaper cuttings, it was scarcely credible he could stand the pace. What was in it for him except the mental exhaustion of juggling his lies (keeping his balls in the air, as he so colourfully put it) and the physical exhaustion of sleeping with four women. Four! I read the article with increasing disbelief. The man had not only married two women, he had also been engaged to two others, both of whom were pregnant at the time of writing.

'You live alone now, I take it.'

He nodded. 'No pretence, no dissimulation. Not any more.'

Interesting as all this was, I couldn't see where it was leading. I didn't need much persuading that living a lie was tiring, I'd tried it on a small scale myself. But Kellock's case, though falling far short of the bigamist's, was on another level altogether. The fact that he was thinking about the matter was commendable as an intellectual exercise, but where was the practical application?

'I can see the problem, but I'm not sure how I can help.'

'You can listen. Talking helps, that's the theory, right? A problem shared is a problem halved?'

'So they say.'

'And here's a thought – maybe I can help you.'

He wasn't sure how, not yet, but it could happen. He made another cryptic reference to his skills. Whatever they were, they impressed him a lot.

'You're a lawyer.'

His face broke into a wide smile and he shook his head.

'You think you're going to need one?'

'It could happen.'

'Well all I can tell you is this: I swim like a fish in my medium.'

'And that medium would be?'

'Electrons, Max, electrons.'

28

Faith and I decided that Christmas would be quiet, one of the advantages of having next to no family. She brought out a small artificial tree from a box at the foot of her wardrobe and placed it in the living room window. Its lights, all white, cycled through a short series of patterns, and to those she added a few simple decorations. It was minimal but effective, and exactly mirrored her attitude to adornment: a little goes a long way. No make-up, the occasional ear-ring and always the skewer through the hair to keep it up, though she had been known to use a pencil as well, especially at work.

Our fare on the day was simple too: steak pie, potatoes, roast parsnip and sprouts. We followed that up with raspberry trifle and pulled a cracker or two. Ignoring the paper hats, we made much of the gifts inside: a pencil sharpener, a spinning top, a metal puzzle and a small torch. As for the jokes, most of them were dire, though Faith found one so much to her liking it is still to be found in her underwear drawer: What do you call Santa's little helpers? Subordinate clauses!

Presents were more of a problem. I solved it by asking her what she wanted, hitting the shops and handing them over wrapped on the day. I knew nothing about perfume, and still less about women's clothes and accessories. She counterfeited surprise touchingly well. By the nature of our arrangement, she assumed she knew in advance everything she was getting, and was duly amazed when she unwrapped a piece of stained glass designed to hang from a sun-facing window. One of Antonia's most delightful pieces, it depicted small garden birds perched on twigs. Her gifts to me were more practical but welcome nonetheless: a digital photography book with DVD tutorials, and The Good Psychologist. At first I took this last to be a non-fiction prod in the direction she hoped I would travel. In fact it was a novel in which the protagonist, a qualified man, gave the reader the benefit of his thoughts on what were the attributes of a good psychologist, a category he was attempting to define.

It was unusual to find us in the living room: it fronted on to the traffic-noise of the street, and though it had a television, we didn't watch it much, preferring to spend our time chatting, reading or listening to the radio in the kitchen. The schedules were crammed with Christmas specials but some plums were better left in the pudding: Eddie Stobart's Christmas delivery for one, and the heavier offering from Sister Wendy on the Art of the Gospel. We opted instead for a DVD of The Artist, accompanied by sherry and shortbread. Valentin's dog had just saved him from a fire of his own creation when our doorbell rang. We considered pretending to be out, but our light would have been visible from the street outside and, anyway, we had a shrewd suspicion who it was.

Hazel had arrived uninvited but bearing gifts. Apart from a box of deep-filled mince pies, her gifts were liquid, and though they might have been considered seasonal, both Faith and I had begun to worry about her alcohol consumption. It had been 'healthy' anyway, but now there were signs of increased intake. She was starting to rely on that dangerous friend the bottle, who was always at hand and never let her down.

Faith believed she was aware of this herself and was eating more to soak it up, so apart from any damage to her liver she was putting on weight, showing the first signs of bloating, which she should nip in the bud while she still could. Otherwise, before she knew it, her prized good looks would be gone never to return. The easy chair certainly felt she was putting it on when, after the obligatory hugs and kisses, she collapsed heavily into it. I didn't see this so much as hear it when the upholstery, suddenly compressed, quietly exhaled as the air was driven from the interior by the impact. It was as close to a sigh as a piece of furniture could get.

'So how are the love birds?'

The love birds were fine, and perfectly okay with stopping the film half way through and listening to Hazel, who painted a bleak picture of her solitary life now the lying bastard had gone. But the house was still littered with too many of his belongings, which constantly reminded her of him. She'd faced him with an ultimatum – remove them, or she would throw them out. And how did he take that, we wondered? Not at all well. He was showing signs of digging his heels in, repeating such spurious points as owning half the house and claiming an entitlement to storage. And that wasn't the only way he was fighting back. We naturally enquired.

'He's sweet-talked a lot of our friends into taking his side. God knows how, they know I'm the injured party, but I'm beginning to think I have an infectious disease.'

Most of her friends had dropped her, not actively, nothing was said, though one of them, Sarah, had told her during a chance meeting in the supermarket that it happened all the time and there was no need to be so strident about it. And that wasn't all. Hadn't we heard? We didn't think we had.

'What about?'

'His web site?'

The more she talked the more we felt sorry for her. She was used to presenting a stylish, confident front to the world, but her confidence was so badly undermined it was taking the style down with it. It is customary to talk about such things in terms of self-esteem, and popular psychology would no doubt have it that hers had been sapped by her husband's betrayal. But the problem, as I saw it, was that the value she placed upon herself should never have depended on his view of her in the first place, nor on their shared identity as a married couple. As they put it these days, she had allowed herself to be validated by him, though it was painfully clear this had been a one-way street. Such power as she had, she had ceded to him. Now he had taken it with him when he left and Henry and Lizzie, without knowing it, passed it between them like a tired balloon left over from the party.

Hazel talked for two hours and sank deeper into her chair with every glass, to the point where we could have praised Henry to the skies and she wouldn't have batted an eye.

'She's in no fit state, you'll have to take her home.'

Given a body's dead weight I knew I couldn't do it without the lady's help, so we brought her round be degrees, stood her upright, though holding onto the back of the chair for support, and fought her arms through the sleeves of her coat. (If only she'd come in her cloak.) Faith helped me with her down the stairs, was rewarded by a deeply felt hug, and waved us off as we started down the street. It wasn't a long way, but it felt like it. When we arrived at her front door Hazel engaged her handbag in a fight to the death. She knew her keys were in there somewhere.

'You're not so bad as they say you are, Max.'

'How bad do they say I am?'

'Oh, you know. The papers and all that.'

When we finally got in, I guided her to the bedroom to sleep it off, but it was so cold it could have doubled as a fridge. It took me all my strength to steer her back to the living room, clear the cats off the couch and park her on it, where she promptly fell asleep. I fetched the duvet from her bed, covered her as well as I could and pushed a cushion under her head. For some reason, I was visited by unpleasant thoughts of people being sick and choking to death on their own vomit, but since she was already lying on her side it wasn't obvious what else I could do to prevent it.

I inspected her fridge. She still had some cold meat, cheese and margarine but her milk was on the turn so I poured it down the sink, washed out the container and put it in the bin. As far as I could see, all that remained were some tins, mostly soup, and half a loaf of bread. If there was a vegetable in the house, I couldn't find it.

Before I left I checked her one last time. Looking at her as she lay on the settee, I experienced the strangest temptation to clean the make-up from her face as she slept and meet her for the first time face to face, to see her rise the following morning and confront the world in her own right, as she really was. Perhaps I wanted her to be more like Faith, or maybe it was an irrational reaction to the can of Nitromors I'd found under the sink

I have seldom been so relieved to get home and shut the door behind me, Faith and I on one side, the world on the other. She was sitting at the kitchen table interrogating her laptop.

'How did it go?' She asked without looking up. 'Put her to bed?'

I described how I'd left her.

'She'll wake with a crick in her neck.'

The least of her problems, I thought, but Faith was probably right.

'So what have you been up to?'

Time to Talk

Faith had been intrigued by Hazel's reference to Henry's web site. It had taken her twenty minutes to track it down. His letter to the press had not had the desired effect because, as far as we could tell, it had no effect at all. He'd got things off his chest and felt no better. Even his friends didn't take their sympathy to the point of publicly declaring their support and at some point, back to the emotional wall, he had decided to carry the fight to the enemy, Max Frei, the man he blamed for all his problems. A friend, possibly Lizzie, had suggested Blogspot, and there it was in all its splendour - MAD MAX SICKS.

The name was lost on me, but according to Faith there had been several Mad Max films and spin-offs such as video games. These had used up the numbers one to five so Henry had gone to the next number up and wittily changed the spelling. We studied it together. The photograph from my flier had been scanned and altered, making it even less attractive than it had been. Quite an achievement. There was something demonic about the eyes and stubble was sprouting on my face. Neither of us knew how it had been done, and neither did Henry. He'd had expert assistance. But the text was another matter. All his own work.

Written in the first person, the words purported to be mine as I advertised my services. I guaranteed to leave you more depressed than I found you, but only if the money was right. I also specialised in stalking my friends with a camera and catching them when their guard was down. And despite my lack of medical qualifications, I wouldn't hesitate to stab you in the back. More worrying was the fact that he had made public both my phone numbers, my home address (the one I had just left), and my place of work (The Warehouse).

Henry's objective was clear: he wanted to blacken my name and cause me as much grief as possible by publishing my contact details. He hoped I would be flooded with nuisance calls and door-stepped by outraged citizens. He had never known my private number, so we had to assume he'd copied it from Hazel's phone on one of the many occasions she'd left it lying around.

'I'll have to change my number.'
'Why? How many nuisance calls have you had?'
'I haven't had any.'
'And what do you infer from that?'

Faith had a point. If Henry's campaign was so successful, why had it failed to generate a single call?

'There's illusion and reality, Max. This stuff is out there,' she said, indicating Henry's handiwork, 'but who is it reaching? Who cares? He's a sad man shouting in a vacuum.'

We later discovered that Henry had opened a Twitter account, also as Mad Max Sicks. Including Lizzie, he had three followers.

Later that evening, when we were getting ready for bed, Faith had a thought.

'Henry knows your number.'

'Yes.'

'But you haven't had a call from him. Why not?'

I hadn't clue.

'I'll tell you why, he doesn't have the bottle.'

I took this to mean that beneath the hurt and anger he knew I wasn't the problem. He was the one who had cheated on his wife. If he called me I'd point that out and he didn't want to hear it.

'And,' Faith said, removing her skewer and letting her hair cascade over her neck, 'if you don't have the bottle you can't leave a message in it, right?'

True, but having the bottle wasn't necessarily a good idea. Hazel had it, and it wasn't doing her much good. We'd have to look after her, of that I was sure, or the woman would sink without trace.

29

During a fallow period such as Christmas and New Year, so little happens you begin to think nothing will and a single small event seems to bear that out. Catherine contacted me in the second week of January and invited me round to Colin's for a working lunch. My latest tax return was due at the end of the month. I didn't know whether Colin would be there or at The Warehouse and didn't like to ask. His card had been attractive but, as always, signed off without a message.

He wasn't there when I arrived. Catherine had soup on the hob and garlic bread in the oven. She assured me that my affairs were in order, just a detail or two she wanted to go over. From the Revenue's point of view, the sums involved were small, but if they believed MacNeil they might suspect I was the Mr Big of the therapy scene, that my income was small by design and turn me over to discover where I'd stashed the rest. But I shouldn't let that worry me: for any question they might have, we had the answer. In fact, I could have claimed more against tax than I had. My return would be submitted online and in good time.

'You're not the tidiest person, are you?'

I liked to think I was tidy in the mind but had to agree.

'Colin's in Dundee. Some gallery or other, can't remember the name.'

'How's he doing?'

'Fine, but he doesn't know what to make of all this. Neither do I. And Max, when you come right down to it, either you're qualified or you aren't.'

I had an answer to that, but knew I had to reserve for the trial. I muttered something about another side to the story and keeping my powder dry. She wasn't impressed.

'That's all very well, but surely you can say something now, at least to your friends?'

'I would if I could, believe me.'

'OK. Well he told me to remind you there's a meeting at The Warehouse next week. Wednesday, ten o'clock. The agenda's a mile long.'

Without a doubt, I would be on it.

The following day the weather changed for the worse. MacNeil phoned. She'd arrived at what she thought was my door and been brought up to speed by Mrs Forsyth, who couldn't tell her where I was living now and wouldn't have if she'd known.

'We need to talk.'

'We're talking now.'

'Face to face, Mr Frei. I'm sure you know what I mean.'

'Is it important?'

'Yes.'

I agreed to meet her at the station. My feeling that matters were coming to a head was confirmed by her closing remark.

'I hope you understand, Mr Frei, that this is a serious matter. If you fail to attend I may be obliged to issue a warrant for your arrest, though obviously that's a road I'd rather not go down.'

There was nothing obvious about it. She'd decided to take it as far as it would go. She ushered me into an interview room where we were joined by DC Hunter. Watching them both at the other side of the table I sensed a certain tension, but without knowing the cause it didn't help me much. Hunter may have felt his superior was making a mistake, which she was, but it could have been something else – she was running him into too much overtime, blighting his career prospects. I would never know. After pointing out that I was entitled to have a lawyer present, an offer I again declined, I was charged on two counts. The first was common law fraud which, as I now know, covers the widest possible range of acting on false pretences. Secondly, I was charged with statutory fraud under the Trade Descriptions Act 1968. Acting as a sole trader, I had provided false and misleading information to potential clients to secure their business. So she was taking the shot-gun approach. If she didn't get me with one barrel, she would get me with the other.

'Well, Mr Frei, how do you respond to these charges?'

'I reserve my position.'

'You're unwilling to comment.'

'For now.'

'You realise this may not look good in court.'

'Assuming we get that far.'

'Oh, I'm confident we will, one way or another.'

I had the impression MacNeil was pleased by my reaction. By not mentioning when charged any defence I might later make, a jury might assume I had something to hide. If they didn't, the prosecution would point them in that direction.

'OK. So what happens now?'

'I pass my files to the procurator fiscal who will decide what action to take.'

'I assume these files include Professor Dwyer's report.'

'They do. But as I'm sure you know I'm not at liberty to divulge the contents to you.'

'Perhaps I should engage my own expert witness.'

'I can't give you legal advice but you're entirely free to do so. It would cost you, though, and there's always the possibility your expert would agree with ours. Anyway, since you're now in the system, I'll need something more substantial than a mobile telephone number. I'm sure you understand my position.'

'You think I'll catch the next flight to Acapulco.'

'Not at all, but I do need to know where you're living.'

I had a problem with that. Articles attacking me had appeared in the press, and the journalist who wrote the first was so well informed he had clearly been tipped off. He had also shown up both at my place of work and my home. While The Warehouse was in the public domain my home address was not. Vincent Cochrane had acted on inside information.

'I hope you aren't suggesting the source was in this building.'

'That's exactly what I'm suggesting, DS MacNeil.'

'The police don't give out information of that kind. Apart from anything else, it's illegal.'

I took a newspaper from my bag and laid it on the table.

'Tell that to Detective Chief Inspector Casburn.'

This officer had been found guilty the day before of misconduct in public office – specifically, for passing confidential information to the press. MacNeil glanced disdainfully at my dog-eared copy of the Guardian.

'This happened in England.'

'And it couldn't happen here?'

'It hasn't happened here.'

There was a short pause while MacNeil glanced at Hunter and wondered what line to take.

'I'm not trying to be awkward here, Mr Frei, I really do require your present address.'

I was sure this was true, but there was no way I was going to compromise Faith.

'And I require a copper-bottomed guarantee that my present address will not be made known to the media. My partner has absolutely nothing to do with any of this.'

'I'm sure he hasn't.'

What to make of this woman and her calculated insults? MacNeil, assuming I was straight, was enrolling me in the gay community to get as far up my nose as possible. She plainly regarded her jibe as a masterstroke, leaned back in her chair and ran her hand through her lank and unattractive locks.

'So am I.'

The stand-off continued for twenty minutes, during which time MacNeil made various veiled threats, mostly hinting at my detention till the matter was resolved. When I suggested bringing in a senior officer she showed the first sign of weakness. He or she would no doubt agree with her stance, but would also discover why I was refusing to cooperate, and that was the last thing she wanted.

'When all's said and done, Mr Frei, I could only give the guarantee you ask for with respect to myself and DC Hunter. You must understand that the information might come out through another channel altogether.'

This had the ring of an escape clause about it. It had to be countered.

'And you must understand that if it comes out at all I shall lodge an official complaint which will cover the previous incident as well.'

'Excuse us a moment.'

The two detectives left the room to commune in the corridor. I heard their voices, occasionally raised, but the only words I made out were 'hard' and 'ball'. Either they intended to play it or thought I was doing so already.

DC Hunter came back alone.

'The boss is far from happy, but as far as we're concerned you have your guarantee.'
'So why isn't she here to tell me herself?'
'She doesn't do backing down.'
'Leaves others to do it for her.'
'You didn't hear me say that.'

30

Meetings at The Warehouse often started late as one or other of the artists was sure to interpret the starting time with creative licence. I timed my arrival for five past ten and proceedings were yet to begin. We assembled in the still empty studio on the ground floor, which was appropriate since, whatever other matters might arise, ensuring adequate rental income was the main issue. I couldn't help noticing that some of the plan chests which Colin had stored along the wall had melted away like snow from a dyke.

I was greeted politely rather than warmly by all except George, who made great play of recognising me as I entered with the suspiciously fulsome praise accorded to those whose celebrity is known but can't be accounted for. He slapped me on the shoulder by way of greeting, though rather too vigorously for my liking, in that jovial, hail-fellow-well-met way of his.

As Janice got proceedings under way, she glanced towards me, acknowledging my presence. Colin was standing at the other side of the room, and so was Catherine: not a worker by hand and eye herself, I could only assume her accounting skills had been called on. Money was tight. They waved in my direction and I waved back. Then someone came up behind me and whispered in my ear.

'We have to talk. After this meeting in your studio.'

It was Lyndsay Craig. Did I imagine that sensation of fresh mountain air as she spoke, or had she just come in from outside?

After various minor matters were dealt with, the question of viability came up. Apart from the vacant studio we were presently meeting in, there were two other concerns. The first was Ceramick who, to my surprise, was present in the room. Why hadn't I noticed him? Breaking the habit of a lifetime, he had not yet said a word and unlike everyone else he was seated, presumably to take the strain off his foot. My line of sight was blocked by Antonia and Vicki.

'We all know that Michael has had his problems and he informed me last week of his intention to return to his ancestral home in Baltimore, where his long-suffering sisters have agreed to take him in.'

'In return for a contribution to the rent, you understand.'

Steve was amazed. 'You come from the States!'

Ceramick pretended to be furious and launched a vigorous attack on everyone from the Pilgrim Fathers to the Daughters of the American Revolution. They'd stolen every place-name they ever had from Europe or, failing that, from the native Americans they'd banished to the reservations. His mini tirade included a round attack on the seventh president, Andrew Jackson, and finished with the point that the real Baltimore, the original Baltimore, was located in County Cork.

So Ceramick had formally lodged his notice to quit – a second empty studio, a consequent loss of income. Then there was our resident photographer. Despite a written request which, Janice said, with a nod in my direction, she now realised may well have gone to his previous address, there was no clear indication of his intention. She would welcome clarification on this point by the end of the week – it was a matter of forward planning. She was about to move on when Albert spoke.

'Excuse me for asking, but no one else is going to – do we really want a conman on the premises, or don't we care any longer where the money comes from?'

I had been prepared for a certain coolness, a nose-numbing nip in the air, but not for an outright frontal assault. Albert, who was getting on in years, inhabited another time when probity in public life was not only admired by cultivated. I could feel myself reddening. Sweat formed between my collar and my neck. Janice was used to the rough and tumble of public debate but I could see that even she was taken aback.

'I think we should be careful here, Albert. We can't believe everything we read in the papers.'

'Fair enough – alleged conman then. How does that suit?'

'Hold on a minute,' George said, 'the last time I looked it was innocent till proven guilty in this country.'

'Good point, George.'

'We're *all* guilty,' Ceramick boomed, from waist height somewhere to my right, 'that's what I was taught, anyway.'

'In sunny, down-town Baltimore?'

George suspected a Catholic education.

'Got it in one, George. Sisters of the Sacred Heart.'

'And another thing,' Albert said, 'these studios are intended for artists, not therapists.'

Vicky weighed in to support me. 'But Albert, therapists can be very creative.'

'So it seems.'

Things were getting out of hand. Though the gathering was small, everyone was talking at once. Janice, who was probably thinking fondly of the loud-hailer in her office, didn't even have a gavel so she brought her foot down hard on the floor, wincing as the shock of the impact travelled up the body to her herniated disc.

'Everyone, please, can we at least be civil!' She waited for a moment or two till the meeting settled down then addressed me directly.

'Max, do you have a view on this?'

I did. They should discuss among themselves, in my absence, whether or not they still wanted me. If they decided the answer was yes, I would decide if I still wanted them – and yes, I'd definitely let her know by the end of the week.

'Thank you, Max. Moving on to other matters . . .'

How could the success or otherwise of the open day be properly evaluated if some of those present failed to submit the requested return? Would those yet to do so – and they knew who they were – please get back to her as soon as possible. And that was the last thing I heard as I left the room,

I climbed the stairs and walked along the corridor to my studio. I hadn't been in it for several weeks. It was cold and cheerless. Worse, if my plants weren't dead they looked it. I hadn't been there to water them and no one had done it for me. I switched the heater on and headed for the kitchenette. Everything was as I'd left it except the biscuits, which someone had taken assuming I wouldn't be back, not the greatest reverse in my life to date. I made a mug of tea, stepped out from behind the screen and almost walked into Lyndsay. Her sheepskin boots had silent rubber soles. I offered to make her a cup, but when she heard I had no milk she decided against it. Neat tea stained the teeth.

'Meeting over?'

'The part that concerned me.'

We went to the window and looked out over the path, the benches and the river.

'I read the story. What's going to happen?'

'I honestly haven't a clue.'

'It would help me to know how much of it was true?'

I told her what I could, pointing out that several clients still backed me. In fact, I was still seeing two, and as a perverse result of press coverage I had one new client and another in the offing.

'You know you can't use this studio for therapy.'

'I haven't since I hit the headlines and don't intend to.'

'So where do you meet them, Max, your clients?'

'Restaurants mostly, pubs.'

'A novel approach.'

'It seems to work.'

We watched a woman with four dogs making her way along the path – a professional dog-walker, perhaps.

'But you can still use the studio for photography, of course, you know that, don't you.'

Lyndsay had tried to find a replacement tutor and failed. Her course was already advertised to run on Saturday mornings. If I was interested it could meet here in the studio. She would provide a detailed course outline.

'But surely you'd require a tutor with qualifications?'

'I would if the course was accredited, but it's not. It's a simple introduction to digital photography for beginners.'

She made it sound easy, and was all the more persuasive because she believed every word of it herself.

'Several of our tutors on the arts and crafts side aren't qualified.'

She went on to refine that point. They might not be qualified on paper but they were by experience, an interesting concept which I filed for future use.

'For example,' she said, 'you'll look in vain for a qualification in origami. In any case,' she added with a wide smile, 'we learn from the paper that you're a noted landscape photographer.'

'There is that.'

My guess was that Lyndsay had her back to the wall. I wasn't her best bet, I was her only bet, and if I didn't agree she'd have to cancel the course, which she didn't want to do. Looking back on it, this was a pivotal moment, though I didn't fully appreciate that at the time. Lyndsay's offer was generous but ill-conceived, so why was it so tempting? Because it came from such a well-intentioned source. I wanted to help her out if I possibly could. But to use her measure, and despite her opinion of my work, I was not qualified by experience.

I'd taken some pictures which Colin had edited and printed. I knew my own camera reasonably well, but if a student with a problem approached me with another make and model I'd be lost. Lyndsay didn't want to fail the students who'd already signed up, but if she recruited me she'd do exactly that. I had entered into counselling after years of study, but if I agreed to Lyndsay's proposition I would become, in another area, exactly what I was accused of being now, a conman, a fraudster and a cheat. So I thanked her for her offer but told her I didn't have enough experience behind me yet and couldn't, in honesty, accept it.

'You can't say I didn't try.'

Never one for songs in a minor key, she struck another positive note before she left.

'You could always continue as a photographer, you know, develop your skills. I'm sure you have it in you.'

As she was leaving, I heard her talk with someone on the stairs. This was the last time we met, and though I didn't know that at the time I was sad to see her go. She was a ray of sunlight on a dark day.

Shortly afterwards, I was visited by Colin and Janice. Meeting either of them was difficult. They hadn't said it in so many words but I knew they felt I'd let them down, so seeing them arrive together was alarming, as if they'd come mob-handed to sort me out. But as interpretations go, this one was hopelessly wide of the mark. A straightforward person himself, Colin didn't know what to make of me any longer, evident from the fact he was finding it so difficult to meet my eye. He had brought Janice with him for moral support.

They wanted to know how I was, given recent events, and to report the results of the meeting. I assumed that Albert's attack would have swayed them somewhat, and so it had, but in my favour. Both of them thought he had gone too far, especially in an open forum, and they had an offer. I could continue to use the studio rent-free till they found a replacement. They would advertise, of course, but it might take a while.

This was a carelessly concealed act of charity. A studio on the ground floor had been empty for months: how likely was it they would find a taker for mine? I was grateful to them for trying.

'You don't have to do this, you know.'

'We know,' Colin agreed, 'but we were thinking the turn-around could start right here.'

It may have been the way he put it, but I didn't like the sound of this; it carried more than a whiff of rehabilitation about it, as if I'd just come out of prison and needed a helping hand to straighten out my life. But I knew he meant well.

'How's it going,' Colin asked, 'with the legal stuff?'

I told him I'd been charged and the papers sent to the fiscal.

'Oh well, you're talking months. It wouldn't surprise me if they mislaid the file and you never hear anything more.'

Colin was trying to reassure me but it was Janice who was closer to the mark.

'Maybe that's not what he wants,' she said, with an enquiring look, 'maybe our friend here would prefer his day in court.'

31

Kellock kept in touch, which surprised me. It wasn't evident that I could do anything for him in a counselling capacity, and it wasn't until we met for our second chat in February of the following year that I realised what was in it for him – someone to talk to who might not know his original name but nonetheless understood who he really was. We met in the same place, the Filmhouse café where, if we arrived in good time, there were always seats to spare. The arrangement saved us the pointless effort of coming up with somewhere new.

He was surprised to learn that though I had lost clients I had retained two and gained another, an actor, a profession from which, it seemed, there was no escape.

'You realise he could be a plant.'

'A journalist?'

'Maybe, or a friend of that guy Henry who wrote to the paper.'

That had not been my impression. Though outwardly calm at first, it soon became clear that the man was disturbed and, after a lengthy trip round the hollyhocks, what he was disturbed about.

'So really, you're relying on nothing more than your intuition that this guy is kosher.'

'Ultimately, that's all we have.'

He looked at me in disbelief.

'For God's sake, Max, get real.' (People told me that so often I was beginning to think they might have a point.) 'Have you never heard of background checks?'

It sounded a tedious process and, anyway, I had no idea how to carry one out. But he was right to be suspicious. MacNeil might have been setting me up, gathering evidence to show that I had continued in my villainous ways despite being charged. If that was the plan, it wouldn't work. On the question of qualification, I had been upfront with him from the start.

'OK, so tell me about this guy.'

He was an actor, young, with stage experience and a few television roles behind him. If he could surmount his problem, he had the prospect of a good career. Ian assumed he knew what the problem was. What else could it be?

'He can't remember his lines.'

'He's homosexual.'

Ian chewed that over for a moment with his chilli con carne.

'I don't get it. Surely that's an advantage in his profession?'

He reeled off a list of well known actors known or thought to be gay.

'Some of them are knights of the realm, for Christ's sake!'

'If I may say so, Ian, that would be of small consolation to him.'

'Enlighten me, then. It doesn't make sense.'

'He can't stand close physical contact with heterosexual males or women of any persuasion. It disgusts him. He even finds it difficult with his current partner, who's getting restive, showing signs of looking elsewhere.'

'The partner has to get his rocks off somewhere, I suppose.'

This was not an expression we used in counselling, but to Ian the solution was simple.

'So he body-swerves parts with sex scenes. Problem solved.'

'It's not as easy as that. If he keeps saying no the offers will start to dry up. Goodbye career. Oh, and by the way,' I added, 'he regards his predicament as evidence of discrimination.'

Ian found that hard to believe. So did I. But in the world according to my client, and conceding that a straight actor might well be offered the same number of roles as he was involving kissing, hugging, groping and the like, only on very rare occasions would that straight actor be called upon to enact them with a homosexual member of the profession. Ian came close to choking on the beer he had bought, as he put it, to damp down the fire. (In fact it was the other way round: he had ordered chilli as a pretext to buy the beer.)

'You've got to be joking.'

'You would think so.'

'But surely it's obvious: most people are heterosexual so most actors are too.'

'I told him that, but it made matters worse. All I had done, he said, was show that he was part of an oppressed minority.'

'It doesn't follow,' Ian pointed out, 'that because a group is smaller in number than another that it's oppressed.'

'You're a great one for stating the obvious.'

We ate in silence for a while before Ian spoke again.

'I've got it!'

He kept me waiting for a moment before revealing the solution with a dramatic flourish of his fork.

'Aversion therapy. Get the guy to snog heterosexuals six hours a day for a week.'

Thanks to his resolutely dead-pan expression, it wasn't always obvious when Ian was joking.

'And where would I find these long-suffering heterosexuals?'

'Ah,' he said, 'tricky one, but I wouldn't look under a stone.'

He didn't claim to have all the answers, which was just as well, but at least he had offered a suggestion. For my part, I believed that my client had a deep-seated problem with sex of any sort and I was not the person to solve it.

'It wasn't Rupert Everett, was it?'

'No.'

When we moved on to matters closer to home, Ian and I had something in common. Like him, I had been through the process – photographs, fingerprints, DNA – and didn't take kindly to it at the time. But Ian had all that and more. His passport was confiscated, hardly surprising given his involvement in large money transfers over international borders. He had also been remanded in custody, something which MacNeil, for all her animus, hadn't tried on me. All I had to do was sign an undertaking to appear in court on the specified date.

'Which is when?'

'Next week.'

'How are you going to plead?'

'Not guilty.'

'Doesn't make sense, my man, they've got you cold.'

'So they like to think, but I have a defence.'

'Don't we all.'

He studied the glass he was holding in his hand as if it might have the answer.

'You realise that pleading guilty would lead to a reduced sentence.'

'Which would compare very badly to no sentence at all.'

'True.'

And if I pled guilty the court would proceed to sentence on the ludicrous assumption that because I was confessing to something I must actually have done it. But in life as real people lived it, defendants sometimes confessed to things they hadn't done. They might be protecting someone. They might feel guilty about something else entirely. All sorts of reasons.

'Right you are, Max, but a guilty plea saves time and effort all round, don't you think? We're talking taxpayers' money here.'

He was right, of course, that was exactly what we were talking. Confess now, no need for a proper trial at a later date, no need to examine the evidence at all.

'In any case, it hardly ever happens.'

'So how about Sture Berglund?'

'Who?'

Ian's horizons were limited to the UK and various sun-drenched locations he thought appropriate as retirement destinations for criminal masterminds such as himself.

'The Swedish man who confessed to over twenty murders, none of which he had committed. He was convicted of eight.'

'Hard to believe. What's this, by the way?'

He was referring to a cyclamen I'd rescued from my studio, the only plant to have made it through the winter. He examined it closely, as if it might it might conceal a hidden microphone which, of course, it did not.

'It's on its way home.'

A group of students arrived and started rearranging the tables. They had to be close to each other, full eye-contact all round, though it wasn't long before they had their smart phones out. One of them, a student of semaphore, was making vigorous gestures of the hand and arm. Why did he bother? What was the point? The person at the other end couldn't see them. This was behaviour I'd observed many times before. Some individuals felt impelled to accompany what they said with gestures which didn't add one iota to the meaning. A subject worthy of study, I thought, but no doubt it had already been done to death in the Journal of Visual Semiotics and several as yet unpublished PhD theses. Perhaps these signals were the equivalent of punctuation marks which, useful as they were, did not themselves embody meaning.

Ian gave our young neighbours a jaundiced look. He wasn't impressed.

'They're probably texting each other. Tell me,' he went on, 'the case against you – is it pretty much what I read in the papers?'

In essence, it was, with the added complication of Professor Dwyer's report.

'I'd love to know what's in it but they won't tell me, not so much as a hint.'

'They paid for it, right? So assume they got what they paid for.'

'Surely an expert witness would be more impartial than that?'

'It could happen, I suppose, but I wouldn't bet the bank on it.'

Mention of the bank made him smile, thinking back to his own past achievements.

'I could do with an expert witness myself.'

'What you could do with is a copy of the report. That way you can prepare your rebuttal ahead of the trial.'

'It can't be done.'

'We're sure of that, are we?'

'They refused point blank.'

'What if I could get hold of it?'

'If they won't give it to me they certainly won't give it to you.'

The discussion which followed took a turn which was almost surreal. Ian agreed, they wouldn't give me the report, but hadn't I noticed? People were forever taking things they weren't given. (That had certainly been true in his case.) I mean, he pointed out, just a couple of weeks ago hackers had taken down the website of the US Sentencing Commission. For him, this was just the latest in a series of such events, all of which had passed me by. I had no idea what he was talking about.

'All I'm saying is there are ways.'

As he explained what he intended to do, I detected a level of excitement I had not observed in him before. Using the IT skills which had put him behind bars in the first place, he proposed to obtain a copy of Professor Dwyer's report. I could use it to prepare my defence, but on no account could I refer to it directly. That would give the game away.

He asked me for the little information I had, primarily on DS MacNeil. The fiscal's office he could find out about for himself. To my dismay, having no paper handy, he wrote down what I told him on a napkin – hardly the cutting edge of espionage, I thought at the time. He could tell I was doubtful.

'Call me simple,' I said, 'but surely they use passwords in legal circles.'

'They do,' he said with a smile, 'but there are ways. You've heard of password crackers, I take it?'

He gave me a quick guided tour with so much detail I started scribbling on a napkin myself, the one I'm looking at now, covering it with arcane references to Haschcat, John the Ripper Pro, Hash Suite Pro and other such unlikely names.

'You have to understand, Max, that a well specified computer can make thirty-three billion password guesses per second.'

'So you're telling me you can buy password cracker programs and it's legal!'

'Hard to believe, isn't it, and some of them are free. But here's the thing, people who rely on passwords need to know how strong they are.'

'So they use these programs to find out.'

'That's the theory, yes, that's why they're freely available.'

Assuming he was right, I could only see one problem.

'What if he sent MacNeil a paper copy?'

'In that case, Max, unless the professor used a manual typewriter, we track down the file he printed it from.'

Since Faith had been working all day, I made our evening meal, which wasn't Cordon Bleu but made up for it by being low on additives and zero in hydrogenated oils. The turbot came from the local fishmonger ('sourced' as they say these days) and peeling the potatoes removed the risk of post-emergent sprays. As for the parsley sauce it was passable at best – the simplest recipe I could find online. It was almost ready when she breezed in, leaving her briefcase in the hall, and made a grab for me at the sink.

I doubt if her colleagues would have believed it but Faith, though presenting a staid exterior to the world, could be remarkably frisky when the mood took her. Which made me wonder why it was that the mood never took her in public places but only in the privacy of our own home. Perhaps, when we were out and about, a certain amount of repression was taking place. I resolved to ask her when she'd had a drink.

'Are we sure this is a good idea?' she asked, after I'd told her what Ian intended to do. 'What if it goes wrong?'

'He seems to know what he's doing.'

'Max, be honest, you don't know the first thing about it.'

I produced my note-covered napkin and placed it carefully before her on the kitchen table. She looked it over for a moment but wasn't impressed.

'This could do with an iron.'

I consoled her with the thought that if anything went wrong he'd get it in the neck, not me. My very ignorance of hacking would be my defence. We were watching part two of a crime programme when Ian phoned. (We hadn't seen part one but didn't let that put us off.)

'I thought I'd better give you some evidence of my ability: you only had my word that I could do the business.'

I walked out into the hall, but Faith had already paused the broadcast. She wanted to follow Ian's moves, the more so since she hadn't met him yet.

'OK.'

'Just wondering, but have you checked Henry's blog lately?'

'He wants us to check Henry's blog,' I said to Faith, who had now appeared in the doorway. I could tell from her expression that this real-life plot had already improved on the murky doings of the fictional detective.

'Stay on the line, we're going through to the kitchen.'

Faith opened her laptop and went straight to Henry's blog, which she had dignified with a bookmark. And there he was, large as life and twice as irrelevant – but now he was wearing a traffic cone and his nose was bright red. And in case the casual visitor failed to spot these clues, a balloon was issuing from his mouth with the words, *I cheated on my wife with another woman and here are the pictures to prove it!*

'Very impressive, Ian.'

'I thought so.'

Faith went to one of the kitchen cabinets and took out the hot chocolate, something she did when she needed to think, the nearest she came to comfort drinking.

'So he hacked Henry's blog.'

'Looks like it.'

'For all we know that might not be difficult.'

Perhaps not, but it hadn't been all he'd hacked. Where had the pictures come from? Only two people had them, Hazel and myself, and hers were prints. He'd accessed my hard drive, perhaps using my email address as a key to the door. And then there were the programs he'd told me about over lunch and many more he hadn't.

Given my ignorance it was a long shot, but I went to the bedroom and switched on my computer, not knowing where to look or what to look for. Signs of tampering? An open drawer I'd left shut?

'Well,' Faith said, 'he can do all the hacking he wants as long as you aren't involved. Nothing,' she said, with unusual emphasis, 'must exist which shows this man in communication with you. No emails, no texts, nothing.'

'Don't you think you're going over the top? You'll be sweeping the place for bugs next.'

Our new domestic arrangement was working well. Though I tried to keep my room tidy, it fell short of the rest of the house, but Faith didn't mind because she never went in. There is always a danger that two people who get on well living apart will not continue to do so living together, but it worked for us. Far from feeling added strain we were more relaxed in our lives than we had been before. Faith still showed minor signs of OCD, such as an obsessive desire to ensure that she'd put on the hand-brake, but in most cases the explanation was simple – whenever she did something physical her mind was elsewhere so she had no recollection of having done it. This irritated her a great deal, so I suggested a simple mental discipline. When she engaged in a hum-drum task requiring next to no thought, she should think about it anyway, bring it to the forefront of her mind. And when she remembered to do this, it worked.

But the fact that we lived together in harmony did not mean we agreed on everything, and the subject we disagreed about most was Ian Kellock.

'You seem to think,' she said, 'that hacking your computer and improving Henry's blog is a major achievement.' I couldn't deny it. 'Well it isn't. Think about it, Max. You use a free firewall, the most basic there is. Any hacker worthy of the name could get past it in his sleep.'

She told me about the technology committee she sat on, one of the disadvantages of her management role. The members were regularly bored rigid by incomprehensible reports from IT staff outlining, in jargon-filled detail, the measures they were taking to detect and prevent unauthorised access to the system. She doubted Henry could get anything past these people. And if the library service was secure, how much harder would it be to access the legal system where data protection was even more important and financial constraints very much less. It was safe to assume they had hired the best.

'As for these password cracking programs, 'she said, holding my tired napkin in front of me, between thumb and forefinger, like a soiled handkerchief ready for the wash, 'they're in the public domain. What they can do is known, as is how they do it, so defences are already in place. Oh, and by the way,' she added as a clincher, 'when your bosom buddy Ian did whatever it was in his previous existence, just remember two things: he was already on the inside, which makes it a whole lot easier, and he was caught. Don't you think you have enough problems already without being mixed up in something like this?'

32

The Grand Opening took place at the beginning of March and it was down to Janice. Finding a lack of takers for the empty studios, she had suggested making The Warehouse into a more attractive destination for visitors by turning the ground floor studio into a café. The proposal was approved by acclaim at a meeting which I did not attend. According to Colin, who brought me up to speed over a quick lunch, it was greeted with great enthusiasm provided Janice took the project forward – weasel words meaning that she did all the work. So Janice had done what she usually did, most of the heavy lifting, while delegating specific tasks to others. One of those was Colin, another Catherine (now pregnant 'by mistake'), and the third a lawyer friend, Lawrence T Scott who, though not active in the hospitality trade, quickly established the legal requirements and ensured Janice met them.

'The hope is,' she explained when we arrived, 'that we'll make some money on this and also have a reasonable conversion rate. By which I mean,' she explained, seeing our horrified expressions, 'that some visitors to the café will be converted into buyers from the studios.'

I looked behind the counter half expecting to see a minister of religion or a colloquy of nuns but the staff, all civilians, were new to me.

'It's a franchise, Max.'

Since Janice was there in a meet and greet role, she left us with Colin who took us, in too much detail, through the improvements required in the ground floor toilets and the difficulties of arranging for disabled access.

'We're not on the rubber chicken circuit here,' he said with a wink. 'Tea, coffee, scones and millionaires' shortbread, though we do stretch to sandwiches.'

'Tables and chairs?'

'Not appropriate for this gathering but don't worry, we have them ready.'

'We hear congratulations are in order,' Faith said.
'Thanks guys, so they are. We're delighted.'

As far as I could tell, he meant it. If not deliriously happy, he was at least reconciled to the development, and when I saw the prospective parents together I detected no sign of strain.

Faith and I settled for a latte and scone and watched as the guests rolled in. This session would probably operate at a loss, as promotions often did.

'Ah-ha, your better half is gracing us with her presence, I see!'

Never one to miss a treat, George had arrived in his usual style. And so had two of my clients who, in a spectacular error of judgement, had been invited to the opening because they were listed on an office spreadsheet as past patrons of The Warehouse.

Mr Armitage was his usual sunny self, doubting whether buttering people up would result in more business and generally pulling the rug from the proceedings. He had just finishing cheering us with this thought when Faith, not finding him to her taste, excused herself and wandered off, to be replaced by Mr Robertson, who had just arrived. Things went downhill rapidly from there. Both of these gentlemen had views on the end of the world. Mr Armitage, knowing that on a longer timescale the solar system was doomed and we mere mortals with it, took such a nihilistic view that Mr Robertson could hardly contain himself.

'The body may die but the soul lives on,' he proclaimed, a round assurance of which Armitage, knowing for a fact there was no God, no heaven and no afterlife, made short work.

I would happily have left them there knocking spots off each other in the hope they would cancel each other out, but as often happens when two people disagree, they appealed to a third party for adjudication, and when I failed to come up with a suitable compromise (impossible, since their views were mutually exclusive) Mr Armitage, as I had suspected he might, went on the offensive.

'You realise, of course, that I'll be appearing as witness for the prosecution.'

'And why would that be, Mr Armitage?'

'Well now, let me see, where to begin? It might have something to do with the fact that counselling is hokum, claptrap, bunk. Sheer pishtushery, the whole thing! I've said it before and I'll say it again, effort expended is effort wasted when failure is inevitable.'

Time to Talk

'Come now, sir, there is always hope,' Mr Robertson said, but Armitage was already making for the door. Since he had told me before that he saw no point in continued existence, I wondered if that was the only exit he was heading for.

'I would like you to know, Mr Frei,' Mr Robertson assured me, 'that I will be more than happy to appear as a witness for the defence.'

I thanked him, assuring him that I would be in touch nearer the time, though I couldn't help thinking that calling him was not without its dangers. The witness box was as close to a pulpit as he was likely to get, and therefore an attractive prospect in its own right regardless of anything he might have to say on my behalf.

I was left alone for a moment or two, adrift in a sea of chatter, mulling over my reactions to these two men. Broadly speaking, I agreed with the Armitage take on the world. Looked at clearly and in the long view, everything was going to end taking our achievements with it. But the analysis was one thing, the emotions which went with it another. As Mr Robertson was fond of saying, there was hope, however irrational that might be. After all, everyone around me at the opening would die, even George, but they weren't collapsing in tears on each others' shoulders. They were talking, often in animated manner and with not a little laughter. And might this not be a key to the difference between the reasonably happy and the depressed: when they looked around them at the world, both dispositions saw much the same things but construed them very differently. A computer analysing these same facts might draw certain conclusions from them but would not be depressed. So, as it usually does, the problem lay with the emotions.

Looking round the room I saw Faith in conversation with Lawrence Scott. I had no doubt that his presence was as much 'an accident' as Catherine's pregnancy. I joined them to hear what he had to say. He had plainly been briefed.

'I hear you have a case coming up.'

Faith gave him an account of the affair and he listened with interest. He was impressed with her grasp of the issue and her ability to summarise.

'You could show some of my colleagues a thing or two,' he said with a smile.

I assumed he was applying the soft soap and flannel, but I was wrong.

'Have you considered becoming a lay advisor to Mr Frei here?'

This was an alarming suggestion. I didn't want Faith tarnished by association with a potential criminal like me, but she leant forward in her chair with every expression of interest, her scone half-eaten on the plate.

'Go on.'

Acting as lay advisor she could accompany me to court, ensuring that any document to which I might wish to refer was readily to hand. She could also advise me, sotto voce, on points of law but could not address witnesses, lawyers or the sheriff. Nor could she impede in any way the smooth running of the trial.

I could hardly deny that a well qualified and meticulous librarian would be an ideal choice for this role. Every conceivable document would be filed and cross-referenced. And if she got her teeth into the subject, she would doubtless supply me with all the relevant precedents from the Declaration of Arbroath to the present day and beyond. She had it all: the training, the resources, the tenacity and the OCD to double-check such a mass of detail to destruction.

'So you're a librarian? Excellent!'

He said it as if he hadn't been aware of it already, but I knew he had and took a dislike to him at once.

'Yes.'

He left us his card – if he could be of any help – making no mention of his hourly rate. I turned it over in my hand.

'Lawrence T Scott. Wonder what the 'T' stands for?'

'Maybe a name he doesn't like?'

I mulled over the possibilities: Terence, Titus, Theodore, Thaddeus, only learning some weeks later that he had no middle name at all but preferred to give the impression that he had.

My reading of what happened was simple. Janice and Colin had decided I didn't have what it took to handle the case myself, so they were putting a lawyer my way. But who needed a lawyer when they had the help of a woman with a mind like a filing cabinet and the focused concentration of a laser? According to Scott, I did, but he would say that, wouldn't he?

Time to Talk

I can't deny that I have always reacted against smooth-talkers, and Lawrence Scott compounded the problem by being too well turned out. I had no idea whether or not his clothing was the height of fashion, but I did recognise expensive gear when I saw it. To add to the impression that this was less a man than a collection of artfully arranged surfaces, every hair was held in place by a discreet but discernible gel, and there was about him a distinct whiff of aftershave. The man was rolling in money and packaged to prove it. I did not foresee then that, despite my adverse reaction, Faith would seek his advice and, for the most part, take it. To this day I have no idea what having recourse to him cost her, but our meeting with Lawrence T Scott, though brief, had one obvious outcome. Faith seized on the words 'lay advisor', sank her teeth into them and wouldn't let go.

33

Faith needed what she termed a Command HQ. Her favoured working place, the kitchen table, wouldn't do since every time we ate she would have to clear away her books and papers and besides, that was where we she sat together and talked. (A naturalist might have concluded that the kitchen table was one of three places in the flat where pair bonding could be observed, the other two being the sofa in the living room and the bed in Faith's room.) My room was out of the question. By my standards it was tidy, by hers chaotic. The only possible location for her nerve-centre (another phrase she used) was the living room. This didn't please her at all since she regarded it as sacrosanct, a place to relax, but there was no viable alternative. It would be pressed into service till the trial was over. For such a pacific person, this military cast of mind came as a surprise, but I was left in no doubt, Faith was mounting a campaign.

She borrowed a large folding table from Hazel, previously used by Henry for cards games with his acting friends, and set it up in the corner of the room farthest away from the television. But even that was fraught. As she sat there perusing her documents, shifting patterns of light from the TV reflected from the inside surfaces of her glasses into her eyes and caused her great distress. Solving this problem entailed some re-arrangement of the furniture. The next problem was only too predictable – noise. She couldn't work when the set was on.

A lightning raid on Radio Shack equipped us with a set of wireless headphones, which almost solved the problem. Faith sat at her table and worked while I watched Horizon in a world of my own. (How big is the universe, string theory, cognitive bias modification.) And it worked, except for the fact that what I saw I no longer enjoyed. In the past we had watched together, a shared activity with the added advantage of close physical contact. Not only was that contact lost but I couldn't watch anything without a feeling of guilt since Faith was not only working through the programme but doing so for me.

I talked this through with her, but the fact that she didn't mind at all was no consolation. It should have been but, as so often happens, emotion trumped logic and I burdened myself with pointless and non-functional remorse.

'It's only for a few weeks,' she pointed out.

So it was, but knowing that didn't help either because, as those few weeks wore on, I realised I had something else to worry about. There was methodical, and there was Faith. The unremitting work she was doing on my behalf, demanding as it did close attention to an excess of detail, was reinforcing her tendency to OCD, exactly the opposite of her intention when she first approached me for help. If I had been appearing for the prosecution, I'd have cited this fact as compelling evidence that recourse to the so-called therapist was counter-productive.

As before, she left with her briefcase in the morning and returned with it at the end of the working day. But now she returned with armloads of documents as well, and these began to pile up on her table. One overcast Wednesday morning I was surprised to see that she'd gone to work in her car. Since she usually walked, this was a rare occurrence. When she arrived back that evening she asked me to bring something up from the rear seat – a metal filing trolley with lockable castors. She put it to good use. Large areas of the table became visible again, and when she wasn't working she rolled it under the table out of the way. A neat solution.

Unfortunately, the law is labyrinthine, not just in its statutes but, every bit as complicated, the process by which legal actions are taken forward. Since Faith was thorough she strove to cover both, attempting to compress into a period of weeks an understanding which members of the profession take years to arrive at. In this she was greatly helped by her proficiency as a librarian and her contacts with fellow professionals. Sources unavailable to ordinary members of the public were easily accessed by her through the National Library and the Library of the Faculty of Advocates. But this ease of access, at first sight so useful, had a down-side: she was amassing so much information I began to fear that much of her well-intentioned effort might be wasted. And this wasn't helped by the decision of the fiscal not to proceed with the charge of statutory fraud MacNeil had hoped for, opting instead for common law fraud – a discovery which sent Faith back to the drawing board, since what she needed now was a handle not on statute but on precedent.

Concerned with the danger of Faith working herself into the ground, I suggested that we eat out more often, which we did on occasion. Nothing grand, but a break from the treadmill was welcome. Colin and Janice visited from time to time, both together and separately, and Hazel appeared on the doorstep with increasing frequency. At first Faith assumed her friend was still distraught and in need of continued support, till the truth dawned on her.

'She thinks it's *me* that needs support! Can you believe it?'

'Her mascara stopped running a while back, Faith. She's worried about you. She thinks you might be overdoing it.'

'And where would she get that idea, Max?'

There was a rare accusatory tone in this question, as if I'd appealed to Hazel behind her back. All I could do was admit it.

'So really, it's you who think I'm overdoing it.'

Hazel was many things, but not a ventriloquist's dummy.

'We're both concerned, that's all. You work all day as it is, working half the evening as well is just too much.'

'Right, okay, so what do you suggest?'

We agreed a way forward over a Saturday lunch at the Two Thin Laddies, whose chorizo and spicy bean casserole kept the cold at bay and stopped us talking shop for at least ten minutes. Our previous agreement was put on hold. I had already identified an online course in psychology at degree level and downloaded the reading list, but my studies would have to take a back seat while legal action was underway. So what was I to do in the meantime? Obvious, she told me. I'd be the one appearing in court, the one answering questions, the one asking them. I needed to know the procedure, not from reading about it but from direct observation. I was to attend the Sheriff Court, take up residence in the public gallery and get to know the ropes.

As for Faith, she was beginning to agree that there was such a thing as being too well prepared. Most of the cases she had been studying concerned defrauding the social security system

– defendants claiming they could only walk three feet with the aid of crutches filmed jogging round the Meadows with a medicine ball. The remainder were mainly business ventures gone sour over missing money and the occasional lawyer siphoning off his clients' savings. None of these had any bearing on me. What she needed was a steer from a professional and that, whether I liked him or not, would be Lawrence Scott, who arrived at our door two nights later dressed for the weather in a quality nap coat. To add a patina of many years' experience, he had with him a tired brown leather briefcase which nevertheless sported the monogram LTS in gold leaf. As Colin might say, he was some piece of work.

Pulling up two more chairs we convened at Faith's table and she gave him the low-down on her progress so far. He nodded sagely once or twice and commended her industry, but after ten minutes or so it was clear he was itching to set her straight. He was just starting to do so when the bell rang. We weren't expecting anyone so assumed it was Hazel, but when I opened the door there he was, Ian Kellock. Since I had yet to tell him my address, I was surprised to say the least.

'Evening, Max,' he said with a smile. 'Hope you don't mind. Tracking you down was the easy part. I have progress to report.'

'You'd better come in,' I said, guiding him past the living room into the kitchen.

Faith was naturally curious. 'Who is it?'

'Ian Kellock.'

They had yet to meet but she was tied up with Lawrence and no doubt his meter was running. Taxis had nothing on him.

'Tell him "hi" from me.'

I made him a coffee and he sat at the kitchen table looking remarkably pleased with himself.

'You were right about the legal lot, remarkably secure. But guess what?'

'You have a man on the inside.'

'Don't be ridiculous, Max. No, but these people at the Kennedy Tower, they're another matter altogether. Very careless, which is really strange when you think about it.'

'Why's that?'

'They're part of the university. God knows how many high-level geeks they have at their disposal.'

'They may consider they're not worth hacking. It's not as if they're air traffic control or the Ministry of Defence.'

'True, but not good enough, my friend. Their research costs a packet so their work should be secure. In any case, they have to comply with the Data Protection Act like everyone else.'

'Right.'

'Anyway, I think I can get you a copy of Dwyer's report.'

'And how would you do that?'

'Ah,' he said, 'that would be telling. No names, no pack drill as they say.'

Spotlight on Kellock, he was loving it.

He talked on for some time, tying me in knots with technobabble (not difficult) and looking for a decision. To hack or not to hack? But until I'd talked it over with Faith there was no way he was getting one, so I said I'd let him know the next day and finally showed him out.

Faith led Lawrence to the door shortly after and as it shut behind him, restoring peace to our household at last, we exchanged looks which might variously have been interpreted as *What next?* and *Thank God for that!* We wandered into the living room, where Faith had covered several sheets of a spiral notebook in her fine hand, and then to our base at the kitchen table to compare notes.

'So what did the great man have to say?'

'He didn't think representing yourself was a good idea.'

'Lawyers never do, it deprives them of work. No doubt he came out with that old one about the man who defends himself having a fool for a client.'

'Actually, no. He was more concerned about the financial aspect. If you represent yourself you won't qualify for legal aid, you do realise that?'

'I have that angle covered.'

'You do?'

'I won't charge me for my services.'

She gave me one of her hard looks.

'And I won't charge you for mine?'

I was about to tell her how much I valued her help but she rose to put the kettle on.

'He only raised the question when I told him you planned to call witnesses.'

'Why, what's the problem? They're both happy to do it.'

After she'd made a pot of camomile tea, presumably for its calming effect, she consulted her notes and told me the bad news. If I didn't have a solicitor acting for me, I'd have to assure the court that I'd be able to pay any witness expenses I might become liable for. Needless to say, there was an elaborate procedure for this purpose. She pushed her notes across the table and looked on as I read them. They were somewhat complicated for my liking but boiled down to two options – depositing a sum of money fixed by the court or lodging a document called a bond of caution provided by an insurance company.

'Lawrence wanted to know how solid your witnesses were?'

'Solid?'

'Can you be sure they'll turn up?'

I was confident Mr Robertson could be relied upon, too good an opportunity to pass by. Jean Ritchie was another matter altogether. She had agreed to attend and was no doubt a woman of her word, but if an emergency arose with her daughter, as happened from time to time, she might not make it unless her sister agreed to hold the fort. I would have to talk with her about that. And Jean presented another problem too. If the prosecution asked if I had been of any use she would have to admit that, thus far, her daughter had refused to meet me. On the other hand, she had refused to meet qualified psychiatrists too.

'I believe they'll both appear.'

'Well, that's good. According to Lawrence if your witnesses don't need to be cited, and it sounds like they don't, this whole bond of caution thing might be avoided.'

'I see.'

I didn't really, but was happy to take her word for it.

'About this Ian Kellock person.'

'He found out where we lived and came round on spec.'

'Why?'

'He thinks he can get hold of Dwyer's report.'

'What did you say to that?'

'I'd talk it over with you.'

'Right, well now that you have, it's not going to happen.'

I may have mentioned earlier in this account that Faith could be decisive.

'I can't think of anything much worse than a being assisted by a convicted criminal breaking the law on your behalf. What if it came out? Where would you be then? And anyway, what makes you think you can't get hold of it yourself?'

'And how would I do that?'

'By asking.'

This blindingly simple solution hadn't occurred to me because of the police reaction when I first suggested it. That, I thought, was that.

'But Max, you wouldn't be asking the police, you'd be asking the fiscal. The prosecution has a duty to disclose the evidence against you.'

'It does?'

'Yes.'

'And the evidence for me?'

'That too – if there is any.'

Later that evening when Faith was already in bed, I looked over her notes. One comment stood out. *If his main intention in defending himself is to broadcast his take on psychotherapy, he should think again. The courtroom is not the place. Small audience, little interest, yawns all round. However compelling his case it will go no further.* And beside this friendly advice from Lawrence, a note from Faith to herself. *Must talk to Max about this.*

I had little doubt she would.

34

In the days that followed, Faith continued her study of the law, I spent several hours at the Sheriff Court observing proceedings from the public gallery, and Ian Kellock sent me texts: I hadn't got back to him with my decision, time was of the essence, a life without risk was no life at all. During a lengthy hiatus at court six (a police witness had failed to attend) I phoned and gave him the good news. He was not well pleased and suggested we meet again at the usual venue to talk it over. Though I felt it was not a good idea, I gave in to his blandishments. In his own dubious way, he'd been trying to help.

Perhaps because we wanted to clear the decks for business we both settled for coffee and a sandwich. Kellock was full of bustle and good cheer, as if his energy alone could bounce me into reversing a decision I'd already agreed with Faith. But Faith wasn't there and couldn't be bounced into anything. Besides, her logic was impeccable and bluster an inadequate response. When he realised he wasn't getting anywhere, which took some time since he did most of the talking, his mood began to change. Next up was the guilt trip.

'You realise I've put my neck on the line for you, Max.'

'I appreciate that, but if anyone's safe from prosecution here it's someone like you on a witness protection scheme. They're hardly going to blow your cover.'

'Someone like me! There are no people like me! How many people do you think there are who could have got you this?'

He slapped a large manila envelope on the table in front of me, looking round the café to ensure he was not being observed by covert operations.

'Go on, open it. You know you want to.'

Paranoia is a dangerous state of mind. As soon as he suggested it I sensed a trap, thinking that if handled the document my fingerprints would end up all over it and I would be implicated in his scheme. Quickly recovering my composure, I opened the end flap and pulled the document out. The title was dry: Report on Maxwell Frei – Anthony Dermott Dwyer. As I looked through it, it became evident there was a problem. The pages were carelessly stapled together at the top left hand corner, presumably by Ian, and there were several instances of strike-through text.

'As you can see, it's a draft, not the finished article, but having said that it opens the door to his thinking. What you have here is the broad thrust of his case against you. With this,' he said grandly, 'you can shaft the bastard. Forewarned is fore-armed, as they say.'

I glanced through the report, put it back in the envelope and returned it to him

'Sorry, I know you've gone to a lot of trouble here but I really can't use it.'

He wanted to know why so I told him.

'It seems to me, my friend, you're under the thumb big time. This woman of yours, a librarian for God's sake, she's spent all her life playing by the rules, playing safe. The book's a day late and she fines you five pounds. You can only have sex during opening hours, never on Sunday or public holidays and it's got be silent. Know the type only too well. There comes a time when you've got to break out. Fight your corner, Max. No else is going to do it for you.'

He was angry but trying to control it. Pushed too hard, Ian Kellock could be dangerous. And there was, perhaps, an element of envy at work. I had Faith. We lived together in harmony, the whole being greater than the sum of the parts. When I climbed into bed of a cold winter evening, I didn't need an electric blanket or a hot water bottle, I had something very much better. Kellock, on the other hand, unless he paid for it on occasion, had no one to keep him warm. I had never been to his flat but he had described it. I could picture him in his living room, bathed in the sterile glow of his screens. His life was constrained and miserable. My problem with the law afforded him a function of sorts and he wanted to exercise it.

'What you say may well be true.'

'It is, believe me, I know. And another thing . . .'

I couldn't imagine that he could have anything to add to his negative critique of my better half, but he had.

Time to Talk

'You do realise what's at the root of all this don't you? You should. You're a self-proclaimed shrink, after all.'

'And what might that be, Ian?' cooling towards him even more, 'enlighten me.'

'Simple. You're a kept man. What is it you say up here, something about paying the piper and calling the tune? She pays, you dance. If you don't she pulls the plug. No Sugar Puffs for Max.'

Afloat on a sea of unrelated images, I nevertheless considered what Ian had just said, and not for the first time. My financial debt to Faith was clear, and so was my obligation to her. I did what I could on the domestic front, short of ironing, which had always seemed to me a pointless activity. But the fact remained that though I was contributing in kind, and apart from the sale of my car, I was bringing in no money. I had already resolved to look for a part-time job which would rectify that while allowing sufficient time for study. And then there was Faith herself. She was happy with the present arrangement – she had suggested it – and despite Ian's dark thoughts to the contrary, she never played the money card. It wasn't in her nature.

'Correct me if I'm wrong, but you haven't even met her.'

'The signs are there. She barks, you jump. She says don't accept this report so you don't. Plain as a pikestaff to anyone but you. Don't get me wrong here, Max, no reflection on your intelligence, but you're so close to her you can't see it.'

There was no future in disputing the point since he had already equipped himself with an off-the-shelf explanation as to why I would reject his penetrating analysis, but he wasn't finished.

'If you ask me, you've spent too much time sitting back listening to your clients' tales of woe instead of speaking out on your own account. You need to be more assertive, Max. Stick up for yourself for once.'

Faith had said exactly the same thing with respect to my dealings with Ian, but I could hardly tell him that so I moved on.

'There's something else.'

He listened in mounting disbelief.

'All you have to do is ask for it! You've got to be joking!'

'Not according to Lawrence T Scott.'

'And who the hell is he?'

'A solicitor.'

'Well, okay, you can always ask, but what happens when they tell you to fuck off.'

'Why would they do that, they have a duty of disclosure.'

'They can do what they like, Max, they make it up as they go along. I haven't told you this before but, confidentially, I was fitted up myself.'

I found this hard to believe, since he'd already boasted of his success in routing large sums of money to overseas destinations.

'That's true, I did, but they had so much trouble proving it they manufactured evidence. And I've got to hand it to them, it worked. In any case, there's something you're forgetting.'

'What's that?'

'You're defending yourself.'

'I realise that.'

'Right, so you're not a lawyer. You're not in the magic circle. They're not going to hand sensitive documents to a layman like you, especially one who's accused of fraud. Unlike the Lawrence T Scotts of this world, you're not bound by a code of practice.' He rose to leave. 'Anyway, I get the message, I can see you're determined to reject the hand of friendship, so on your head be it.'

He left me unsure whether his parting shot was a prediction or a threat, and a second coffee failed to neutralise the bad taste in my mouth. I was about to leave when I glanced at the afternoon's shows and ended up buying a ticket. When the film finally started, after the customary deafening ordeal by advert and trailer, my reading of the title was borne out. Side Effects. A psychiatrist prescribes medication for his patient, but the medication has unexpected results. Well now, there's a first, I thought, like prescribing meds for depression which have the useful side-effect of increasing suicidal thoughts. Whether the director had such things in mind I didn't know, and distracted by thoughts of my own I lost the plot and left before the end.

It occurred to when I was home that seeing this film on my own was something of a regression to my bachelor habits of old. Faith might well have wanted to see it too. So later that I evening I confessed, expecting a rebuke perhaps, or an expression of disappointment. Instead of which she hugged me, whispered 'silly boy' in my ear and went about her business.

But there was, as it were, a postlude to the day. The following morning after Faith had left for work, the doorbell rang. The postman had a package for Frei and needed a signature. A closer look at the envelope showed it was indeed addressed to Maxwell Frei, but the next line read, in large capital letters underlined twice, 'aka RAGING MOUSE'. Very witty no doubt, and a way to make his point. I would have the report whether I wanted it or not. Ian Kellock, criminal mastermind with too much time on his hands, didn't take no for an answer.

35

In the weeks preceding the trial, various documents came my way from the fiscal, the first being a list of witnesses who would testify against me. One was Mr Blake who, as a man of impeccable academic credentials and a library to match, might be expected to take a dim view of anyone who claimed a qualification he had not earned. Whether he would say as much on the stand I had no way of knowing. Nor did I know, given his insecurity, that he would be able to go through with it without his wife at his side. Time would tell.

The second was Mr Armitage. What to make of him I wasn't sure. Since he believed we were all doomed in the long run, what reason could he have for dooming me in the short? But one thing neither could claim was that I had made myself rich at their expense. The third witness named was Professor Dwyer, who could doubtless be depended upon to defend his report if called upon to do so. The addresses of all three witnesses were withheld by redaction, presumably to guard against the possibility that I would arrive on their doorsteps, baseball bat in hand, ready to rattle their jaws or otherwise 'persuade' them not to attend.

Two weeks after the witness list a second packet arrived. Requested by me, this was a copy of Dwyer's report. I was on the point of going to the kitchen to read it but, on impulse, borrowed one of Faith's spiral notebooks and left the house with both, ending up in the Elephant House, as close to the library as I could be and still sit down with a coffee.

With hindsight I can see that I treated the report like an unexploded bomb, removing it from the house as quickly as possible before it went off. And my destination was no accident either. I hoped to talk over my findings with Faith at lunchtime. It was only when I was seated and ready to begin that I realised I hadn't brought a pen. Leaving my papers on the table to keep it booked, I dashed to the nearest newsagent, bought a ballpoint and ran back.

To my relief, nothing had been removed, though my coffee had cooled somewhat.

As might be expected, I looked first for such positives as I might to find. And they were there if I looked hard enough, but qualified so heavily they came across as damning with faint praise, doubtless the author's intention.

Although Mr Frei has applied himself to his reading of the literature with reasonable success there are nevertheless considerable gaps. This is only to be expected since his labours did not benefit from professional direction. As his present grasp of the subject demonstrates, there is a significant difference between study per se and a course of study, the latter being structured to ensure a) that nothing essential is omitted b) that the student acquires a command of the subject through participation in tutorials, the submission of essays and the taking of examinations and c) that the correct weighting is given to the various branches of what is, after all, a large and diverse subject.

Out of a paragraph whose sole purpose was to justify the academic approach, the only plum I could extract was 'reasonable success'. Hardly a ringing endorsement. It got worse.

The following areas of weakness may be noted: clinical practice, knowledge of results from recent analytic techniques such as FMRI scanning, and any approach having at its centre human sexuality. I would go so far as to say that when it comes to the question of sex Mr Frei is fastidious to the point where he might be considered to have a problem in this area himself, something he may be aware of since he has always refused to take on clients where sex is an issue.

This made uncomfortable reading. The list of weaknesses was certainly correct, but what did it prove? Could the great man put his hand on his heart and claim that there existed the psychologist with no area of weakness at all? And nowhere in his report was there any attempt to list my strengths. The professor had not been retained to look for them.

As for the question of sex, I still remembered the slight tone of surprise, quickly suppressed, when I'd mentioned Faith. What did he think we were up to under the duvet, looking for a missing rubber duck? And yet he had a point. Based on what I had read, there were precious few men of my age who had slept with only two women, the first of them only once. Nor could I deny a feeling of revulsion at the thought of sexually transmitted diseases. And even now I remembered the first cause of my confusion when I wandered, at a tender age, into the bathroom of my uncle's house. My cousin, then aged four, was having a bath. She was clearly enjoying it, and so was I till my uncle remarked that what I was doing was dirty.

What a perplexity entered the young mind then. We bathed to clean ourselves but having a bath was dirty, how could that be? And as the years wore on, water came back to haunt me. Wash your hands before you leave the toilet. What was I to make of this insistence on hygiene but that the genitals were a source of infection best kept to ourselves? Which, in the main, was exactly what I had done. But though the professor may well have had a point, it had absolutely nothing to do with my grasp of psychology. Was my dirty washing to be aired in the public forum of the court? Would I be hung out to dry on this irrelevance? I hoped not. It didn't bear thinking about.

Excepting the professor's analysis of my attitude to sex, most of what I read came as no surprise. But the same could not be said for his conclusions. An evaluation of my competence was only to be expected but, here again, he appeared to believe he had opened a window to my soul and was not above looking in. And who did he see when he did? A man whose name had not come up at any point during our discussion.

Mr Frei has, in effect, set himself up as the Ivan Illich of psychotherapy. Just as Mr Illich advocated the de-schooling of society, so Mr Frei wishes to counter what he regards as psychology in its institutional aspects. He takes issue with the many competing therapies which presently exist, believing that each client is unique and demands a tailored response. Though his scope is very much narrower, he is at one with the sentiment expressed by Mr Illich when he wrote 'The institutionalization of values leads inevitably to physical pollution, social polarization, and psychological impotence'.

I had heard of Ivan Illich, but that was as far as it went, so I had no idea how just this comparison was. As luck would have it, I was yards from the library, so a desire to research the man led me in the direction I was going and Faith found me in the reference section taking notes from The Limits to Medicine and Disabling Professions.

'My word,' she said, resting her hand on my shoulder, 'what have we here, an anarchist in the making?'

We decided that we'd both had enough for the time being, needed to get off the treadmill for a while, and lunched together at the Balcony Café. It was good to relax, talking together about nothing of importance. Should we come back at the weekend to check out The Vikings? I thought not. Their seafaring skills enabled them to travel, but what did they do when they arrived? They murdered monks, raped nuns, and laid waste their kitchen gardens.

'But Max, this is a major exhibition. Some of the artefacts are amazing. Surely you should come to a judgement *after* you've seen the evidence – you'd expect nothing less at your trial.'

It was hard to argue with this point of law, and in case I needed reminding the National Museum was uncomfortably close to the Sheriff Court, the entrance to which, as we passed, was populated by the usual assortment of waifs, strays, unfortunates, offenders and smokers.

As usual, it was Faith who thought of it, though it should have been me: Dwyer's draft report was lying on my window ledge, not hers. We sat at Henry's table and compared the two documents paragraph by paragraph, line by line and found what we were looking for - significant differences. There were several occasions when the professor had simply improved his expression, making his meaning more clear. But those were not the changes which interested us. Where, in the final version, I had applied myself to my reading with 'reasonable success', in the draft I had been 'remarkably successful'. What a watering down was there! And the draft contained a significant paragraph absent in its entirety from the final version. He had come to a conclusion on the question of fraud, a bold move given he had met me only once.

I come now to the question of fraudulent intent, considered from the psychological rather than the legal perspective. Was it Mr Frei's intention to defraud his clients? I would argue that it was not. Before offering his services as a therapist, Mr Frei studied his subject over a period of years and arrived at settled view. The fact that this view may be challenged does not alter the fact that it was, and is, genuinely held. If his intention had been to obtain money by deception, devoting years of his life to study was not the way to go about it.

We had just located this paragraph when the lights went out. Opening the front door we saw that the problem was not restricted to our flat since the stair lights were also down. Faith walked to the living room window and reported that the street lights were down too. Just as obvious, and much more welcome, was the sudden cessation of noise from the many television sets in the surrounding flats.

Faith found two candles and a box of matches under the kitchen sink and we sat at our table, quite the conspirators, plotting the way ahead. Our phones were off, the Entryphone system at the main door couldn't work without juice, so no one could reach us till the fault was fixed. We could work without interruption. Conditions were perfect for hatching a plot, but what was that plot to be? The more we discussed it, the more distant it seemed.

Compared to the draft, the final version of the professor's report was considerably more damaging to me because of what it left out. There were two possible explanations for this: the professor had refined his view from one draft to the next, always possible and hard to disprove, or someone had reminded him why he had been asked to write it. We both inclined to the latter: the professor had been leant on. And it need not have been heavy. It might have been suggested to him, in a quiet moment, that a conclusion as to fraudulent intent was beyond his purview. Whatever the cause, we were left with the problem of what to do about it. Raising the question of the changes would involve an admission that we had the draft, at which point the question of how we'd obtained it would certainly arise. Not from the fiscal's office, which would never have sent us a draft, especially one they had never had in the first place.

Not from DS MacNeil, who would rather spit in my eye than help me in any way. And not from the author, of course. The draft had been obtained by nefarious means. We couldn't make use of it.

When power was restored later that evening, we switched on our phones and retired to the living room. Faith had a voicemail from Lawrence T Scott. He hoped they could meet. I had one from Ian Kellock. He'd come round that evening but couldn't get through the door, and so had a very attractive woman – it hadn't been all bad. Faith phoned Hazel in alarm, but she hadn't been the woman in question. She did, however, keep Faith on the phone for half an hour, about par for the course.

'Why is it,' Faith asked as we were going to bed, 'that gas central heating needs electricity to work? What's the point,' she demanded to know, 'in having an alternative source of energy if you can't use it!'

The bed was cold but we soon sorted that.

36

We passed through the rotating door of the Sheriff Court and joined the queue at security. It was Thursday the sixteenth of May. What little metal I had, I placed on the tray and walked through. Faith, who prepared everything in advance, had gone to the trouble of selecting a bra with the minimum of metal, but even so was concerned that the tiny hooks at the back would trigger the detector. She needn't have worried, though it took some time for the guard who met her on the other side to check the briefcase containing her mini library of files. Her philosophy was simple, better safe than sorry. If it might be relevant, have it to hand. Dressed in a sober suit, she looked for all the world like one of the busier solicitors with several cases pending, none of them simple. By my usual standards, I looked respectable myself. Faith had borrowed a suitably sombre tie from Hazel who, as she would, asked her why I needed it and duly appeared in the public gallery to see it in action. She assured us, with some regret, that Henry wouldn't miss it. Following his new lease of life with 'that woman', he had taken to sporting colourful cravats.

I had been in the building several times before but Faith had not. Like me, she was struck by the invention of the architect, who had provided a multiplicity of views through several levels, the lighting improved by penetrating shafts of light from long glass cupolas in the roof. From the higher levels, it was possible to look down through several floors below, take in the hum of conversation and observe the interested parties: the solicitors with their gowns and folders, and their clients, sometimes agitated, often supported by family members and friends. From the marble floors to the polished wooden banisters, no expense had been spared, an indication of how seriously society regarded the law or, perhaps more likely, how seriously the law regarded itself.

We walked along the main hall and descended the stairs to court seven, where proceedings began at nine-thirty. We sat in the public gallery and we were not alone. To my relief, the silver-haired gentleman from the Evening News had bigger fish to fry (not very difficult) and so was missing from his usual front-row seat. Two cases were called before mine, neither of them up-lifting. A man who had caused an affray on a train had no recollection of the blood-curdling threats he had made, or so it suited him to say. According to his solicitor, alcohol had caused him to behave out of character, though it could just as easily have been argued that alcohol had showed him in his true colours. And then there was Miss Mutch, an unfortunate woman who had arrived at the door of a friend's flat when a drug bust was underway. Asked by an officer if she had anything on her, she had admitted to having some valies and was charged with possession. Before she was called, she told us she was having trouble sleeping. The doctor had refused to prescribe Valium, her remedy of choice, so in desperation she had turned to a dealer. Up to this point, as far as the law was concerned, this lady had led a blameless life, yet now the law was pursuing her for a few blue tablets worth fifteen pounds on the street.

As she left the well of the court, I entered. Was I Maxwell Frei, otherwise known as Anderson? I was. And was it still my intention to plead not guilty? It was. Having established why I was accompanied by Faith, the sheriff indicated that he was happy with that, on the understanding that she made no attempt to participate in the proceedings.

The fiscal depute, a short individual with a matter-of-fact manner, made the case outlined in the complaint. He was a man devoid of drama, which I couldn't but feel was a good thing, his preference being to let the facts speak for themselves. And what were these facts? I had advertised my services as a psychotherapist, which I was not, and fraudulently relieved a number of clients of sums of money by way of an hourly rate. He proposed to cite as evidence a flier produced on my behalf and a screenshot from my website as it appeared at the time. He was prepared to call three witnesses. He handed copies of his productions to the clerk, who passed them on to the sheriff.

'Looking at the flier, my lord, you will note that Mr Frei describes himself as a psychotherapist. You will also note that he claims a qualification in psychology and, to give added weight to that claim, the flier contains a reference to a professional organisation, the BACP, and its register of qualified practitioners. Any member of the public seeing this document would conclude that Mr Frei was a qualified psychotherapist. I should perhaps point out that The British Association for Counselling & Psychotherapy defines its role as "to enable access to ethical and effective psychological therapy by setting and monitoring of standards". Mr Frei does have a university degree, but not in psychology, and a search of the BACP register shows that he is not on it.'

'And the screenshot?'

'It contains much the same information as the flier, My Lord.'

At that point sheriff turned to me.

'If you were represented, Mr Frei, your solicitor might choose to agree these productions with his friend,' indicating the fiscal depute. 'Do you wish to challenge either or both?'

'No, My Lord.'

I thought I detected a faint smile at that point, as if the sheriff noted I was playing the game with sufficient knowledge of the rules not to waste the court's time. The fiscal depute then moved on to his witnesses.

'I wish to call Mr George Armitage.'

Mr Armitage was summoned from the adjacent witness room and got off to the best possible start by contesting the existence of the deity and refusing to take the oath. I could almost hear the sheriff groan inwardly and Faith, delighted with this development, gave me the lightest poke in the ribs with her elbow. The witness having solemnly and sincerely declared and affirmed, the fiscal depute asked his questions. Yes, Mr Armitage had believed me to be a qualified psychotherapist. He had attended three times in all, the first of these sessions being free, the remaining two being charged at thirty pounds each. He was down a total of sixty pounds, not including time spent travelling to and from the appointments and the wastage of petrol.

The sheriff, clearly annoyed, intervened at this point.

'This is not a small claims court, Mr Armitage.'

The witness acknowledged that and the fiscal resumed. Was it the opinion of Mr Armitage that my services had assisted him in any way? No, it was not.

Invited to question him myself, I observed that the fiscal depute had not enquired what problem it was that caused him to seek my services, and suggested that he had been driven by a sense of impending doom. The witness agreed that was the case.

'So, Mr Armitage, would you say that this sense of impending doom is wholly irrational or does it have some logical basis?'

'As I'm sure you know, Mr Frei, there are cosmic forces at work.'

'And how could you have thought that I might be a match for these forces?'

This gave him pause for thought.

'Well,' he said, 'it's not so much the forces themselves as how we deal with them, isn't it?'

The sheriff wanted to know, in brief, what forces Mr Armitage was referring to, and received a reply including the death throes of the solar system and the continued expansion of the universe to the point where all the lights went out and we were left in total darkness.

'Not that we'd be there to see it, of course.'

'If I understand you aright, Mr Armitage,' the sheriff said, 'these events would not occur next week or the week after.'

'On a larger time-scale altogether, sir.'

'I see. Any further questions, Mr Frei?'

He could only have hoped that the answer was no, and I obliged him.

Mr Blake was less colourful. Glancing frequently at his wife in the public gallery, he agreed with the fiscal depute that professional qualifications were of the utmost importance.

'You are a qualified man yourself.'

'I have a degree and a doctorate. After all,' he added, to the surprise of the fiscal, 'who here is not properly qualified, apart from the accused, who is yet again pretending to be what he is not!'

The sheriff took exception to this remark.

'Mr Frei has chosen to exercise his right to defend himself. There is nothing improper in that.' Having established that Mr. Blake was also down to the tune of sixty pounds, the witness was passed to me. Yet again, the fiscal depute had neglected to ask why the witness had consulted me.

'My wife was concerned. She felt I was spending too much on academic texts.'

'Did you agree with her?'

He looked anxiously in her direction, and I had the impression that if she hadn't been there he might have denied it.

'Yes, I suppose I did.'

'So really, Mr Blake, you felt your degrees and diplomas were not enough.'

'I may have done, but at least I had them, unlike some I could mention.'

'No one here is denying that, Mr Blake.'

Professor Dwyer was neatly attired in a dark three-piece suit, probably the one he wore to funerals. The fiscal passed a copy of his report to the clerk who passed it to the sheriff.

'I don't know if Your Lordship has had time to read this document.'

According to his lordship he had, though where he had got it from was a mystery to me.

'Professor Dwyer, you conducted an interview with the accused at some length.'

'That's correct.'

'And your report is based on that interview.'

'Yes.'

'Would I be correct in saying that your purpose was to establish whether or not the accused, though not professionally qualified, was competent in the subject he professed?'

'Yes.'

'And what did you conclude?'

'That when it came to knowledge and understanding he had a qualified competence.'

'When you say a qualified competence . . .?'

'He had read extensively over a period of years and, with a few significant gaps noted in my report, had a working know-ledge of the literature.' 'But that alone did not qualify him to set up as a practitioner.'

'He lacked the experience required of a practitioner.'

'If I read your report correctly, Mr Frei is somewhat radical in his approach. You portray him as a psychological Ivan Illich at one point.'

'He rather tends in that direction, yes.'

'So in a nutshell if you would, what can we take that to mean?'

'He is distrustful of off-the-shelf solutions be they medications or specific therapies. He prefers to treat each client as an individual rather than label him with a diagnosis from the pages of the DSM.'

'The DSM?'

'The Diagnostic and Statistical Manual of Mental Disorders.'

'So really, Mr Frei starts afresh from the ground up with every client, aware of but preferring to ignore the accumulated knowledge of mental health issues built up by you and your professional colleagues over the years.'

'I would have to agree with that, yes.'

'And tell me, professor, how practical is that approach?'

'In an ideal world, perhaps, where both the practitioners and their clients have no limitations whatsoever on their time it might be suitable for some. But we are far from inhabiting such a world.'

'Finally professor, is there any sense in which Mr Frei might be said to be deluded?'

'Not in the clinical sense, no.'

'In some other sense, perhaps?'

'Well, we might say that he has more knowledge of his subject than he has of himself.'

'And for the therapist self-knowledge is a pre-requisite.'

'I would say so, yes.'

Professor Dwyer regarded me with equanimity as I rose to question him.

'You mentioned medications at one point. The BMJ reports there were 46 million prescriptions for anti-depressants in 2011, a rise of 9.6 percent that year alone.'

'We can agree that the figure is high.'

'Some would say too high.'

'And others would not. There is some discussion as to how effective these medications are over the population as a whole.'

'I would put it to you that where a drug is effective there is always a secondary market.'

'A secondary market?'

'The drug is sold on the street.'

'I see.'

'We can find many drugs on the secondary market – marijuana, ecstasy, cocaine, heroin – but what we don't find are selective serotonin reuptake inhibitors. What would you infer from that?'

'Unlike the other drugs you mention, SSRIs are only available on prescription.'

'True, but so is diazepam, and there is clearly a secondary market in that, as we have seen earlier today in this courtroom. I would suggest, Professor Dwyer, that that there is no secondary market in anti-depressant medications because, despite the high level of prescription, they are ineffective for the majority of patients.'

'You are suggesting that these medications are over-prescribed.'

'I am suggesting that they are, yes, by your professional colleagues and on an industrial scale.'

The professor chose not to contest this claim, knowing as well as I did, and probably better, the number of research papers broadly supporting this view. However, I could see the sheriff was growing restive.

'Mr Frei, what you say may well be true, but it has no bearing on whether or not a fraud has been committed. If you have a case to make on the subject of qualifications the court would like to hear it.'

'Can we take it as read professor, that in your view psychotherapists should be professionally qualified?'

'Yes.'

'And if they are professionals, that the success of their interventions can be measured in positive outcomes.'

The professor went into the expected rigmarole about the difficulty of determining outcomes in the area of mental health.

'From what you are saying, professor, there is no reliable measure of success in your field?'

'Such measures are very difficult in mental health, for the reasons I have just explained.'

'In which case,' I suggested, 'you could not demonstrate that a knowledgeable amateur is any more or any less effective than a professional.'

'Unless the amateur's results were disastrous.'

'Not even then, professor, unless you are claiming that professionals, by dint of their qualifications, never have disastrous results.'

Since he already knew I had several such cases up my sleeve he did not contest this point either.

'I am not claiming that, no.'

'The author of Hamlet had no qualification.'

'I would assume there were no degree courses for playwrights in his day.'

'I was thinking more of his understanding of how the mind works, his psychological insights which, for an unqualified man, ran very deep.'

'That may be, but as far as we know he never set himself up as a therapist charging thirty pounds an hour.'

'And yet, professor, this amateur has been quoted many times by luminaries of your profession such as Dr Freud in connection with, for example, the Oedipus complex.'

'That is true.'

I decided to risk one last throw of the dice.

'During the composition of your report, did you, at any point, address the question as to whether or not I had harboured any fraudulent intent?'

'A reading of my report will show no such reference.'

'Since the purpose of these proceedings is to come to a view on whether or not a fraud has been committed, your failure to address this point is strange to say the least.'

The professor looked so uncomfortable I was considering pressing home the point when Faith, from a sedentary position, gave me a sharp tap on the ankle. On no account could I reveal my possession of the draft.

'As I say, I did not address that question.'

'In that case, I invite you to do so now. Was it your impression from our interview that my behaviour was motivated by fraudulent intent?'

The professor looked across to the fiscal depute: no help there, he was pretending to leaf through his papers.

'I cannot offer a definitive judgement on this question on the basis of one meeting, but with that proviso, my answer would have to be no.'

Of my own witnesses I would only say that Mr Robertson took the oath in ringing tones as though his life depended on it, and Jean Ritchie, though she plainly found the experience an ordeal, did her best to answer the questions asked. She agreed that when the subject of DBT had come up, I had stated I was not competent in that therapy and so could not offer it. Was this consistent with fraudulent behaviour? Not in her opinion, no. And both averred that I had helped them, Mr Robertson lauding my indebtedness to the Good Book along the way. The fiscal depute, having established that I had not met her daughter, asked Mrs Ritchie how I could possibly have helped her. A reasonable question. She answered by pointing out that life with her daughter was a constant source of stress which she found easier to deal with as a result of her visits to me.

'So if I understand you correctly, Mrs Ritchie, you visited Dr Frei seeking help for your daughter but came away with help for yourself.'

'That's right.'

'In which case you weren't getting what you paid for.'

'In a way I was – at one remove, if you see what I mean.'

'I'm not sure I do.'

'Dr Frei helped me help her.'

And it had all been going so well.

'Dr Frei? That's what he called himself was it?'

'No. That's how I thought of him.'

'May I ask why?'

'I don't know really. That's how he came across.'

As is usually the case, there was considerable coming and going from the public gallery. On the only occasion I was distracted enough to look I caught a glimpse of Hazel, who gave me an encouraging smile. But to my dismay, two rows behind her was Ian Kellock whose attitude, and he always had one, could not be discerned from his expression. And who should be there by the doors, chatting to the policeman, but the kenspeckle figure of Lawrence T Scott, complete with hair gel and gown.

When the fiscal depute rose to sum up, he did so with economy. Both my flier and my website gave a wholly false sense to those who read it, and witness testimony confirmed that. The inclusion of information about the BACP gave the impression, without saying so directly, that I was accredited by that body. Most damaging of all was the fact that these documents claimed a psychology qualification when in fact I had none. And on that subject, he had reason to believe that I was now embarking on a degree course in psychology. Why would I do that if I really believed no qualification was needed? In prosecuting this case, the Crown was acting in the public interest by seeking to ensure that those who offered a service to the public in this difficult area were properly qualified to do so.

In my defence I pointed out that even the witnesses for the Crown had conceded that my first session was free and subsequent sessions charged at the rate of thirty pounds per hour. Study of the market would show that this rate was unusually low, which I had set to reflect the fact that I was not formally qualified. It was hardly the action of a man intent on fraud to study his subject for several years and charge so little for his services.

Turning to the productions, and with respect to the BACP, I had made available on both documents a link to their site from which prospective clients could find out for themselves whether or not I was registered. I further pointed out that there were nine protected titles which included the word 'psychologist', I had used none of them and no other titles were protected. Therefore, in describing myself as a psychotherapist I was in breach of no statute or regulation. My last point concerning the documents was that nowhere in the text, contrary to the assertion of the fiscal depute, had I claimed a psychology qualification.

This caused, as I had expected, not a little consternation. The evidence was there for all to see. But as they looked more closely I saw the penny drop, first with the sheriff then with the fiscal. The word I had used was 'qualifiction', the accuracy of which, when I thought about it, always caused me a frisson of delight, and never more than at this moment. A small pleasure which was not to last.

A court officer (contracted out) led me back to my position in the dock to await the sheriff's ruling. He spent an age rifling through his papers and I found the wait unnerving, the more so since, earlier in the morning, I had seen a defendant led away in handcuffs. Faith had returned to the public gallery and was sitting with Hazel, but because they were directly behind me I couldn't see them and there was no comfort to be had from that quarter. For the first time in months I felt on my own.

When the sheriff finally looked up over his glasses and spoke, he reviewed the evidence in some detail, though he needn't have bothered. I only had ears for his decision which I thought, no doubt unfairly, he was delaying as long as possible to prolong my anxiety. But his judgment, when it finally came, was a great relief and one which, despite my outward display of assurance, I had not been confident of.

'I find Mr Frei that, on balance, though your behaviour has left a lot to be desired, you did not behave with fraudulent intent and, further to that, I do not believe the public interest was well served in bringing this case before the court.'

I was free to go and so was he.

37

There was some talk on the pavement afterwards about where we should go to celebrate, something I wasn't eager to do. I had not been led away in chains to the nether regions, but nevertheless felt a little flat. Looking back on it, the reasons were obvious. The sheriff had made a point or two in his concluding remarks which deflated the balloon somewhat, but at a deeper level was another question – what was I going to do now? I had spent months preparing for this day and now it was over. Nothing so immediate lay over the horizon. The next targets I hoped to hit were several years away and much less dramatic. I had been riding the crest of a wave which was bound to break as it neared the shore and here I was, washed up in more ways than one, left by the receding tide to dry on the sand like an old piece of driftwood or storm-tossed frond of seaweed. After the climax comes the anticlimax, after the peak the trough.

We walked along Chambers Street, still discussing the alternatives, and ended up in Biblos by default: one of many establishments mistaking underlit for intimate, I had passed it many times but never entered. Despite Faith's professional interest in books, she had not been tempted either, but Hazel and Lawrence were regular patrons. That was something they had in common, could there possibly be anything else? I had grown fond of Hazel over the last few months. She could be histrionic at times, but had a good heart and a generous nature. Who wouldn't warm to a woman like that? As we settled at the table I resolved to keep a weather eye on Lawrence.

I don't know how it happened, but Hazel and I ended up at one side of the table, Lawrence and Faith on the other. At first this appealed to me, since the table would protect our still vulnerable friend from unwelcome advances, but after a while the disadvantage dawned. Faith spoke quietly at the best of times, and Lawrence lowered his voice to match. I was sure they were having a useful conversation, but apart from stray words such as 'fiscal', 'sheriff' and 'Max' I couldn't make out what they were saying, and a constant stream of chat from Hazel didn't help. Her spies were keeping her well informed of goings on at 'the house of ill repute'; a divorce was now on the cards; she had been impressed by my demeanour during the trial; if I needed any more ties I knew where to come. I tried and failed to filter all this out and discover what, if anything, Lawrence was saying about me.

'You did it!' Hazel exclaimed, giving me another vigorous hug to the point of putting my neck out. 'Well done that man!'

She beamed at Faith, who moved a glass out of harm's way and agreed.

'He certainly did.'

One thing puzzled me though. How did the fiscal know I was planning to get a qualification? His witnesses didn't know and neither did Dwyer.

'Good point,' Hazel asked, 'how did he know?'

Faith looked at Lawrence. 'I believe I mentioned it to you.'

'And you move in legal circles,' I added, hoping to stitch him up.

Lawrence looked frantically towards the bar, hoping our food was on the way.

'I may have let something slip. I have a friend in the Crown Office – not the fiscal depute dealing with your case, I hasten to add.'

'But your friend would know him.'

'Of course.'

'That's it, then.'

Hazel was less than impressed. 'Lawrence, that could have harmed his case.'

'Oh, I don't think so. If anything, it went to show that our friend Max here has a serious interest in his subject, hardly the attitude of a man intent on fraud. If I'd been the fiscal I wouldn't have brought it up. In any event,' he added, regaining his composure, 'it plainly didn't harm his case, did it? He was acquitted.'

And then the soup and bread arrived. Faith didn't talk while eating and Lawrence soon gave up trying. I couldn't help noticing that, for a smooth operator, he had a very poor technique. Every time he presented the spoon to his mouth he breathed in, slurping loudly as he sucked on his potato and leek. I don't know what

Time to Talk

Faith made of it, but I didn't like it one bit. Just as he was finishing, his mobile rang. He glanced at the screen, looked worried, rose and excused himself. He really had to take this call. We saw him on the street outside pacing up and down and gesturing as he spoke. Shortly afterwards, offering his apologies, he left with the promise to keep in touch. Late for a court appearance? A shortfall discovered in one of his client accounts? We would never know.

'Seems like a nice lad,' Hazel said as he left, reminding me of the obvious. She could have given him ten years. Presumably, Lawrence had younger fish to fry. What had I been worrying about? Where was my brain? The answer to that was simple - overtaken by a strong and irrational dislike.

The three of us finished an enjoyable lunch and rounded it off with a celebratory drink. Hazel was genuinely happy for me and reminded us of little details which we, in the well of the court, might not have noticed. The clerk had plainly had a heavy night and kept on stifling yawns, the bar officer had been seriously under-employed during the entire proceeding, and the policeman had pounced on a man in the public gallery who'd been reading a newspaper – not allowed, it seemed.

'And you know how they're always going on about justice being seen to be done? Well I think it should be heard to be done as well. Some of these people, the sheriff included, verged on the inaudible. And there's no excuse for it,' she added, 'they all had microphones!'

'You're not thinking of a fresh career as a lawyer, are you?'

Not for the first time that day I felt a light tap on my ankle. Faith was reminding me that Hazel had never had a career, let alone a fresh one.

'Just ignore him, Hazel, everyone else does.'

'Actually,' Hazel had something on her mind but was reticent to tell us, 'I was considering something – not the law, of course, nothing like that.'

It took her a minute or two but Faith coaxed it out of her. She had taken up writing again, something she had first attempted many years before. Her reluctance to tell us was due to the subject matter. Hazel had started a romantic novel and it was going well.

'I think that's wonderful, Hazel, don't you Max?'

- 259 -

I did, but found myself entertaining the obvious thought that through her imagination she was attempting to meet a need currently unfulfilled in her life.

'I'll want someone to check it over before I try to publish it. I know it's asking a lot, but I was wondering if you two . . .'

'We'd be delighted.'

I decided to get my retaliation in first and gave her a hug.

'Good for you. What's it called?'

'No laughing.'

'We wouldn't dream of it, would we Max.'

This was less a statement than an instruction.

'Behind the Scenes at the Theatre of Love.'

So Henry, whether he liked it or not, would have another starring role. I loved it.

The unexpected news that Hazel was writing a book distracted me a bit and Faith a lot. Before I knew it, my exploits earlier in the day had been forgotten in favour of an in-depth tutorial on the subject of physical versus electronic publishing and the respective merits of various file formats none of which I had heard of.

'That's all very well, but won't my agent handle all that?' Hazel asked.

'If you do it yourself you won't need one.'

Hazel was doubtful. She found it hard enough writing the thing, marketing it was something else again.

'Oh I don't know, Hazel,' I said, trying to reassure her, 'I can just see you in the signing tent after the reading.'

She rewarded me with a vigorous push to the shoulder.

'Now you're just pulling my leg.'

But the news that Hazel was writing a book had day-changing consequences. Faith, who knew a thing or two about the subject, suggested heading for the library. A great deal of useful information was available for writers. She knew, she'd collected some of it herself following numerous requests from interested members of the public. Hazel took her up on the offer.

'You could be my agent,' she suggested, as we walked back the way we had come and as though there were nothing to it.

Faith declined on the grounds that agents were a dying breed, withering on the vine as self-publication took off. But she could help, and she would.

Time to Talk

'I feel a bit bad about this, Max. This should be your day, not mine.'

'You shouldn't,' I told her, and then, in a rare thought-for-the-day moment, assured her grandly that, after all, the day belonged to us all.

'Well, yes, but still . . .'

Faith and Hazel crossed George IV Bridge and made for the library, chatting together in a remarkably animated manner. I watched them enter the building with regret. Clearly, Hazel had touched on an area of interest. By way of compensation, Faith had whispered in my ear the promise of a night to remember and I had headed home, but when I arrived at the door I felt no inclination to go in. On this occasion, I didn't want to be alone with myself, and what would I do there anyway? I was in no state of mind to watch television, let alone pursue the dry and dusty study of psychology. And though, at a subterranean level, I must have made the decision without knowing it, I found myself heading towards Lothian Road and entering the café just as the lunchtime crowd was thinning out.

As I sat down at table with my coffee and a caramel shortbread, I glanced round to ensure that Ian Kellock hadn't followed me in. I couldn't quite shake the idea that he was savvy enough to track my movements via my mobile phone even when it was off. Was this possible? I had no idea, but assumed it might be. If people in Afghanistan could be taken out by drones controlled from New Mexico or California then tracking me, a much simpler task, had to be within the bounds of possibility. Why anyone would bother was another matter altogether, though in Kellock's case the motive would surely be to show that he could do it. Still hoping to win approval, he was yet to grow up. *Daddy, look what I can do!* Very good, Ian, now go and play with your toys and leave me in peace.

After a minute or two sipping my coffee and nibbling the shortbread, I concluded that all I was doing was massaging myself. I didn't need food or drink, I'd just eaten. The coffee gave me something to do with my hands and reassured any onlooker that I was genuine, a bona fide customer. The food and drink were a source of comfort, particularly the shortbread with its quick fix of chocolate. And yes, I was missing Faith. All I had of her right then was her spiral notebook with its account of the sheriff's closing remarks.

Before they faded from my mind, I intended to note what I remembered of the trial, though remembering when you are an actor in events is more challenging than remembering as a detached observer. I was sure there were things I hadn't noticed and other things I'd forgotten, even, on occasion, the precise order of events. And of course, at no point was I observing myself, which didn't make the task any easier. Nor did the people at a neighbouring table, who were discussing a film about a projectionist at an art house cinema. It was folding and he was out of a job. Which seemed an uneasy subject to be discussing at this particular venue, but as far as I could see the Filmhouse was thriving and in no danger of closing. As for projectionists, that was another matter. I could only assume that they too, like literary agents, were a dying breed as more and more directors turned to digital cameras and manufacturers stopped making film. The craft of projection was one of a growing list of skills no longer required by the digital age.

It is surely important to pin down memories before they fade, as they will. If you go to the moon what's left to do but come back again, and after you have, as the years pass by, all you will be left with are memories playing in your head like footage from a film with no sound. And even those will fade, as the projectionist in your head falls asleep on the job and is finally shown the door. You know you went, but why did you bother? The immediacy of the event is lost and gone forever. Or if the moon's too far, take Tuvalu. You remember going all those years ago, that's fine, but is it still there or has the steadily rising sea taken it back? And even if it is, it may have changed so much you needn't have bothered. Remember it as it was or go back, but don't pretend you know it any longer.

Starting with a fresh page, I noted that the fiscal depute had chosen to ask me no questions. Probably because he knew what my answers would be, he had preferred to rely on his productions and his witnesses. I had the impression, later confirmed by Lawrence, that the sheriff had extended me considerable latitude, not in how I comported myself (as Hazel would have it) but in the area of relevance. But that had not inhibited him when it came to his concluding remarks, noted in detail by Faith, which was just as well since I was unable to do it.

Some of my defence, in his view, smacked of the barrack room lawyer. The fact that I had referenced the BACP in my flier without claiming to belong to it did not impress him at all. Any student of psychology, as I professed to be, must have realised that the average reader would have drawn from this the false inference that I was registered with the body in question, even though at no point did I make that claim. He was particularly dry when referring to my use of the word 'qualifiction'. I plainly regarded this as very clever, a masterstroke which, in a way it was but, again, one did not have to be a psychologist to realise that people read whole words, not the individual letters making them up. If that were not the case we would never get to the end of a book. He therefore concluded that my flier and website, though technically accurate, nonetheless gave the misleading impression that I was qualified, though he accepted my point concerning protected titles.

He then went on to consider my behaviour as attested to by the witnesses. There was no question in his mind that I had applied myself seriously to the study of my subject. Two of the witnesses felt I had failed to help them, but from their testimony it was clear that I had tried, and it would not be difficult to find equivalent cases from the clientele of qualified professionals. Further, two of the witnesses had testified in my favour so, effectively, these testimonies cancelled each other out. Nor was there any question in his mind that whatever I could be accused of it was not an attempt to get rich quickly. Indeed, that had never been part of the complaint against me. I had clearly tried to provide the service advertised and any financial gain was minimal. Finally, he was aware of no precedent from a com-parable case obliging him to convict.

By the time I had completed my notes, the film critics had their diaries out, both paper and electronic. It seemed they were agreeing the date of their next meeting. Watching them at work it occurred to me that perhaps Faith and I were a bit too sufficient unto ourselves. We had a small social circle and met our friends from time to time but really, though we benefited from that and liked them a lot, at some deep level we didn't need these people, they were not essential to us. It was Faith and I against the world. But this was not necessarily a good thing. Unlike the film buffs at the next table, we lacked a defined social role. And if that was true of us as a couple it was even more so of me since Faith, by virtue of her job, at least had a social role at work.

And then, in a flurry of handshakes, hugs and kisses, my neighbours were gone and my cup was empty. I felt the need for another, which I nursed as I considered what the sheriff had said. There was no getting away from the fact that he had been right: the conceit on which I had set so much store was of no importance at all. Far from being a get-out clause, it was little more than juvenile wit, a wordplay of no significance, yet I had regarded it as the lynch-pin of my defence, so much so that I had confided it to no one, not even Faith, in case word of it somehow got out. A sobering thought. As for his passing remark that he was pleased to hear I was now embarking on a recognised course of study, it confirmed for me the way I should be going.

I reached into my jacket pocket and took out my phone, which had been off since I entered the courtroom. Faith might be trying to contact me by now, her session with Hazel over. And sure enough the device lit up with an incoming message, but it was not from Faith. FESS UP, FREI, WE BOTH KNOW YOU USED IT!

Kellock, without turning up, had invaded my interlude in the café, and he was right. If I hadn't known what the professor's final version had left out, I would not have drawn from him the damaging admission that whatever else he might say he had found no evidence of fraudulent intent. And who would know that better than a qualified man with letters after his name?

38

The weeks that followed were quiet, though not without event. Faith's boss, Mr Gilchrist, on extended leave of absence for several months, passed away at the end of May. Faith and I attended the funeral, where it soon became clear there were very few relatives present. This was confirmed several months later when his staff discovered, to their surprise, that he had left several of them bequests, Faith being one. She assured me she had not known him well, which put her in a large group. He had never encouraged any degree of closeness but had, it now appeared, thought highly of them from a distance.

Faith was then faced with a choice, whether or not to apply for his job when it was advertised: she had the qualifications and experience. But on reflection, and talking it over together several times, she decided it wasn't for her – too much admin, too many meetings. She had her fill of both as it was. She lived with this decision for several days and it still felt right. Which meant that it was. Her only regret was passing up a pay rise, but thanks to her we were making ends meet as it was, though I didn't see why should she do all the work. She didn't mind, but I did. Being a kept man for several years was not the way to go, however much cooking, cleaning and laundering I might do.

My attempts to find part-time work were looking good, and I soon narrowed it down to two possibilities: security and hospital portering. I was attracted to the first not because I am big and strong, quite the opposite, but because the opportunity I first came across was as a night-watchman on a building site. I liked to think I could sit in my Portakabin, drinking tea and studying course-books while glancing out the window from time to time to ensure that no one was making off with a mortar silo or a block of flats. How accurate this fantasy was I never discovered, since Faith took exception to any possible overnight absence from the marital bed (as she always referred to it, though we were not yet married).

'No way, Jose,' she said, which put paid to that.

I applied for and secured a job as a porter in the ERI. Though concern was expressed that I was over-qualified and might not stay the course, my employer had little to lose. The training involved was on-the-job and minimal, so their loss would be slight if I left. Getting there was another matter. It was possible but difficult by bus, and we soon agreed that since Faith didn't need it for work, I should use her car – which I have to admit I had been doing for several months before we thought to check the wording of her insurance. Still, though I was bringing in much less money than she was, I was at last contributing to the household economy and, according to Hazel, not before time. She said she was joking, but I wasn't so sure.

Hazel made good progress with her book and recruited us both to read it as it progressed. I found this difficult. The strand of the plot dealing with Henry's betrayal worked well and retribution, when it came, was in the form of a virulent STD which not only removed him from the scene but also provided an opening for our heroine's new love interest. Very neat, though she said so herself. And it soon transpired that Anne fancied Josh, the new arrival, actor and man about town. Good, but all she needed to do was say so. I soon tired of the frequent references to his muscles, chest, strong features and penetrating blue eyes, a reaction I should have kept to myself.

'Frankly, Max, and no offence here,' she said, rising to her full five feet one inch, 'but a threadbare hospital porter is hardly representative of my target audience. You know what I think?'

'No.'

'You wish you looked like that. You're jealous.'

In the light of this response I withheld my second concern, namely, that the detailed descriptions of sexual congress later in the book verged on the comic.

Faith avoided such difficulties altogether by restricting herself to the safer areas of syntax, punctuation and layout, and pointing out the occasional inconsistency, such as a minor character's name mysteriously changing half way through a chapter. Both of us felt the title was too long. To our surprise Hazel agreed, and reduced it to The Theatre of Love.

At that time, though Hazel didn't know it, Faith was about to take on a second book, the present attempted record of events – on condition that I gave her complete editorial control. She would take it as she found it, but had no intention of getting embroiled in endless arguments with the author. This policy presented her with considerable difficulties, not least because she featured in it herself. From what she had read so far, she drily observed that I was too keen on the parenthesis for my own good and concluded that her best course was to leave the content intact while correcting any factual errors she might find. And then, ever the librarian, she proposed to add a critical apparatus consisting of an afterword and notes. Women like Faith are few and far between.

DS MacNeil made a brief appearance in the Evening News. She had been suspended on full pay (we all should be so lucky) on suspicion of having perverted the course of justice by fitting up a suspect. The man was a well-known dealer who, for the best of reasons, she wanted to keep off the streets. Having enough evidence to do it would have been the preferred method.

The trial of Mr Olatunde did not take place since that enterprising man, despite having been relieved of his passport, somehow passed through the hands of the UK Border Agency and made it back to his home in Nigeria.

As for myself, I take the occasional photograph but have abandoned any pretence of becoming a photographer. In these dark times when all and sundry have a mobile phone, digital camera or both, everyone and his uncle is a photographer and leaves numerous pictures on websites to prove it. And so the value of the photograph is reduced by inflation. In any case, the competition is too hot and the motivation lacking. My studies have since begun in earnest and I have every intention of completing them.

To Colin's evident delight, Catherine gave birth to a daughter and Janice, ever helpful, having hired a van for the day for her own creative purposes, kindly delivered my oriental screen to the door on her way past. It is now posing an attractive obstacle in my room, but I take pleasure in looking at it, especially in a good light.

Afterword

The author has based this memoir on his memory of events and his own notes. On several occasions he has supplemented these by reference to voice recordings of meetings. Otherwise, where direct speech is concerned he has followed Thucydides in attempting to convey the essence of what was said without claiming to be quoting verbatim.

He has given me carte blanche to deal with his narrative as I think best. Because I feature in it myself I have resisted the temptation to change any part of it since one change can so easily lead to another.

I have not felt it appropriate to burden this book with a full scholarly apparatus. The notes below are intended to amplify or explain certain points as they arise in the text.

The author has included a number of literary references, several of them silently. These are identified in the notes.

Faith Gordon, Edinburgh, April 2013

Notes

CHAPTER 3
ONE CAN'T BUT TOUCAN: Michael was harking back to a series of Guinness adverts featuring this colourful bird.

The hippocampus: a part of the brain which plays an important role in the consolidation of information from short term to long term memory.

CHAPTER 4
DSLR: digital single lens reflex camera.
GPS: global positioning system.

CHAPTER 5
The Rangoon Printmakers Expo: an invention of the author.

Napiers: a well known herbalist in central Edinburgh.
The Edinburgh Sleep Centre: situated on Heriot Row, Edinburgh.

CHAPTER 6
Still Life With Bible and Scissors: George Leslie Hunter (1879-1931)

The ontological argument for the existence of God: an argument first advanced by Anselm of Canterbury in 1078. God is defined as 'that than which nothing greater can be conceived', the argument proceeding from that point.

CHAPTER 7
Though the author describes Faith's appearance as 'severe', women's clothing was not his forte. A more accurate term would have been 'businesslike'.

Creative Scotland: successor body to the Scottish Arts Council.

CHAPTER 8
Amour courtois: otherwise known as courtly love, amour courtois is an idealised form of love found in the literature of the Middle Ages in which a knight or courtier devotes himself to a noblewoman who is usually married and feigns indifference to preserve her reputation.

The Games People Play: Eric Berne (Penguin)

The Science of Mind and Behaviour: Richard Gross (Hodder Arnold)

CHAPTER 9
BPD: borderline personality disorder, a disorder of the personality deemed to be on the border between neurosis and psychosis.

Sleeping pills: the author had been taking an interest in the efficacy of sleeping pills. In one of his notebooks he writes: 'They increase total sleep by twenty minutes or so, not a lot. The more you use them the less effective they are. What's the point?'

CHAPTER 10
The Gallery of HMS Calcutta: a painting by James Tissot, now in the Tate Gallery, a particular favourite of the author.

Listings by category: in fact, the author had compiled lists under five different headings intending to aggregate them later: textbooks which covered the subject in its entirety; course books used by university psychology departments; books dealing with specific aspects of the subject; books dealing with the various types of therapy; and books aimed at the popular market which might nonetheless be of value.

Maslow: in his 1943 paper 'A Theory of Human Motivation' Abraham Maslow posited a hierarchy of human needs.

La Maja Desnuda and La Maja Vestida: two paintings by Francisco Goya of a model in identical pose. In one she is naked, in the other fully clothed.

Hot Stuff Monthly, Killer Babes: these magazines appear to be inventions of the author.

CHAPTER 11
One must be pedantic to be accurate: the author attributes this reference to the novel 'The Man Without Qualities', by Robert Musil.

Gansie: a traditional knitted sweater.

The rule of thirds: a method used to locate centres of interest in a visual image. The image is divided by two vertical and two horizontal lines, the centres of interest occurring where the lines intersect.

CHAPTER 12
Robert Ferguson (1750-1774): a Scottish poet who died in an asylum at the age of twenty-four. He is variously thought to have suffered from depression, religious melancholia, or both.

Biblica and The Tablet: publications of the Catholic Church.

CHAPTER 13
Multiverse: a term first used by the American philosopher and psychologist, William James.

De l'Amour: published by Stendahl under his real name, Marie-Henri Beyle. The author's copy is heavily annotated. In his notes he compares De l'Amour and the Memoirs of Hector Berlioz as being similar examples of the destructive effect of the romantic attitude to love.

CHAPTER 15
RSA: The Royal Scottish Academy.

CHAPTER 16
Gawain: a reference to the medieval poem Sir Gawain and the Green Knight, in which the Green Knight walks with his own head under his arm.

TNT: the chemistry teacher in question was the late Terence Nigel Thake.

CHAPTER 17
Daniel Deronda: a novel by George Eliot.

CHAPTER 18
The Hypostasis of the Archons: the Reality of the Rulers, a Nag Hammadi text.

CHAPTER 20
Pamela: a reference to Pamela Stephenson Connolly, resident sex therapist to readers of The Guardian newspaper.

Penthouse Porn Awards: an invention of the author, who was unaware of the AVN Awards (Audio Video News) and probably still is.

CHAPTER 21
T'ing: a traditional small pavilion (Chinese).

Casimir the Great (1310-1370): King of Poland.

CHAPTER 22
Joseph Heller (1923-1999): author of Catch 22.

Franz Kafka (1883-1924): author of several works and master of the impossible situation.

ICP: 'Lothian integrated care pathway for people who may attract a diagnosis of personality disorder.' The copy in the author's possession is dated November 2010.

Mental Welfare Commission: The Mental Welfare Commission for Scotland.

Niel Gow (1727-1807): Scottish fiddle player and composer.

Chapter 23

'The world is a comedy to those that think, a tragedy to those who feel': Horace Walpole in a letter to Sir Horace Mann, 1770.

The Tragic Sense of Life: the author refers to a book of this title by Miguel de Unamuno.

Henryson's fox: a reference to the Morall Fabillis of Robert Henyrson, specifically to The Taill how this foirsaid Tod maid his Confessioun to Freir Wolf Waitskaith, lines 770 -771:
'Methink no man may speke a word in play
Bot now on dayis in ernist it is tane."

Regression to the mean: a reference to the fact that intelligence cannot be bred. If the parents are at the high end of the spectrum, their children are likely to be intelligent, but less so than their parents.

The Amateur Immigrant: Robert Louis Stevenson (1879-80). The reference to pies may be found on page 64 (Tusitala Edition).

Wilhelm Reich (1897-1957): Austrian psychoanalyst and author of such classic texts as The Sexual Revolution (1936) and The Function of the Orgasm (1942).

Chapter 24
Art Blakey, John Coltrane, Herbie Hancock: jazz musicians.

Chapter 25
The current proceedings: a reference to the Leveson inquiry into the culture, practice and ethics of the press.

By dint of abstruse research he would steal from his own nature all the natural man: a reference to section six of Dejection: An Ode, by Samuel Taylor Coleridge.

*'And haply by abstruse research to steal
From my own nature all the natural man'*

The marriage of flesh and air: a reference to the poem 'Life Is Motion' by Wallace Stevens.

As Frank said of apples, women like that don't grow on trees: a reference to the TV series MASH. When Major Frank Burns is asked for more apples, he replies that apples don't grow on trees.

CHAPTER 26
Perhaps the poet had it right when he referred to the imagination as the one reality in this imagined world: a reference to the poem 'Another Weeping Woman' by Wallace Stevens.
*'The imagination, the one reality
In this imagined world.'*

That melancholy, long, withdrawing roar: a reference to the poem Dover Beach, by Matthew Arnold.

CHAPTER 27
This guy : Alexander Roy, a business development manager, who married Morven Wylie at the Dunblane Hydro Hotel in Perthshire while still legally married to another woman. After living with Miss Morven as her husband and while still married to his first wife, Roy set up home with two other women, proposing to both and getting them both pregnant.

CHAPTER 28
The Good Psychologist: Noam Shpancer (Abacus).

The Artist (2011): film directed by Michel Hazanavicius. Often described as silent since there is no dialogue, the film features music and sound effects.

CHAPTER 29
Detective Chief Inspector April Casburn: this officer was found guilty of a count of misconduct in public office by jurors at Southwark Crown Court and was jailed for fifteen months.

CHAPTER 30
Andrew Jackson (1767-1845): seventh president of the United States, he has been accused of infringing the rights of native Americans by forced resettlement.

CHAPTER 36
Ivan Illich (1926-2002): Russian philosopher and social critic. The quotation is from the introduction to Deschooling Society (1970).

CHAPTER 37
'A Useful Life' (2010): Uruguayan film directed by Federico Veiroj.

Printed in Great Britain
by Amazon